SEIDR'S AND SWORDS

MARIE LEFORTE

PANTHEON PRESS

TRIGGER WARNINGS

Seidr's and Swords is an adult Viking-inspired fantasy set in a mythic, war-torn world where violence, trauma, faith, and passion coexist. While sensitive subjects are handled with care and narrative intent, some scenes and themes may be distressing for certain readers.

This book contains depictions or references to:

Graphic violence, warfare, and battle trauma (including blood, injury, and death)

Religious and mythological themes inspired by Norse paganism, including ritual practices, sacrifice, and divine intervention

Slavery, captivity, and exploitation

Psychological distress, trauma responses, and post-traumatic stress

Grief, loss, and the death of loved ones

Torture, cruelty, and abuse of power

Magical corruption and body-horror elements

Romantic and sexual content between consenting adults

Off-page references to past sexual assault and grooming

Emotional manipulation and morally complex character dynamics

Themes of fate, faith, mortality, and personal agency

Reader discretion is advised.

This novel is intended for mature audiences (18+)

PRONOUNCIATION GUIDE

Character Names

Skúli — *SKOO-lee* — From Old Norse *Skúli*, meaning "shield" or "shelter."

Alura — *Ah-LOO-rah* — A name symbolizing light.

Eirik — *AY-rick* — From *Eiríkr*, meaning "ever-ruler."

Astrid — *AH-strid* — Means "divine strength."

Freydis — *FRAY-dees* — meaning "noble goddess."

Björn — *BYORN* (rhymes with "yawn") — Means "bear."

Locations

Drakensvar — *DRAH-kens-var* — "Dragon's Keep"

Vardengrim — *VAR-den-grim* — "Grim Guardian"

Hayhjem — *HAY-yem* — "Home of the High Meadow."

Eyrie — *AIR-ee* — Eagle's nest.

Vargheim — *VARG-hame* — "Home of the Wolf."

Áelfrheim — *AELF-r-hame* — "Home of the Alva."

Concepts & Mythic Terms

Seidr (Seiðr) — *SAY-der* — Norse magic of fate-weaving, foresight, and spirit-calling. Practised by seeresses and priestesses.

Dreki — *DREH-kee* — "Dragon."

Yggdrasil — *IGG-drah-sill* — The World Tree that binds the realms together.

Blót-Jörd — *BLOAT-yord* — "Sacrifice-Earth."

Cultural & Magical Titles

Stormborn — One touched by stormlight or divine magic, feared or revered for their power.

Ulfhednar — *UHLV-hed-nar* — Norse "wolf warriors."

To my readers,

Demi said it best.

Sorry not sorry.

(This is a soft introduction to the series.)

Yfirland
Vargheim
Vardengrim
Drakensvar
Dreki Pass
Velskarr
Hallegard
Rotundvik
Hayhjem
Sunnuholen
Eyr

PROLOGUE

Before the storm, there was silence.

Not peace. Never peace. But a stillness, as if the world were holding its breath, waiting for the gods to bleed again.

The old magic had rotted beneath the stone and ashes, buried by the iron hands of men and the silence of traitorous kings. Only the echoes remained. Whispers in the shadows of bloodlines long forgotten.

But fate does not die.

Under the glowing silver light of the eclipse that reflected off the water's edge, a priestess shrouded in robes carried something precious against her chest. To a passing stranger, it might have looked like nothing more than offerings to a temple. But she knew what she carried was far more dangerous and far more sacred.

The storm that raged in the mountains had nearly torn the temple roof away. It was an unnatural, dark, old magic forcing its way through the realms while the gods cried out. Thunder boomed, rain hammered the glass, lightning scorched the earth, setting trees ablaze. Many had died as the magic ripped its way back into this world, and none would be safe if she couldn't get the child she carried to safety. Wars would come. Kings would kill for her. Most people would want to harness this power for themselves, to fulfil their desires and take control. And there were those who believed this child was a curse, and others who saw her as their salvation.

Once in a millennium, a silver-blood eclipse graced the skies, bringing both destruction and salvation. It was devastatingly beautiful, but the priestess had no time to stop and admire the beauty of which the gods had bestowed upon them that night.

There was only one reason for an eclipse like this: Sköll or Hati–the wolves who hunted the sun and moon–had caught their prey, and magic was leeching into the realm. The same magic that had been gone for generations. Magic long thought dead.

That could mean only one thing.

They were coming.

Across the continent, far from the storm, in a mountain keep, a boy crouched in the straw of a dimly lit stable. His breath misted in the cold as he reached for a shivering wolf pup, its eyes still closed, left behind by its mother.

Nothing so much as breathed as the boy lifted the pup into his arms and cradled it awkwardly against his chest. As he did, a low thrumming heat pulsed beneath its ribs, so faint he almost thought he'd imagined it. The same silver light that crowned the moon, haloed the pup's fur, and for a heartbeat, it was as though the creature were outlined in runes too old for memory. The boy blinked and they were gone.

He bent close as if speaking to an equal rather than an animal and whispered a vow into its tiny ear, a boy's promise spoken with the weight of a man's truth.

"We'll look after each other, you and I, Björn."

The same silver light touched his hair as it did the waves that drove the priestess forward.

Shouts echoed across the shore, the thundering sounds of horses hooves racing on the compacted sand. But the priestess pressed on, her arms tightening around the swaddled infant. Tiny fingers curled in the folds of cloth, and for a heartbeat, the priestess thought she felt the air around the child hum with something ancient.

She reached the pier and spotted the Karve waiting, its crew tense and restless. They had risked everything to help her escape.

Her shoes made no sound against the wood as she all but leapt into the boat, urging them to push off. She prayed to Freyja that the sea would let them pass. The oceans were known for being treacherous at the best of times, but on a night like this Jörmungandr would be hunting, eager to devour this magic for himself and claim the right to start Ragnarök.

Still, they had to try.

Though she had outrun it thus far, the storm was headed their way. Lightning flashed at the edge of the pier as the riders closed in. The oarsmen grunted as they heaved the heavy oars, propelling them away from danger.

Four riders shrouded in darkness watched as the Karve evaded them, they'd been sent here to kill the priestess and destroy what she was fleeing with. The priestess looked back at them, noting the way the shadows seemed to swallow them. They drew back their bows, releasing flaming arrows that hissed through the air, some burrowing into the Karve's hull, others finding flesh.

The steersman called for them to keep rowing, throwing one of the deceased overboard as he took their spot. The oarsmen rowed harder, calling on the gods.

"Onward to Valhall! If we die tonight, let it be for purpose!"

Fire caught, unnaturally hot and fast. The priestess knew they wouldn't make it. There was only one way left to save the child—and it would cost her everything.

She began to chant, her voice low and dangerous, speaking words passed from mother to daughter, never written and never meant to be uttered.

"Shut your mouth woman!" The steerman snarled, fear in his eyes. "You will commend us all to death. Our souls will be lost forever and never reach Valhalla!"

"There are other halls," she called out before continuing.

Thunder crashed. Ravens descended from the sky, perching even on burning wood. The smell of singed feathers filled the air. The priestess scattered stones and bones onto the deck—they split and bled where they fell, runes glowing red.

Her voice cut through the noisy darkness.

"Freyja, Lady of the Vanir, I kneel in your name beneath the stars that watched the first men die.

Hear me now before the storm awakens and delivers its final blow. Before the blood of the child stains the stones of fate.

From the shadowed edge where the sea swallows the sun, shall she be torn, child of stars and storm begun.

Bloodline forgotten, yet older than flame, hair like frost-wrought silver, eyes none dare name.

Send the child to safety so that she one day may return, though the path will be shrouded and difficult to discern."

The wind screamed, the world tilted, and then the child was gone.

CHAPTER ONE
ALURA

Beneath me, the ground felt soft, yet not like my bed. My sweet, fluffy bed that I had spent entirely way too much money on. But this wasn't that. This was soft like when I would lay on moss in the summers. My ears rang, my head pounded as if the storm from last night was still whirling inside me.

Wait...was I dead?

I had been in my apartment by the ocean, looking over photos that I had taken of an excavation site. I was preparing for my masters in archeology, specialising in Norse era history specifically. But there had been something wrong with the grave we had found.

There had been no body.

A grave with no body meant that they knew they were not going to come home, and 'they' were a 'she' because Priestesses always were. It had been a weird finding for us, definitely the first my two superiors had ever seen. But the thing that I didn't understand was, who made the grave for her?

I forced my eyes open, despite the sunlight stabbing at me, I rolled onto my side and took in my surroundings. Crisp leaves crackled underneath me, forming a soft bed that did little to ease my pounding head. I was somewhere unfamiliar.

The glade around me was alive with the distinctive colours of autumn. Golden and orange leaves fell around the deep, green grass. Only a moment ago, I'd been on the beach. And now I'm here.

I pressed my palms into my eyes, willing myself to wake up from this nightmare and to be back in my apartment, surrounded by the familiar hum of research papers and the smell of coffee.

But the forest held me in place. Alone.

Judging by the sun's position, it was probably late morning, though my memory placed me on the beach late last night, exhausted from fieldwork. There had been some kind of weird phenomenon.

There had been a storm. I'd always loved storms. They calmed me, made me feel like I was being watched and cared for. So I went to it, standing on the sand as the waves beat against the shore.

I should have stayed home. I should have continued the work that needed to be done. I had worked my whole life to get to where I was. To get my hands on the things that called to me in unexplainable ways. Instead, I had left. I had shrugged on my coat ignoring the faint rune shaped birthmark that sat on my collarbone and I had gone to the beach.

The sky had lit up during the storm, glowing silver runes etched themselves into the darkness above the water. There had been a voice, an ethereal voice telling me that it was time to come home. Calling me Storm-Born. Lightning had struck the sand, scrawling outwards as more silver runes created an intricate pattern.

The vegvisir.

The way home.

A chill bit through my jacket as I returned to my senses. At least it was still intact. Thank the gods for small mercies.

Disoriented, I forced myself upright on shaky legs and scanned the ring of trees. A narrow path led left and I followed it, hoping it would take me somewhere familiar–or anywhere really. Birds called out, each note making me snap my head around nervously.

Newfoundland had bears. Wolves, maybe cougars. Good boots were my only advantage, the ones I'd chosen over my usual sandals.

I was no rookie. Four years of university, two years of archeology fieldwork, and a master's scholarship. I'd survived on grit and logic, not luck. I'd make it out of here. I had to. I just needed to follow the trail. Obviously there were people nearby, the trail was well worn, carved into the side of a hill.

I missed the familiarity of my work bag, a satchel that slung across my front when I was in the field. In it, I always carried a knife and bear spray. But now I was defenceless, and panic began to set in as I walked.

The trail curved upward. I pushed past the exhaustion gnawing at my legs, but a sudden rustle behind me made me freeze. A shadow? Just a trick of the light filtering through the trees, I told myself. But in the canopy of trees, there's plenty of shadows. The unease lingered.

I tried to shrug it off as I continued along the trail. My footsteps grew heavier as I trudged along but I was determined to get out of here in one piece. Wolves, bears and people would be the least of my problems if I was out here after dark. Without shelter, I was sure to freeze.

Finally, at the crest of the hill, I stopped. Sighing in relief, almost sagging. Below, water snaked through the valley, and in its curve was a village. Wooden and stone walls surrounded it, with a massive gate partially open. The half-timbered houses were tightly packed, their thatched roofs sloping steeply. A towering hall loomed in the back, and small boats dotted the riverbank.

Thunder rolled overhead, closer now, and rain began to fall. My stomach churned as a primal unease settled in my chest. The village looked...Norwegian? No. Not Norwegian. Norse.

Impossible.

I'd visited the fjords on a university trip once, but I lived nowhere near Norway. How could it resemble the reconstructed village that I'd visited while doing my degree?

Doubt clawed at me, as always. Orphaned, alone on a beach as an infant, surviving against odds most would crumble under. I'd built my life on logic, on evidence, on work I could control. And now, standing at the edge of a village that shouldn't exist, I was beginning to question everything.

Rain soaked through my jacket as I descended the hill toward the gate. I pulled my hood up higher over my face, bracing myself for whatever I may find down there.

People came in and out of the large gate as I approached, carrying various things in baskets. The gate itself was huge, with a lookout perched on top.

Everyone paused as my hood slipped back, letting my hair spill free. Gasps arose from the villagers. Voices shouted in a language I barely recognised. Guards poured out, spears and axes glinting in the rapidly disappearing sunlight.

Something was wrong.

I glanced at the people and noticed their clothes. Tunics and woolen dresses, some embroidered and some plain. Hair kept out of their faces in elaborate braids.

"Shit."

I spun and ran, abandoning reason for survival.

I raced for the cover of the trees, stumbling over my own feet, pushing myself further than I'd ever pushed myself before. Exhausted and hurting, I propelled myself into the tree line.

Branches tore at my jacket as I raced through the canopy of birch and spruce trees. I was in their world, and they knew every corner of it. My lungs burned, my legs threatened to collapse. Arrows whistled past. One lodged in a tree mere inches from my head.

Pain flared in my ribs as I tripped on a root, tumbling down a slope. Leaves, pine needles, rocks–everything hurt. But I didn't stop.

My throat burned, a metallic taste filling my mouth, and my heart beat so fast that I swore it was going to explode out of my chest. A painful pulse throbbed at my temples as something shifted underneath my skin.

Rain battered down in sheets now, drenching me as I tried to find the will to keep moving. I needed somewhere to hide. I scanned the area until I found an alcove in the embankment. Half crawling, half scrambling, I reached it. Footsteps halted nearby. Voices in a foreign, yet familiar, tongue—words like *andskoti* and *handtaka*.

Enemy and capture.

The scent of dampened earth infiltrated my senses as I tried to breathe quietly. In the distance I could hear birds crying out. Raven's perhaps. It sounded like they were alerting them to where I was hiding. Maybe they were mocking me.

I stilled, waiting for the party to give up and leave. Each moment left my heart beating so loud that I swore they were going to hear it. That they could feel it radiating through the earth. But, the footsteps began to recede, and I slumped in exhaustion and gratefulness.

I thought that I was going to be a goner, that they would have killed me, but now I was reeling, my mind was running wild with the different possibilities of what could have happened had I not found this small spot.

When I was certain that I was alone again, I crawled out of the alcove and took a deep breath. The first real one since I'd crawled in there, when the threat of my head was still great. I stared at the embankment that I had fallen down and cursed softly, I was not getting back up that way.

I looked around, scanning my surroundings as I tried to find where I could go next. The cold bit into my skin, the rain soaking me to my bones. Pine and disturbed earth were the only things I could smell.

I jolted as a rustling from behind scared me. I turned to see a man, dressed in a tunic with a leather vest. He stared at me curiously. Pointing to my hair, and softly speaking, "*Stormborinn.*"

His voice was filled with a soft kind of wonder, almost like he was in awe of me standing before him. But that couldn't be right. I tried to recall some of the Norse languages I'd learnt.

"Hvar er ek?" I asked him. *Where am I?*

I kept my eyes on him, narrowed in fascination.

"Hayhjem," he answered before everything went dark.

CHAPTER TWO
ALURA

V oices echoed around me like broken pieces that didn't belong to me. Too close, too warped, like echoes rebounding off of cave walls. They promised me things I didn't want to hear. Things that made no sense. My head throbbed, a sharp pain radiated from the base of my skull as if someone had hit me there. I tried to move, but my wrists screamed as something coarse dug into my raw skin.

Panic surged. My eyes flew open.

I was lying on a straw-stuffed sack that scratched at my skin beneath my clothes. The air was thick with damp earth and mold, the scent of smoke lingering like a fire was burning nearby. Shadows clung to every corner, and when I moved, I felt the chilled air seeping through my clothes and into my bones.

A cell.

My breath came in ragged gasps. My logical brain tried to reject this, to rewrite what was happening into a dream.

A field trip gone wrong. Anything but this. But the roughness of the rope, the biting cold, the ache in my head–all of this cemented that this was real.

I pushed myself upright, wrists bound awkwardly before me, and blinked at the heavy wooden door. A lock glinted dully in the flickering torchlight beyond. Somewhere in the hallway outside, voices carried.

Captured. Prisoner. Death.

I caught the words. Just fragments of things I'd studied for years. In my spare time, in university. No one should speak Old Norse fluently anymore. And yet, here it was, alive, surrounding me, and being whispered like a curse I was forced to bear.

Surely this was a psychotic break. My mind was playing tricks on me. Maybe I'd finally broken under the pressure of it all. The fieldwork, the storm, the isolation. It was the logical explanation. And yet...it didn't feel like madness. It felt real.

I struggled against the rope, twisting my wrists, trying to find the slack. The more I fought, the deeper the fibers bit into my skin. I hissed in pain, slamming my bound hands against my knees in frustration.

"Shit!" My voice cracked against the stone.

The cell gave nothing back except silence, and the slow drip of water somewhere in the dark. I swore the shadows bent closer, as if answering my fury.

I forced myself to breathe, slow and steady.

Survival first. Panic later.

Exhausted, defeated, and frustrated, I lay back down with tears spilling from my eyes, while I tried to make out more of the words floating from down the hall. I don't know how long I laid like that, cold and shivering while trying to make out faint words.

I'd heard mention of Thor and Odin, which left me wondering where I was.

Who were these people?

I became lost in a vortex of swirling thoughts, trying to make out more words, trying to gain knowledge that would help me survive this.

A voice grunted at me. I glanced toward the cell door, seeing a man standing there in a plain tunic and breeches. "*Stattu upp*," he grunted at me again.

I could just stay here. I could stay lying down and refuse to move, but I wanted to live. I didn't want to anger them, especially because I didn't know who these people were or what they're capable of. But I had an idea.

I got up and walked over to the door that he unlocked quickly, grabbing me by my elbow, and half dragging me down the corridor until it opened into a large space that was filled with people.

The great hall reeked of smoke and sweat, the tang of spilled mead mixing with the salt of sea-worn furs that hung along the beams. Torches flickered in their sconces. Long tables spanned the length of the hall, groaning beneath lavish spreads of food–not just what was needed to sate hunger, but mountains of roasted meats, cheese stacked high as shields, and bowls of fruit imported from warmer shores where snow never touched the ground. Candles sat atop the tables in clusters, their wax bleeding down the ornate holders fashioned into the shapes of serpents and beasts.

The sheer abundance seemed less meant for feasting and more for flaunting.

Fire pits blazed down the centre of the space, their warmth mingling with the stench of grease. Hides of rare animals were strewn carelessly across benches and the floor, their pelts too fine to be trampled by boots yet threadbare from neglect.

A dais stood at the far end, where two thrones loomed. Not mere chairs, but carved monuments of dark, heavy wood, their backs lined with knotwork so elaborate it seemed no mortal hand should have the patience for it. Gold had been set into the grooves, catching every flicker of firelight. High above them were carved ravens, with jewels set into their eyes, probably meant to represent Odin's. Furs of white bear and black wolf lined the seats, and behind them hung a massive tapestry, the threads thick, dyed in pigments expensive enough to feed an entire village. They depicted a snake coiling endlessly around itself, devouring its own tail.

From a side passage, two people emerged. One, a woman, with dark brown hair that was twisted up into several intricate braids that fell down her back, strung with beads of silver and amber. Her face was pinched, her eyes cold and cruel as she looked over me with disinterest. Her clothing was finely made, with bold colours and intricate designs, the hems heavy with golden embroidery.

The other, a man, with long dark hair that was starting to turn grey. It was not braided or worn in any way that showed he needed it off his face. His beard, however, was braided into a single braid bound with a gilded cuff. His tunic stretched over his middle, its fabric woven with patterns that only the richest traders could have brought from distant shores. He looked to be in his fifties, either proof of surviving many battles, or of avoiding them entirely.

A King and his Queen.

"Velkominn," the man shouted across the silent space. *Welcome.*

The word clicked into place in my mind like a key sliding home into a forgotten lock.

Velkominn. I had read it once, scrawled it in the margins of a textbook when I had been slaving over written evidence with Professor Haldor. He'd tapped the word with his finger, leaned in close, and murmured the syllables slowly, his deep voice curling around the sounds until I had whispered them back.

"Good," Professor Haldor had said, lips turning upward as his eyes lingered too long. "Again."

I had flushed, stammering through it a second time, his approving wink had made me burn hotter than the fire in this room.

And now—here, across this strange space—the sound lived. Not just ink on a page, not just the ghost of a memory, but a living word, shouted in a tongue I should not have known, and yet did.

The King began to speak again and I only caught certain phrases and words, my mind having to work twice as hard to translate everything. The King asked for others to come forward and speak. I noticed the man who'd spoken to me before I'd blacked out.

Though I was not confident in what he was saying, I'm pretty sure he said something along the lines of *'she has the right to be here.'*

That wasn't a popular sentiment.

An uproar erupted from across the room and people shouted words like *'witch'* and *'death,'* but threaded in were other words I knew well–*coin, price, slave.* Voices rose above each other until the whole room began to sound more like a battlefield, not calling for blood, but for profit.

"She is rare!" One man shouted. "Look at her eyes. Like no woman of our lands. Foreign blood fetches a high price!"

"A thrall like her could buy us three ships," added another.

The word *ships* lodged in my chest. They weren't talking about me as though I were a woman standing before them, but as though I were cattle on display, my worth measured in what could be traded in my place.

I was still held firmly by my elbow, not giving me a chance to escape, to get lost in the chaos as fist fights began to break out around the room. I wanted to shrink back, to melt into the shadows along the borders.

The King frowned, his forehead wrinkled as he pinched the bridge of his nose. His wife, who sat beside him, revelled in the chaos that was brewing. I wondered just for a second if things were so boring around here that perhaps this was entertainment for her. She enjoyed this, watching people fight over scraps of power and possession.

The King flicked his hand, almost lazily, and one of his guards stepped forward. For a heartbeat I thought the man who had spoken for me might be spared. Then steel rasped free, a blur of motion–

The blade punched through his chest.

The sound was worse than the sight of it. A wet gasp, a choke as his body bowed around the steel. His eyes went wide, shocked as if he couldn't quite believe what had been done to him as he locked them on mine.

A ragged shriek tore out of me before I even realized why I was screaming. My stomach dropped so violently it felt like the ground had given way beneath me. I couldn't stop staring, couldn't look away from the blood spilling dark and heavy down his tunic.

He had stood for me–for me–and they had cut him down like he was nothing.

The guard yanked his blade free with a wet rip, and the man crumbled, a sack of meat collapsing at the King's feet.

My vision blurred, my ears roared. This was the truth of this place I had been dragged into. Here, defiance wasn't argued against. It was butchered.

And the King sat above it all, smug, certain, basking in the power of knowing no one would dare raise their voice again.

The room descended into silence once again. The King's wife–displeased with the room's sudden disappearance of entertainment–whispered something to her husband. I stared at her curiously, watched as she tapped her fingers on the carved arm of her throne.

As if she could feel me watching her, her head swivelled, bird-like and unsettling, and her cruel gaze landed on me. Our eyes met in a clash of fury.

I refused to break contact first. I tried to have a look of defiance on my face, to show her that I wasn't afraid. But I was. I think I just came off as stupid instead.

Her gaze snapped back to the body on the floor and she ordered someone to clean up the mess. Two men stepped forward wearing plain tunics and pants. Slaves.

They dragged his body out, the sick sound of him sliding away left my mind reeling.

I was in danger.

I tried harder to listen into the discussion, to decipher the words that were being spoken. I wasn't stupid, I'd trained for this and studied for hours upon hours. In my spare time, in the university libraries. I'd studied this language and although I rarely used it, I knew the knowledge was inside me somewhere.

Another man stepped forward and I tried harder to make out what he was saying. "Her kind are dangerous, she cannot live."

A woman stepped forward next, her brown hair loose around her shoulders as she glanced at me cautiously. "If she had any magic, she would have used it already. Numbers are dwindling. We need more thralls. Look at her, she will fetch twice the gold of a common one."

Slaves.

I wasn't just a prisoner. I was a commodity.

They were talking about selling me into slavery. It was a better option than death, but barely. Being held captive would give me time to find a way out. It would give me time to work on some kind of plan...if I lived long enough. I knew how slaves were treated and it was not with kindness.

There were different levels to slavery of course. I could be sold into prostitution given my unique looks. I could be sent to a farm, forced to work under the sweltering sun in the fields or domestic chores. But the worst kind would be to work for the King himself. To work under the man who's keeping me captive. None of that was even including if I got sold to foreigners.

The King was beginning to grow tired of the commotion. He stood from his throne, raising his hands to silence the chatter once again.

"My people," he began, a smirk written across his face. "You are right, she has no power so cannot be a witch. But she is rare. Useful." His smile spread, turning predatory. "Better to give her as a gift. To the Shamed One. Let her deformity earn his loyalty."

Cheers erupted throughout the room. I could make out the distinct rhythmic sound of stomping feet echoing out. I couldn't help but to breathe out a sigh of relief that I wouldn't be put to death.

"Do not feel so relieved so soon, *Stormborinn*. The Shamed One is as cruel as he is unforgiving. Death would have been a mercy." The man holding onto me bristled, his voice low enough that no one except me could hear him.

"What?" I asked.

"You will find out soon enough."

CHAPTER THREE

ALURA

I was marched back to my cell as the hall began to clear out. My guard made no further attempt to speak to me and the longer the silence stretched, the more I thought about what it was that he had told me.

Once I was safely locked back in the damp cell, I tried to formulate a plan to get out of here. Perhaps if I could manage to escape, then I could find my way back home. I just needed to make it back to that clearing. At the very least I would die a free woman instead of a slave for some weird cult.

I checked every nook and cranny, trying to find some way out. The floor was compacted dirt and, without something to dig with, I would break my fingers before managing something big enough to poke my head out of. The lock that kept the door inaccessible needed a key and there was no way I'd even be able to attempt to pick the lock. None of the walls had any loose spots that I could try and take advantage of either.

I wasn't getting out until somebody let me out.

I was defenseless, alone and cold.

I sat, defeated, against the back wall and glared at the cell door that separated me from my potential freedom–or my potential demise. Dying whilst attempting to gain my freedom would be better than just sitting here and waiting for my inevitable fate.

It might have been hours or minutes before the King arrived. He appeared on the other side of the door, peering his face through the small slats. He wore a cocky grin, in the way a serpent would smile if it could. He opened the door and stood before me, unworried. I was no threat to him, and he knew it.

"You should be thanking me." His gaze turns hard as his eyes raked over my body, making me shiver in disgust, heat flared inside me as my anger grew.

"I should...what?"

"Thank me." We stared at each other for a second before I shook my head in disbelief. "I could have killed you. I could have made you a concubine. Yet, I let you live and stay untouched. Do you not wonder why?"

My throat tightened. He already looked at me like I was a prized horse, and I hated the answer before he gave it.

His grin sharpened. "Because you are worth more un-spoiled. A rare prize must not be tattered. Men would throw away their coins for a woman like you. Your eyes, that strange look of yours. You are no common thrall, girl. You are coin walking and breathing."

"I...know," I say through gritted teeth, my language skills were rusty, though I was getting better every day I stayed in this cursed place.

"What is your name?" He asked me.

The question made my stomach twist. Not because of the words themselves, but because of the way he said them. He knew it was not a question at all, but a command. It's like he already knew the answer, and he was only waiting for me to hand it to him, to give him a piece of myself to claim.

I pressed my lips together. I didn't want to give him that.

His grin sharpened. "Ah. Silence. You think that protects you?" He leaned closer, close enough that I caught a whiff of his scent. Wine and smoke, hanging off his breath. "I will have it from you eventually. Your name. Your loyalty. Perhaps even your heart, if I wish it. Even if I need to cut it out of you myself."

"Open me," I said. "You will get nothing from me."

The laughter that burst from him chilled my blood. It was soft, not cruel. Amused. Like he was chuckling over a child who'd fallen over their own feet. The sound rattled through me, stirring something deeper—something sharp that drummed against my ribs like a caged storm.

"Girl," he said at last, tilting his head. "Do you think I speak in jests? You are alive because I allow it. You are unsullied because I wish it. I could end your life with a word, and yet here you stand, breathing."

My jaw clenched, but I forced myself to not look away. The air between us prickled, fine as static, though I could not tell if he felt it. I whispered, "Why?"

His grin faded into something sharper, more calculated, like a blade's edge. "Because you are more valuable to me alive. Not only valuable, but *profitable.* Why kill you when I can trade you? Why break you when I can parade you? I will give you to the Shamed One. And in return you will make him loyal to me, or kill him. That is the worth of you."

"Why?" I asked again.

"He is doing something in those mountains. I am sure of it. Plotting against me. Trying to take my throne. I send scouts and their heads are sent back to me, but I have no proof if it is his doing or the spirit's haunting the mountains and forests. His people won't talk no matter how they are tortured. And I am growing impatient."

His grin widened again, cruelly. "If he does not want you, then I will keep you. You will bow and serve and make me richer for it. Your beauty alone is enough of a prize. A treasure Kings kill for. And so, I offer you a choice."

He spread his arms, almost generously. "Bow to me. Pledge yourself. Your power, your silence, your obedience and loyalty. Do this, and you will live. More than live, perhaps. You will thrive. You will be seen as favoured." His voice lowered, turning silky yet venomous. "Refuse me and I will not just kill you. I will make you watch as I break the innocents one by one until you beg."

My palms burned with heat, though I haven't moved them. My skin buzzed like something was searching for release. The walls seem to close in, pressing against my chest. He had wrapped his threat in choice. But I saw it for what it was. A leash. A noose.

"You think he..." I thought for a moment. "...will trust me?" I asked.

"You are an outsider. No one will think you are strong enough to be a spy, smart enough. You barely speak our language."

"I–" The word cracked out of me sharper than I intended- ed, and the air seemed to shiver. His eyes flickered, but he said nothing.

"Choose wisely," he said, stepping back with a mock bow, his grin returning. "I can be a generous King. Or a merciless one."

The King's voice lingered long after his footsteps had faded.

Choose. Choose wisely.

The words etched themselves inside me as if they were carved there. No matter how I turned them over, they remained sharp, impossible to twist.

I sat alone in the cold cell, my hands still knotted in my lap, knuckles white. The brazier's fire had burned low, and the shadows it threw against the walls twisted like reaching hands. I wanted to rise, to scream, but I felt heavy. As if I were rooted.

I thought of the Shamed One.

I had not seen him, not met him. I only heard the whispers. Slaves with downturned eyes, voices lowered to hushed warnings as they slipped passed.

"Best not to look too long," one had muttered. Another had sworn he was not even a man anymore, but something else. More man than beast. Kinslayer had been thrown around more than once.

I tried to tell myself they were just cruel rumours.

I pressed my palms to my eyes until sparks of colour burst behind them. Breathe, I told myself. Just breathe.

But each breath tasted of iron and smoke.

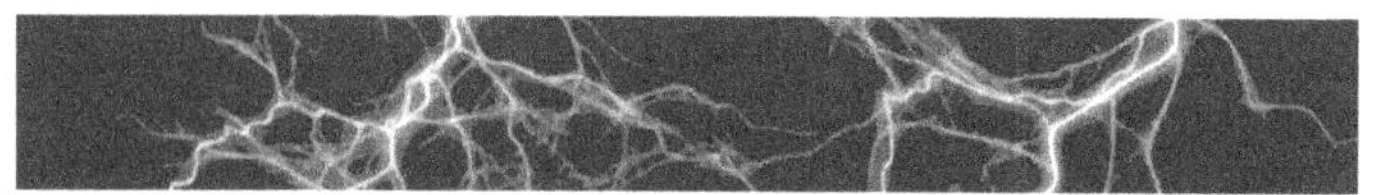

The next few days passed in a haze that felt both endless and too short. I was not summoned, not touched, not spoken to. Yet the King's presence was everywhere. The guard's eyes lingered too long on me. The slaves that brought me food placed it down quickly and scurried away, as if afraid of being seen in my company.

I was left in silence, sentenced to my own thoughts, the cruelest of companions. I tried to not think of freedom, the word itself feeling more like a trap. Like bait being dangled in front of me.

Yet it was there. A choice. He had given me a choice.

But what choice was that? Accept his offer, become his instrument—or refuse and be broken.

One night, sleepless and raw, I found myself whispering into the dark, "Would it not be better to die?"

My voice cracked on the last word, shame washing over me.

Only silence answered.

On the fourth day, they came for me. Two guards escorted me through a narrow passage I had never walked before. The air grew colder with each step. Each breath clouded in front of me, though I swore the chill was sharper around me than them.

When the door opened, I smelled the iron tang of blood before I saw it. There, strung up from the rafters was a man no older than twenty. His body was bent, twisted as though bones had been broken. His hair hung filthy and caked in blood. His eyes...gods his eyes, they burned with hatred when he saw me.

I stumbled backward, colliding with the guards. They did not move to steady me, only shoved me forward again. The jolt sent a pulse through me, and for a heartbeat the torchlight guttered, shadows flaring long along the walls.

The King stepped into the light, and I hated how he looked at me. Like this was going to be what broke me. This was going to be what made me agree to his cruel and twisted offer.

"Do you understand, girl?" His eyes glittered. "I offer you more than life. Refuse..." He gestured toward the man strung up. The man whimpered like a wounded animal. "...and you will envy him."

I couldn't speak. My tongue felt heavy, the air thick in my throat, as though the air itself waited on my answer.

"What will it be?"

I nodded, unable to speak, the lump in my throat difficult to swallow. "Yes."

"Your name," He demanded, the word not coming out as a request, but as a man demanding ownership.

"Alura."

The King smiled. "Perfect. Alura, you depart tomorrow."

That night I couldn't eat. I couldn't drink. I curled on the straw filled sack, drawing my knees to my chest and stared at the stones until my vision blurred.

Freedom. Chains. Leash. Noose.

They circled me like carrion birds. And with each word, I thought I heard the faint crack of thunder, muffled, distant, like it was stalking the edges of my mind.

When I did finally sleep, it was no mercy.

I dreamed of a storm. The sky splitting with lightning, the waves of the ocean rising in tall towers. The wind tore at me, but I did not fall. It lifted me, held me, as if it knew me.

And there, on the cliff's edge, a wolf stood. Its fur as dark as midnight, its eyes a burning green.

It did not move toward me, just stared at me steady and unyielding.

"*You are not his,*" an ethereal voice whispered.

The wolf lifted its head and howled. The sound tearing apart the storm, scattering the darkness.

For a moment, I felt it. The echo of something wild, a promise older than the King's throne. It rushed through me like lightning through metal, leaving my skin tingling as I jolted awake.

CHAPTER FOUR
SKÚLI

Being called out to Hayhjem was more than just an insult. It was King Skargrim Vornirsson telling me—and everyone else—that he had power over me, that I needed to heed his call.

For now at least.

It was a three day ride if I pushed my horse, closer to five if the weather turned. Dreki Pass was dangerous even at the height of summer. As winter crept closer, it became treacherous. The mountains surrounding my home stood far taller than almost any other range on the continent. They were a natural defence, the reason why my ancestors had settled there. Enemies had only two choices: brave the pass or attempt to row ashore through the inlet. Either option led almost certainly to death. It had taken nearly a hundred winters before Drakensvar finally fell into enemy hands.

Surprisingly the ride was quite enjoyable—if only because the King's men were not at my back. This time, I was spared their cruel jests and the weight of their leering gazes. The journey through the pass was uneventful despite the handful of lizards that tried to run between my horse's feet.

I was pretty sure he crushed one or two.

I made camp on the other side of the pass, hobbling my horse so he did not wander too far in search of green grass—what little remained of it. Sitting around the fire on my bed roll, I fed small sticks into the meagre flames.

Morning came swiftly. I packed up quickly, continuing on. We stopped by a lake that night, watering my horse and stretching my legs. I washed as best I could, though my thoughts were elsewhere.

A nearby village greeted me with cold stares, as expected. The last time I'd passed through here, I had accidentally burned down the tavern during a brawl. Not my fault, really. My reputation preceded me, and nothing I did would change their minds.

At least back home, I had my people. They knew me. Even disgraced, I was welcome in their homes. Treated like family. I would never be able to repay that kindness.

The final day was the climb from the lake to Hayhjem. Half the journey was a steep incline, but my horse was built for it.His coat as black as my own hair with white feathering along his legs, compact and muscular with endurance for long rides. We had an understanding: he took care of me, and I took care of him.

As I reached Hayhjem's gates, the guards were stoic, rigid, watching my every move and waiting for a reason to execute me on the spot. I gave them none. I was used to this—the way they shuddered as I rode past, the scrutiny, the expectation that I would falter underneath it all.

All eyes followed me as the city fell quiet.

One of the lessons my father taught me when I was very young was this: give your enemy an opportunity, and they will seize it without hesitation.

I kept my head high, carrying myself like everyone here was beneath me—which was not difficult. They called me the Shamed One, but it is they who were steeped with shame. They had cast aside the gods that once kept this land flowing with magic and warmth. It was why their summers had been growing shorter with every generation, why their fields struggled to yield enough to sustain their people.

Drakensvar had no such issue.

From the corners of the streets, I glimpsed the truths no one dared mention aloud. Children with hollow cheeks, ribs pressing beneath tunics too small. Women hauling water from wells with trembling arms. The sick and aged leaning heavily on walking sticks to make their way home.

And yet, the great hall loomed as though it belonged to another world entirely.

The stench of wealth hit me before I had even entered. Furs, scented oils, roasting meats and candles so plentiful their smoke curled in spirals above the heads of the people inside. Torches burned bright along the walls, glinting off the gilded vessels stacked high with wine and mead. I could see it, every extravagance displayed to showcase the king's indulgence while the people starved within the stone walls.

It was not until I stopped just outside the great hall–one of the smallest I had seen–and dismounted my horse that I felt a small pang of worry.

Usually, Skargrim summoned me every six moons or so, just to remind me of my place. It never unsettled me in the way he intended; it merely pulled me from work back home that mattered. This was different though. I had stood in this hall barely two moons ago. To be summoned so soon meant something had changed.

Something dangerous brewed behind these walls.

A thrall came forward, dressed in his undyed tunic and pants, a simple cloak pinned at his shoulder. He gave me a warm smile. "I will take your horse."

I handed over the reins reluctantly, watching as he led my horse away, whispering something in his ear that made him snort. A small kindness—a reminder that even in a city built on greed, compassion endured.

They were not all monsters here.

Inside, the hall revealed itself fully. Skargrim's great hall was a dragon's hoard of indulgence. Long tables bearing platters of roasted meat, stacks of bread, and vessels of mead that would keep a village fed for a week. Candles flickered, furs lining every chair. Jars of honey gleamed in torchlight, shining like captured sunlight.

The King sat atop this stage of greed, smirking as if every indulgence before me were mine to envy.

Walking past them all, I heard only the crackling of the fire in the pits. It was eerily quiet, but as my eyes scanned the hall, I could not ignore the truth. People outside were starving while this room overflowed with the blood of their labour. This display was meant to remind me of the cost of defiance.

Instead, it only stoked the fire of fury within me.

I stopped before the dais.

Skargrim's gaze followed me like a predator studying its prey. He looked triumphant, though I could not tell what he thought he had won.

We remained silent.

He waited for me to kneel, and when it became clear I would not, he huffed in disapproval.

Footsteps shuffled behind me, the space filled with on-lookers, eager to witness either my humiliation or punishment.

"Welcome back, Skúli Ulfsson," Skargrim said, his voice dripping with condescension.

"Thank you for having me," I replied, my tone edged with deliberate arrogance.

"I have called you here to bridge the divide between us. Just because I have stripped you of your title and seized your lands does not mean we must remain enemies."

I arched a brow. "What do you want? Or did you just summon me here to gloat?"

He laughed, it was a hacking, breathless sound. "A gift."

"A gift?" I asked, suspicion sharpening my tone.

My mind ran wild with all manner of cruelties he could inflict upon me. An exotic venomous serpent, perhaps to see how long I could hold it with my bare hands before it struck. Maybe it was a bucket of shit, I had seen that one before.

One of his men disappeared, returning moments later, half-dragging a figure towards us. My gaze followed, and I stilled, caught between disbelief and a reverence I could not explain.

It was a woman.

Her hands were bound in front of her slight body, thrown at my feet. Silver hair framed the storm brewing in her eyes—grey and blue with flecks of silver catching in the dim light.

She glared up at me, defiance burning despite her position. Yet something about her felt *wrong*. Not because of the fire in her gaze, but the weight behind it—as though she carried something in her chest that wanted to break free.

Old stories stirred at the edges of my mind. There were whispers of only one child ever born with silver hair. Born beneath an eclipse. Hidden away before anyone could reach her.

Skargrim's grin widened as he presented her, like she was a commodity, a rare and valuable piece to flaunt.

"What is that?" I demanded.

"Your new thrall," Skargrim said coldly. "I trust she will be of great use to you."

His gaze lingered on her, like he was appraising a fine horse at a market. He measured her strength, her youth, her spirit. Everything about her was a commodity to him.

I could not refuse. Yet anyone with sense could see what she was. A spy. She was not here to serve me; she was here to watch, to report. And yet...there was a pulse beneath her fear, a current I could not ignore, like the air itself stirred when she moved.

"Thank me," Skargrim prompted.

"Why should I?" I crossed my arms, looking down at her. I could smell the fear beneath her rage. "You know our stance on thralls in Drakensvar."

"I think it is time you rejoin the rest of the world. She is yours now. Perhaps she could help you expand your farming so that you can pay your taxes."

Offended, I scoffed. "We always pay taxes. Even to a usurper."

"I am raising them. And I want more than gold." His smile was thin. "Bring her back so I may see her progress in one moon." *Fucking asshole.*

"Thank you," I ground out between gritted teeth.

Skargrim waved me away, eager to see me leave..

I crouched beside the woman, extending a hand.

"No," she snapped, recoiling.

"No?" I raised an eyebrow at her. She was a small thing. "Get up."

Reluctantly, she obeyed, following me out of the hall where my horse awaited. Each step past the lavish display of excess and toward the gates hardened my resolve. Skargrim would never understand true strength. Greed blinded a man to the cost of what they hoarded.

I wanted to reassure the woman—to promise safety—but there were eyes and ears everywhere, and the clothes she wore marked her as an outsider. Still, every step she took carried a rhythm that made the air feel taut, like a bowstring drawn tight.

I could not shake the thought that she was unlike anyone I had ever met.

Behind me someone spat the word *Kinslayer.*

I did not falter.

She eyed the horse nervously, and I chuckled.

"No," she repeated, then almost childlike and broken, "I...can walk."

She spoke our language poorly, but it was something. I had no intention of befriending her—but letting her suffer under my watch would only hard Skargrim another weapon.

Even so, I found myself studying her as if she were a puzzle I was not sure I wished to solve. There was a weight in her gaze, as if she were carrying something the rest of the world had forgotten.

"You need to get on. Let me help you. It is too far to walk and we have a few days to ride to get there."

I laced my fingers together and got down onto one knee. Reluctantly, she hoisted herself up and got on, looking uncomfortable and unsteady. Her closeness prickled something in me—not fear, not desire, but recognition.

A thread of fate, fragile and undeniable.

I swung up behind her, pulling her close as I took the reins. Her back pressed into my front, hair brushed my face, and the hairs on my neck rose like we were in a storm.

We began to depart, but not before the thrall whispered a final goodbye. "Farwell for now, Storm-Born."

CHAPTER FIVE
ALURA

S *torm-Born.*

The name echoed on the wind, carried on gusts sharp enough to cut me to the bone. I was barefoot, my toes curled against the jagged cliff, skin stinging in the icy air. Snow spiraled around me in silver flakes, clinging to the thin linen dress that hung from my shoulders. The cold bit at me through the fabric sharply, and still I couldn't move.

"It's just a dream," I whispered, though the words dissolved the second they left my mouth. "Just another dream."

I'd been having them—these dreams—all my life. Echoes of something both achingly familiar and utterly foreign. Maybe I didn't belong to whatever place this was, but I felt its pull all the same..

The cliffs plunged into nothingness. If I fell, the rocks below would claim me–if I was lucky. If not, the sea would swallow me whole, breaking me against itself, and leaving me floating nameless amongst the waves.

I wrapped my arms around myself, trying to rub warmth into my frozen skin, but it was futile. The sun was sinking, slipping behind distant cliffs, yet the world refused to turn dark. The sky hung suspended, streaked in pinks and purples. Like time itself was caught in the same dream.

A sudden gust struck me hard enough to drive me to my knees, nearly shoving me over the edge. My hair whipped around my face, stinging my cheeks. My heart hammered, desperate to tear free of my ribs.

Then there was music.

Low, at first, only a murmur. Then, a rhythm—pulsing like blood through the cracks in stones. A chant. Voices in unison. The sound weaved itself through the storm, through the marrow of my bones, and called me to it. I strained to listen, but the words blurred, slipping out of my grasp.

Lightning raked across the frozen sky. It didn't strike with thunder, but with intention, carving luminous runes into the clouds. Symbols burning bright, ancient, before vanishing in the same breath.

"Storm-Born."

The voice was clear now. Feminine. Ethereal.

Too close. Too far.

"You came home. But you are not safe yet." My throat tightened.

"What do you mean?" I cried out. "I don't have a home!"

"You have always had a home, Storm-Born. It is here. With us."

"Who is *us*?"

There was no answer. Only the relentless wind. The endless chanting. My fists clenched. None of this made sense. I didn't have a home. I had been abandoned—left with nothing more than a blanket wrapped around my body, discarded on the shore to die with the tide.

"Not discarded," the voice breathed, cutting through my thoughts. *"Saved."*

A sob lodged in my throat, but I swallowed it back, shaking my head. This was a dream. A trick. My mind was trying to weave meaning out of madness. I was a graduate, for gods' sake. I was supposed to be writing my master's thesis, not thrown back in time, slipping into visions where the sky carves itself in runes and ghostly voices tried to tell me who I am.

"Not back in time."

I froze. "What?"

"Elsewhere. The answer you seek lie with the last Ulfhed-nar."

Wolf Warrior.

The words struck me like a lightning strike.

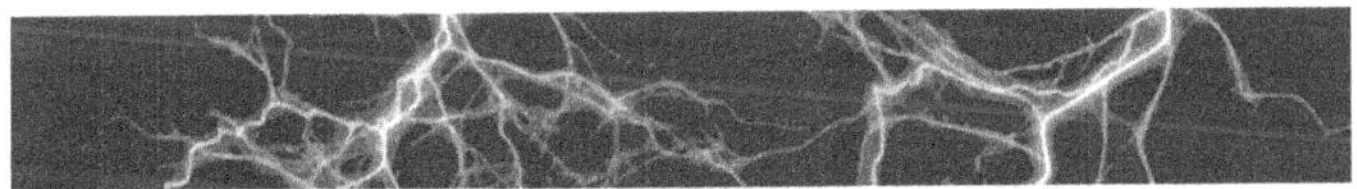

I woke with a gasp, lungs heaving, my skin slick with sweat despite the freezing air. Frost burned my cheek. I drew my jacket tighter under the furs that were draped over me.

The night air felt charged, the air humming faintly, like the remnants of a storm that had lingered too long. My breath fogged in unevenly, and for a moment, the fire's flames flickered violently.

I rubbed my arms, telling myself it was only nerves, but the hair on my arms stood on end—as if something unseen had brushed past me.

Across the fire, Skúli's eyes caught mine.

The embers between us popped and hissed, sending a thin coil of smoke into the pre-dawn dark. Beyond the fire's light, the woods pressed close, too silent. Too watchful.

"Bad dream?" His voice was low, roughened by the fire smoke.

I swallowed, forcing my heartbeat to slow, my skin still prickling. The voice's words echoed in me still, gnawing at my last bit of reason.

The answers you seek lie with the Wolf Warrior.

I didn't know if I could trust it.

I didn't know if I had a choice.

"Yes," I said finally, my voice hoarse.

Silence stretched between us. His gaze dropped back to the embers, unreadable. I couldn't look away. Some of it was mistrust–I'd been a fool to sleep unguarded near him–but part of it was something else entirely.

Something far more dangerous.

His hair caught the faint glow of the firelight, black with red undertones, braided neatly down his back. The fur cloak draped over his shoulder made him look half-wolf, half-shadow. Black tunic. Leather chest plate. Tattoos ghosted across his arms from beneath his sleeves. And his weapons–twin scabbards crossed over his back, an axe strapped to his waist.

He was built like a man who had known battle more intimately than peace.

He looked older than me, but not by much. Early thirties, perhaps, though the hard lines of his brow made him seem carved by years heavier than his age. His skin was bronzed from sun or sea, his body strong, and when his eyes lifted back to mine, the fire turned them to amber.

Something in me faltered.

Melted.

I hated it.

"Can I ask you something?" I said quietly.

He grunted—something between permission and irritation.

"Where are we going?"

"Drakensvar."

"Is...is it nice?"

He sighed. His gaze travelled the length of me, lingering just long enough for him to tighten his jaw before he looked away.

"It is the most beautiful place I have ever seen," he said at last. Then, sharper, as though he regretted speaking to me at all, "Get some sleep."

I must have looked too long.

"Has no one told you that staring is rude?" He added, mocking.

Heat crept up my neck. I ignored it. "What is your name?"

For a moment, I thought he wouldn't answer.

"Skúli."

Shield. Too fitting.

"Skúli," I repeated.

He nodded once.

"Drakensvar," I said quietly, testing the word.

His shoulders lifted in a shrug, as though that explained everything.

It didn't.

Nothing about him explained anything. He kept his words clipped, his thoughts locked behind his guarded expression. Four days on the road and all I knew was that he disliked people—and he disliked me. Every villager we passed spat at his feet or turned their eyes away. Every night he refused to sleep, blades always within reach, as though he daring me to try my luck against them.

Maybe he was right not to trust me. One day, the King would likely order me to kill him.

I wasn't sure yet whether I'd obey.

It would be a shame, though. He was too beautiful for an ugly death. The scar on his lip. Freckles across his skin. Those high, cruel cheekbones. He looked like something claimed by the gods themselves.

Untouchable.

I wondered if he had a wife. Someone who braided his hair for him. Someone who saw a softness in him that he refused to show the rest of the world.

I scolded myself for the thought.

"You should sleep," he said suddenly. Quiet, but not gentle—a command disguised as advice. I scowled but before I could argue, his eyes rolled. "Sleep."

I lay back down, grumbling under my breath.

If I had to spend another four days with him, I'd happily throw myself off the nearest cliff. And judging by the mountains surrounding us, there were no shortage of those.

The pass loomed ahead. We would cross it tomorrow.

I drifted into uneasy sleep, wondering what waited on the other side.

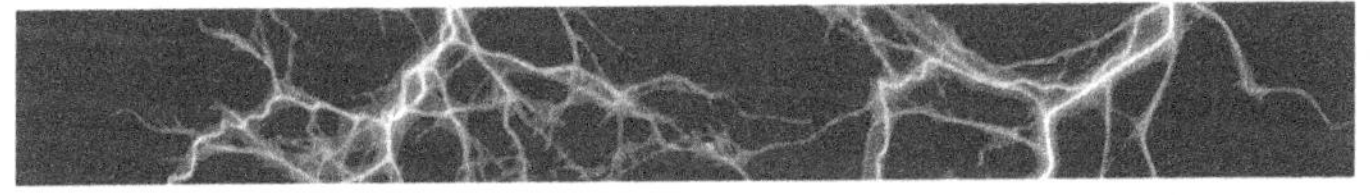

I woke up to hands on me. Shaking. Pulling.

Before I could draw a breath to scream, I was shoved out of my bedroll. Cold slammed into me as I stumbled upright to see Skúli already on his feet, blades gleaming in each hand.

"Get behind me," he muttered, eyes locked on the dark.

"Do not tell me...what to—," I hissed.

The sound that followed silenced me.

A growl. Low. Deep enough to almost vibrate the ground beneath us.

"Just fucking get behind me," he snapped.

I obeyed, my throat dry as stone.

Then I saw it.

"Is that a bear?"

He didn't answer.

"That's a *fucking* bear," I said in English.

He glanced at me then, briefly, then turned back to the monster.

It was enormous. Bigger than any bear had a right to be. All ribs and claws, hunger shining in its wild eyes. Its paws alone could crush me flat without effort.

"Do they come this close?" I whispered.

"Shut up," he growled.

The bear huffed, lumbering closer, the firelight catching the sharp gleam of its teeth. Skúli raised both blades, shifting his stance low, balanced. I noticed then the size difference—one sword long, the other half its length. He didn't reach for the axe at his hip.

His body bowed slightly, arms raised, never breaking eye contact. The bear growled again. The sound rattled my bones.

Then—

A snap of twigs behind it.

The bear spun, roaring and a figure darted out of the trees. Hooded. Fast as a shadow. An arrow sang past the bear's shoulder, and in the same breath the figure drew twin draggers, circling with lethal grace.

Skúli glanced back at me—just for a moment. His eyes searched mine, hard and unyielding, as if looking for something. When he didn't find it, he turned away.

"Stay," he muttered, and charged.

What followed was chaos and art all at once.

The hooded stranger and Skúli moved in tandem–like a practiced dance–never speaking, keeping the bear penned. Daggers flashed silver, carving shallow wounds that only enraged it. Skúli's blades struck deeper, controlled, always retreating before the bear's claws could rake him open.

I couldn't look away.

My heart thundered against my ribs, fear mingling with something darker, something that burned just as sharp.

The hooded figure lunged in close, driving one blade into the bear's eye. Blood sprayed, hot and dark. But the beast did not fall. It screamed and turned on them, jaws gaping.

Skúli was faster.

His long blade sank into the beast's shoulder. The shorter sword was thrust up, driving beneath its jaw.

The roar broke into a choking gurgle. The bear staggered once, then collapsed in a shuddering heap.

Silence crashed down around us, heavy as the body at our feet.

The stranger straightened, breath fogging in the cold air. Their hood slipped back with the motion.

First, I saw a tumble of red hair, wild and gleaming in the pale sunrise.

Then I saw the pointed ears.

CHAPTER SIX

ALURA

"Astrid!"

Skúli's voice rang out, sharp in a way I hadn't heard from him before. "Are you hurt?"

His long strides ate up the ground between them, his hands immediately cradling her face like a man checking for cracks in a precious blade. He turned her gently, scanning for wounds.

"I am fine." She shoved him back with a light punch to the shoulder, laughing—but there was steel beneath it. "I was hunting when I saw the bear creeping up on you."

Skúli's jaw flexed. "You were alone beyond the ridges. Alone. You could have been killed, Astrid–" His voice dropped, lower, heavier. The kind of voice you obeyed. "You did not take Björn with you."

Her smile only widened, all teeth. "The deer have left the valley until summer. I needed to find something for the winter stores. Now we have it." She jerked her chin toward the carcass.

Skúli exhaled through his nose and pulled her close, pressing his forehead to hers. For a moment, I felt like an intruder and stepped back, giving them space.

I started to pack up camp the way I've seen Skúli doing it for the last four days. I was slow and clumsy but I managed while they finished their reunion.

Their voices rose and fell in low argument—his protective rumble, hers quick and defiant. From where I knelt I couldn't quite make out the words, only the tone.

She seemed too young for him–ten years, maybe–but there was no heat of lovers between them. The way he touched her was tender, but in the way of family.

I packed clumsily, stealing glances at the pair. Protective. Stern. Indulgent. He listened to her even as she defied him.

When they both looked up at me, I realised I'd been caught staring. I wished the earth would swallow me whole.

They approached together, Astrid laughed at something he murmured before stopping directly in front of me. She crossed her arms, narrowing her eyes as though trying to intimidate me.

"I am Astrid," she said, playful but sharp. "You are?"

"Alura."

She nodded then let out a sharp whistle. Two horses trotted out of the cover of trees that were nearby– neither of them were ours.

"I will tie the bear to the horses and drag it through the pass," she announced to Skúli.

While she busied herself, Skúli took over my–very awkward–packing with efficient ease. When he mounted, he pulled me up in front of him, his arms circling my torso as he gathered the reigns.

He leant down, his breath brushing against my ear. "Hold on, Alura."

The way he said my name made my pulse stutter. I gripped the saddle tighter as the horse surged forward, Astrid trailing behind, her horses dragging the carcass with a steady scrape.

The pass narrowed, the cliffs hemming us in, moss clung to slick stone. The air grew damp and heavy. The sound of hooves echoed off the walls. My stomach knotted at the thought of one misstep sending us tumbling, but the horses moved with a calm precision—as though they'd done this a hundred times before.

"So, Alura," Astrid called from behind us, "what are you doing here?"

I twisted around to answer, but Skúli cut in.

"She was a gift."

The word struck harder than I'd expected. Gift—handed over, owned. My breath caught for a fraction of a second, sharp and humiliating. I hated that my body leaned instinctively into the warmth of his arms even as my chest burned.

"I can speak...for myself," I said, too quickly, stumbling over my words.

Astrid snorted. "You sound like a child. And you are not from here."

It wasn't a question. Just fact.

"She was given as a thrall," Skúli said, bitterness sharpening his words.

Astrid hummed thoughtfully. "We have no use for her," Astrid said lightly. I turned to face her then, she tilted her head, eyes narrowing in thought. "Though..."

Her gaze slid over me, unhurried. Assessing what use I could be.

"I could," she finished. "Will you give her to me?"

Skúli stiffened behind me, his arms unconsciously tightening around my waist. His horse halted and he met Astrid's gaze.

"No."

The word was final.

Astrid muttered something under her breath, but didn't press. We continued through the mist. When the path widened, we stopped to rest.

Astrid began the grisly work of breaking down the bear with efficient precision, her movements sure. The knife flashed in deliberate strokes.

I tried not to watch. And failed.

The smell came first. Warm iron and musk, sharp enough to infiltrate my senses. The sound followed. Wet and grizzly. I swallowed hard, forcing myself to breathe through my nose.

Skúli kept his distance, leading the horses to water.

"Hold this," Astrid said, pressing a cloth bag into my hands.

It was heavier than I expected. Warm. My fingers curled before I could stop myself.

She moved with startling strength and skill, her hair a copper flame against the pale sky, her pointed ears marked her as something else. Something almost ethereal.

She smeared blood across her cheek, laughing at my grimace. "Winter does not care about squeamishness."

I nodded, though my stomach rolled. This wasn't cruelty. It was necessity—and somehow that made it worse.

When she tossed me the rolled hide, I caught it awkwardly.

"Keep it," she said. "Winter is cruel here."

By the time the meat was tied onto a sled that Skúli and Astrid fashioned from branches, I was sore and weary. When Skúli lifted me back onto the horse, I felt his gaze lingering on me.

"Are you alright?" he murmured, voice low.

"I am fine."

"You are sure?"

Before I could answer again, Astrid piped up from behind. "She said she is fine, cousin. Leave her."

Cousin.

The word clicked into place.

I glanced back at him, surprised. "Cousin?"

"Yes," he said simply. "Astrid is my aunt's daughter."

No wonder. The tenderness. The protectiveness. Blood-deep, not romantic.

Skúli offered no more explanation, and I didn't pry him for it. There would be time for that later—I was certain of it.

Mist thickened into drizzle, Astrid swearing colourfully behind us. Skúli urged his horse to go faster, and I watched eagerly as we began the descent of the last part of the pass.

Then the valley opened before us.

My breath caught.

Green stretched wide below, broken by fields of crops and grazing herds. Mountains cradled the land, their snow-tipped peaks carved with terraces where more crops grew. Homes scattered the valley floor, smoke curling from thatched roofs. Karve lined the shore, men and women unloading cargo, children waving from doorways. A boy grinned at me, something small and scaly perched on his shoulder.

This was Drakensvar.

Not the haunted shell whispered of in Hayhjem, not a den of monsters—but a place that was alive with colour, warmth and order.

As we neared the water, I noticed the way the houses were built up on stilts. Others clung higher along the hills. I assumed we were heading towards a house near the shoreline, instead we veered off left toward the mountainside.

We passed under a gate made of iron, stone pillars on either side and a wooden battlement high above us, all guarding a structure carved into the rock itself.

I stared at it, awe stealing my breath for a second.

"What is that?" I whispered.

Skúli's voice was steady and certain.

"Home."

CHAPTER SEVEN
ALURA

The cavernous space was colder than the night air outside. Our footsteps echoed as we entered, dragging the sled behind us. Shadows clung to the carved stone pillars, broken only by a few sputtering sconces along the walls. The hall was vast, with ceilings so high I could hardly see where they ended. Six hearths lined the room, cold and dark, and each breath I took bloomed in a pale fog before vanishing.

At the far end stood two thrones.

Not like the King's in Hayhjem with ravens crowning the backs and gilded finery that screamed for attention. Wolves were carved into one and a dragon into the other. The figures were precise, fierce, and deliberate. They loomed in silence, commanding respect without ornaments or indulgence.

Unlike the King's hall, this one was vast but unpretentious. The walls were sturdy stone, unpainted, showing the natural grains and textures of the rock. Beams of dark wood crossed the ceiling, polished by hands rather than coated in gold or lacquer. The tables were long and simple, solid oak, lined with plates and cutlery that were meant to be *used*, not admired. Furs lined the benches—soft, worn, chosen for warmth and longevity.

There was a quiet order to everything.

Every item had its place. Every carving, every beam, every bowl, spoke of care and tradition. Purpose. The air itself felt different, cleaner, steadier. As if the hall itself respected those who walked its floors. There was no gold to blind, no riches to tempt or corrupt.

This place did not demand awe.

It demanded respect.

Something skittered across the floor–too fast to see clearly. My heart jolted before I forced myself to breathe.

A rat, I told myself. Just a rat.

We took the left doorway and dragged the sled into what must have been the kitchens. Astrid went straight to work, humming softly as she carved the meat with ease. Skúli muttered something about a drink and vanished deeper into the hall.

Useless at butchery, I drifted back to the main chamber.

The vastness pressed in on me now I was alone. This hall was meant to be full of life, of laughter and feasting—yet all I could hear was the hollow echo of my own steps. It made me feel small.

I touched one of the carved pillars. Each bore a face above a small shelf, offerings long since turned to dust. Each an attestment to the craftsmanship that went into carving them. One in particular caught my attention.

A woman's face framed with a woven band, cats at her side, eyes steady but kind.

Freyja.

Walking through here felt nothing like Hayhjem. Where the King's hall throbbed with greed and the unspoken cost of starving mouths, this place breathed balance. Power here was not flaunted. Strength was earned, not bought.

A low growl rumbled behind me.

I spun around, blood rushing, heart hammering.

A wolf stood a few paces away.

Massive. Black. Its eyes glowed an unnatural green, sharp and intelligent. My knees threatened to buckle, but I didn't step back. A strange sensation crept across my skin—a faint, electric awareness. Like we were made of the same thing. The shadows around the two of us seemed to deepen, as though they bent toward us.

It growled again. A warning.

"Björn," a voice commanded. Skúli's. "That is enough."

The wolf lowered its head and padded past me, silently, disappearing toward the kitchen.

My heart didn't slow, instead it raced harder. I felt like I'd just stared down death itself. Shivers ran across my skin, like the air had thickened around us.

My hands shook. "What...was that?"

"My wolf," Skúli said simply, stepping into view. "He is protective of me."

I turned back toward the pillar, forcing myself to breathe, to still my hands. I did not want him to see how close I felt to breaking.

"That is Freyja," he told me.

"I know," I whispered.

His footsteps grew nearer until I could practically feel his presence at my back. For a moment the sconces flickered, though there was no draft. A warm current brushed my skin, almost like something was pulling me toward him.

"Goddess of love, beauty and fertility."

"Yes." His voice was low now, close. I could smell the mead on his breath. "And war and magic."

A pause lingered between us like he was debating his next words. Deliberate. Dangerous.

"And sex."

I turned to face him, heat rushing to my face. "I am not–I cannot."

"I was not offering," he said, a faint smile tugging at his lips.

The air between us tightened, heavy. He broke it, pressing a cup into my hand instead. Honey wine. When our fingers brushed, a small, electric tingle shot up my arm, and the warmth that followed had nothing to do with the drink.

We drank in silence. Somehow, impossible, it felt almost safe.

When I shifted, restless, Skúli noticed immediately. His brow creased and without a word, he led me through the right-hand door, up a carved staircase. The stone hallway above was lined with doors, each marked with an animal. Fox, bear, eagle. We stopped before one etched with a moose. I noticed the door just beside it bore both a dragon and wolf, unusual among the others.

Skúli opened the door, gesturing for me to go inside.
I froze.

A carved bed piled high with furs stood in the centre of the room. Firelight danced over intricate knotwork etched into the walls. Candles flickered on low tables. Food and drink waited by the window.

After cold cells and the hard ground, it felt like a dream.

"You did not have this in Hayhjem," he said, settling into a chair.

"I got the...floor and dagmal." I shook my head, overwhelmed. "This is good."

"It is not much," he said, his voice laced with a stern kindness. "But it is yours."

I sat carefully on the edge of the bed as the words sunk deeper than I had expected. "Thank you."

His expression hardened. "We need to talk."

"Are we not talking now?" I folded my arms and forced a smile to mask my nerves.

He ignored me, passing me a tray of food.

It was delicious. Bread, some kind of stew and a cup of ale. It was not fancy but I almost let out a moan when it entered my mouth. I forgot that I was somewhere foreign, possibly in enemy territory and that I shouldn't have just torn into the food without thinking.

"There are things you need to understand about Drakensvar." His tone was gruff, deliberate, as though he were choosing every word with care. "First—we do not keep thralls. This is a free city. The only of its kind."

I froze, spoon halfway to my mouth. "So I am...not a slave?"

"Not exactly." His gaze sharpened. "But that does not make you one of us either." He leaned forward. "What did Skargrim promise you?"

My heart slammed against my ribs painfully. He was watching me too closely, waiting for the twitch of a lie. I scrambled for something safe, something simple.

"Freedom," I said at last.

"Freedom," he echoed, then barked out a laugh that held no joy. "Freedom in a free city. I told you—I have no use for slaves."

His words should have felt like salvation, instead, they felt like a trap. Silence stretched between us, broken only by the crackle of the fire. Skúli rose, as though the conversation was finished and turned toward the door. Desperation made me speak.

"Wait."

He stilled.

The truth hovered on my tongue–sharp, dangerous. But I couldn't tell him. I forced out a kind of half-truth instead. "Skargrim...he thinks his scouts are being killed." I hesitated, then added, softer. "I do not know why but he is...afraid."

His eyes narrowed on me, searching my face for the lie. I kept my gaze steady, though sweat prickled at the back of my neck.

"They are," he said with a shrug, but sat back down.

I swallowed hard. "Why?"

"For the same reason we have always done what we must," he replied. He didn't look at me when he spoke, staring instead at the fire. "Because I will not let him see what we are doing here."

"What are you doing?"

Skúli stopped breathing for a moment. Then, he looked at me—really looked at me—and something resembling a smile tugged at the corners of his mouth.

He rose, moving toward the door again, and with his back to me, murmured something so quiet that I was not sure I heard him at all.

"We are living."

CHAPTER EIGHT
ALURA

I woke to the faintest light creeping over the valley—pale gold bleeding into grey. The hall was quiet, colder than I expected, the embers of the fire long dead. Beds empty.

I hadn't heard Skúli leave. No shuffle of boots. No murmured words.. Just silence.

For a moment I stayed where I was, wrapped in furs, listening to the faint sigh of wind against the stone walls. But the silence felt different today. Heavy.

I'd barely seen Astrid or Skúli over the past few days. They were out before sunrise and often didn't return until long after the sun had set, if at all. I wondered what occupied them. Where they went, who they met. I'd asked Astrid once if she would take me into town.

She'd refused.

Skúli says you cannot go.

I'd been told that I wasn't a slave. No one had said I wasn't a prisoner.

In some ways, it felt worse. Free to wander the halls, forbidden to leave them. Given work, but no direction. Kindness, yet no permission.

Björn, thankfully, I had avoided. The freakishly large wolf stayed close to Skúli, a living warning. Skúli insisted he wouldn't hurt me.

I didn't believe that for a moment.

At the foot of my bed, folded nearly, waited new clothes. Soft tunics. Warm trousers. Clean dresses. Thick woollen socks.

Skúli had provided, even if he wasn't here.

My fire was already lit, flickering shadows along the walls—a quiet kindness I hadn't seen. I washed quickly, my hands were cold under the small basin of water, the soap leaving a faint scent on my skin. I dressed quickly, slipping into the underdress, sighing as I ran my fingers over the hem of the sleeves that reached my wrists. I pinned the apron dress together next, then pulled on my soft leather shoes. I brushed my hair, tying it back tight with a thin strip of weaved fabric.

There was bread in the kitchen and a flask of water. I took a piece and gnawed at it while I watched the mist curling across the fields, smoke from distant hearths drifted in ribbons across the morning sky.

I tried to remember that I was here for a reason.

I was here to spy for the King.

But spying was not what the sagas I'd studied had promised. There were no secrets spoken aloud, no maps left carelessly around. Conversations tangled with names I didn't know, places I couldn't yet place. Half the language slipped through my fingers no matter how hard I reached for it.

I listened anyway.

Servants trading gossip by the well in the courtyard. Warriors grumbling over mead. But all I got were scraps. Mutters of debt, of raids that had failed, supply lines thinning. Whisper about me—the stranger, the curses that followed.

I tried to hold the pieces together in my mind, to shape them into something sharp enough to carry back to the King, but they shifted each time I reached for meaning.

Once, I had thought myself clever for having studied the sagas and the old tongues, proud that I could speak half a dead language. Now it only made the failure sting more sharply. Knowledge was not the same as understanding, and understanding was not the same as betrayal.

And understanding was not betrayal.

Each time I reminded myself of the bargain I had made, the bread tasted like ash in my mouth.

When the hall doors opened, Astrid strode in. She moved with ease, her armour catching the early light, her hair braided back neatly. Her eyes swept over me like she was measuring me.

"You look like you have been waiting," she said, voice flat.

"I...I was," I admitted. My stomach twisted. "I wanted to thank him-" I gestured to my clothing "-where does he go?"

She smirked, faint, and circled me. "You will learn. Everyone has their hours. Some leave before dawn. Some do not return until sunset. Waiting accomplishes nothing." Her gaze hardened. "Work does."

She led me into a small workroom, a small room just off the kitchen. Tools, tables, half-finished projects, hides and baskets were scattered around.

"These need mending," she said, dropping a bundle of clothes into my arms. "Properly."

I eyed the sloppy stitching. "The last person was careless."

Astrid let out a laugh. "Gods, I hate mending."

I sank to the bench, letting my hands do the work while my mind wandered. Hours passed. I stitched, I cut, I folded. My hand ached, my back felt stiff. But the work kept me grounded. I could control the cloth and thread in a way that I couldn't control anything else in this place—the valley, the house, Skúli.

When midday came, Astrid returned, carrying a loaf of bread and a flask of water. She set them in front of me. "Eat. You need strength."

I nodded, tearing the bread carefully, my mind calculated each movement. Show competence. Stay alert. Don't falter.

I could sense that both Skúli and Astrid were always watching—even when they weren't here. I could feel the suspicion pressing against me like an invisible weight.

After eating, Astrid pulled me outside. "We are going to tan the hide," she said, motioning toward the bear skin we had brought home. My stomach twisted at the memory. The scent of iron still clung faintly to it.

She showed me how to stretch it over a wooden frame, how to scrape the fat and remaining flesh with a knife. The rhythm was methodical, almost meditative.

"This is not just about preserving meat," she said. "It is about respect for what the animal gave. Do it poorly, and you waste its sacrifice. Do it right, and you honour it."

I followed her instructions carefully, the smell of the hide strong in my nose. Her hands were fast and sure, her movements confident. I worked slowly, trying to mirror her precision, aware that my every move was being judged.

She corrected my angles once or twice, showing me the proper way to pull the hide taut without tearing it.

"You will need patience," she said, standing back. Her eyes were as sharp as a hawk's, scanning me. "And your full attention. Haste is useless here."

I nodded, my hands learning discipline as my mind wandered. The tasks kept me grounded, though sometimes the humming beneath my skin threatened to rise, stirring like restless embers.

But my thoughts always circled back to Skúli, to the man I was supposed to spy on.

Where he went. What he guarded. Why his absence unsettled me more than his presence had.

That was the cruelest edge of it—the guilt. Every time I caught myself wondering where he was, or listening for his footsteps, a weight pressed down on me. I was supposed to observe, to report, to protect myself by keeping my distance.

But he had been kind.

Not loudly. Not foolishly. But enough to blur lines that needed to remain firm.

Astrid left me to finish the work, warning me to stay inside after we cleaned up. "Stay put. No wandering. There are things at night that do not take kindly to strangers."

I nodded even as unease prickled through me.

As I moved inside the hall later, I heard it–scratching, soft but deliberate, coming from the shadows and I froze.

The sound moved along the walls, up and down, never close enough to identify, never far enough to ignore. I followed it with my ears, tilting my head, but I couldn't figure out what was making it.

Mice? A lizard? Or something else entirely?

My stomach clenched. I wanted to call out, but I knew better. Astrid was around somewhere but she was not a friend. She was another pair of eyes judging me, waiting for me to trip over myself so she could catch me.

By the time the sun dipped low, painting the valley in orange and purple, my muscles ached from the day's work. I was covered in dirt and dust, my fingers sore from stitches and scraping. And then I heard the sound I'd been waiting for all day.

Boots echoing on the stone floors.

Skúli.

He didn't speak at first. Just stood in the doorway, tall, silent, eyes sweeping over me.

"Good," he said at last. "You learned something today."

I met his eyes carefully, swallowing the lump in my throat.

"Yes," I replied carefully.

Every word I spoke was chosen and measured. I had learned, yes–but I had also learned what to say, what not to say. He didn't trust me, and I couldn't trust him either.

He moved toward the stairs, glancing back at me.

Later, dinner was on the table. Simple but nourishing. Bread, stew with vegetables, and a cup of ale. I savoured each bite, mindful, grateful. Skúli sat opposite me, his eyes flickering me like he was testing my intentions before returning to his food.

"Thank you," I said quietly. "For the clothes."

He didn't immediately respond, and I felt my pulse quicken. The silence stretched between us. Finally, he gave the faintest of nods, eyes narrowing slightly as if gauging my sincerity.

"You are welcome," he said, tone gruff.

I nodded, lowering my gaze back to my food. The bread was thick and hearty, and I tore a piece off slowly. I could feel him watching.

"Are you comfortable here?" He asked, almost casually, but there was an edge to it. Like he actually cared if I was comfortable in his hall.

I swallowed the urge to roll my eyes or give a flippant answer. "Yes," I said carefully. "It is...enough. Better."

He grunted, a sound that could have either been approval or disapproval. I couldn't tell which. I took another bite, letting the silence settle.

"You have been busy today," he said finally, stirring his bowl of stew. "Astrid has you working hard, I hear."

"Yes," I said, cautious. "I am...learning." My voice was calm, neutral. But I allowed a small truth to slip in. "She is patient."

He snorted, the barest hint of amusement. "Patience is not something anyone would have guessed she possesses."

I managed a small, polite smile. "She...knows what she is doing."

Another pause.

I kept my hand still, resting lightly on the table, aware of how close he was, yet how far. Trust was a currency neither of us were willing to spend yet.

Finally, I dared to ask, keeping my tone light and measured. "Do you often leave early?"

He glances up sharply, his eyes narrowing. "Sometimes," he said shortly. "When it is necessary."

I nodded, saying nothing more. Questions were dangerous and I had to learn to use them carefully.

We ate in silence after that, the fire crackled, both of our movements were careful and deliberate. And though neither of us said much, there was an understanding. The careful truce we were navigating.

I finished the last of my food and set down the spoon, my eyes briefly meeting his.

"Thank you" I said again.

Not just for the meal.

He didn't respond, but there was the faintest tightening of his jaw, a brief pause he took before he stirred his bowl again, that told me he had heard.

And that was enough for now.

CHAPTER NINE
SKÚLI

Drakensvar had taken in many strangers over the years. Few had unsettled it so quietly.

The snows were not here yet, but the wind carried a sharp edge that bit through even my thickest of fur cloaks. Winter was coming.

Already, the sky hung low over Drakensvar—grey, heavy, pressing down on the valley—and the trees whispered of storms yet to arrive. I rode along the ridges above the valley, Björn at my side, sensing the stirrings of unease before I even saw the movement below.

"They are here again," I muttered under my breath, spotting the figure crouching behind a rock outcrop, barely moving, almost part of the stone itself. A scout. One of Skargrim's, I would wager—desperate enough to risk venturing this close to our walls.

Björn growled low in his throat, stepping closer to me, his hackles lifting.

"Calm, Björn," I murmured, stooping to rest a hand briefly against his neck. "I will handle this."

The scout had not yet seen me, but I was not about to wait. I urged my horse down the soft slope, landing silently behind the spy. When he finally noticed me, his breath caught as his eyes widened sharply—prey realising it had been marked too late.

"You do not belong here," I told him flatly. No need for threats; the fear in his eyes was enough. "Tell your master he will not find what he seeks in Drakensvar."

He stammered, useless words spilling out in a flurry I barely caught, but the message was clear enough. Skargrim wanted information. He wanted to know the state of our walls, the strength of our people, and perhaps even the movements of my people.

I turned him away, letting him stumble back up over the ridge. He glanced back over his shoulder at the wolf at my side. Björn's green eyes seemed to pierce deeper than any spear or sword.

"Wonder how long it will take for the next one to come," I muttered. Björn pressed his nose against my arm, nudging me as if he understood the weight I carried.

The locals had begun whispering.

Whispers I could not ignore.

Alura. Dangerous. Cursed.

I had seen the way they flinched when she passed them in the hall, how conversation stilled a breath too long. I did not fault them for it. The world remembered things longer than people did.

And yet, I could not bring myself to treat her as they believed she should be treated.

There was something about her. Something that tugged at a part of me I did not like to name. Not her strength, nor beauty alone, but a presence that both unsettled and intrigued me. As though she occupied more space than her small body should allow. As though something watched the world through her eyes.

I did not trust that feeling. I trusted it even less because I could not name it.

Every glance she cast my way, every word she carefully picked reminded me that she was not one of my people. And in times like these, outsiders were dangerous—whether by intent or by accident.

I rode back toward the city, Björn beside me, silent and sure as always. My hands tightened on the reins and the wind carried the scent of smoke mingled with the tang of pine and moss.

This city was mine to protect, and yet I felt a gnawing frustration that I could not do it properly. The city was mine to protect, and yet the crown was not mine to wear.

How do you protect your people when you are not permitted to lead them?

Björn growled low again, and I stopped, looking toward him. "Do you think I am failing them?" I asked quietly. "You would tell me, would you not, old friend?"

His green eyes met mine, unblinking and unwavering. In the only way he could, he made me feel that he understood. That we could understand each other without words.

"I do not like this," I admitted. "Not being in command when I should be the one to make the calls, to decide what is right, to see it done. And yet...here I am, watching and praying that what I do is enough."

He looked at me, almost as if to say that the world does not wait for doubts. I exhaled, trying to loosen the tension coiling in my shoulders.

The snow would come. Winter would demand more of us, and I would have to be ready.

The next days were long, filled with patrols, meetings and the constant, gnawing awareness of the spy's presence. Every shadow, every movement caught in the corner of my eye, made my hand drift to the hilt of my axe, only to relax again when I realised it was nothing more than a branch or a passing hawk.

And Alura–her presence complicated matters further. I caught her moving through the training yard, tending to tasks Astrid assigned her. Her movements were deliberate, careful—never wasted, never hurried.

I noticed how she watched everything. Listened more than she spoke. That unsettled me more than open defiance would have.

The air around her felt...charged. Not dangerous, but expectant. Like a storm waiting to decide whether it would break or pass us by.

Stay grounded, keep distance, I told myself.

But distance, I was learning, was not always easy to keep, nor did it lessen risk.

But I had to believe that she was not a threat.

Not yet at least.

At night, I found myself sitting by the fire in my chamber, Björn at my feet, watching the flames dance. I thought of Alura again—not as a threat, but not as harmless either.

I reminded myself of my oath.

Protection. Guidance. Strength.

She was under that oath now.

That knowledge settled heavy in my chest.

A sharp scratching echoed from the eaves, pulling my attention upward. Björn's ears twitched as he growled softly. The shadows shifted, but there was nothing to see. Just wind, just the creak of old timber. I rose, walking to the window, peering into the darkness. My fingers drummed along the stone sill.

How do you protect people when threats are unseen? When danger comes wrapped in whispers and shadows? When even the ones who walk beside you cannot fully be trusted?

Björn pressed against me, warm and steady, I rested my hand on his head. "We will do what we must," I murmured. "Winter is almost here, and when it is, we must be ready."

The next morning, I rode before the sun had risen, scouting the northern ridge where the snow would gather first. The cold stung my face, but the clarity it brought was worth it. Every tree, every rock, every hidden path that I knew could conceal danger. Every step could be the difference between life and death.

As I rode, I thought of Alura again. Not as a threat, but as a variable. Her presence was a puzzle, her intentions hidden behind careful eyes and measured words. I would watch her, yes—but more than that, I would observe. Because Drakensvar was my responsibility, and the people trusted me to see what others could not.

The trails were quiet, crisp with the scent of pine. I made my way back to Drakensvar, my eyes scanned for danger.

As I descended the last hill before the village, I spotted a small gathering near the edge of a road.

A man knelt, clutching a bolt of cloth and shouting in distress, while another stood over him, his chest heaving with anger. Their voices carried on the wind, sharp and bitter, threatening.

I slowed my pace, then dismounted and stepped towards them. The two men froze, their quarrel forgotten for just a moment. I raised a hand, and everything silenced.

"Enough," I said. "Both of you."

The standing man opened his mouth but I gave him a sharp look. "You will speak your grievance, and you will do so without anger. If you cannot, I will settle this for you."

The kneeling man spoke first, explaining how a few heads of goats had wandered and been damaged. He blamed the other for negligence. I listened, nodding then turned to the second man, letting silence demand his version of events. His story was different, but not untrue.

"Both of you are at fault," I said finally, after I had deliberated the turn of events. "But this land belongs to all of us. You will make amends, and you will do so with respect, not anger. Disputes solved with fists do nothing but weaken us."

I gestured to the kneeling man. "Return the animals to pasture, tend to those harmed. You," I said, turning to the second, "help him. You are stronger, yes, but strength alone is not an honour. Honour is in how you use it."

Both men bowed their heads. The tension between them melted, replaced by a fragile respect for the law I loosely represented.

As I turned back toward my horse, I could feel it in the wind. The quiet acknowledgement of the people nearby, who had watched from a distance. Respect was not demanded with fear or gold. It was earned—with fairness, with restraint, with the willingness to listen.

And every step I took home reminded me why my people follow me willingly.

By the time dusk rolled over the valley, I had returned. The city was lit, warm and flickering, a reminder of what we were defending. And though I felt the gnawing weight of uncertainty, I knew that we would endure. We had to. We would face this together, and no spy, no outsider, no shadow would take this from us.

I dismounted at the gate, giving Björn a rough pat on the shoulder. "Keep watch while I check on the walls."

He growled softly in acknowledgement, his eyes catching the lantern light. The bond between us was unspoken, absolute. In a world full of unknowns, it was a certainty I could rely on.

As I walked the battlements, listening to the wind moan through the towers, I realised that the coming winter would be more than just snow and ice.

It was a test of resolve, of vigilance and trust.

And I would need every ounce of it to protect this city—and the people who called it home.

Even from those who, for now, walked beside me.

CHAPTER TEN
ALURA

I had been awake for hours, listening to the faint rustle of servants, and the occasional clatter of hooves from the stable below. Winter edged closer each day, the air carrying an icy sharpness that made my chest tighten when I breathed. Beneath my skin, a faint spark of warmth flickered as I drew a careful breath, steadying myself.

Björn padded silently into the hall, his black fur almost blending with the shadows along the stone walls. I froze when I noticed him, my pulse quickening as he stopped a few paces away, his head low, green eyes fixed on me. There was no aggression—only watchfulness—and that unsettled me more than a snarl would have. Every step he took seemed deliberate. And yet, beneath the unease, there was a strange allure to him. A whisper of connection.

He was magnificent, and I couldn't help but feel that maybe he could understand me.

"Good morning," I whispered.

Björn's ears twitched, and he let out a low rumble in response. I exhaled slowly, telling myself not to overthink it, he was just a wolf after all. A very large one.

The doors at the far end of the hall opened, and a small procession entered, their boots echoing against the stone floor. Nobles from neighbouring lands. Their rich clothing, embroidered with gold and gems, glimmered in the firelight, a stark contrast to Drakensvar's great hall. The scent of perfume and rare spices trailed behind them, sharp against the clean scent of smoke and pine.

They murmured amongst themselves, polite but distant. Their glances turned toward me more than once.

One noble's gaze lingered too long, measuring and appraising, like I was a prize to claim. Another muttered under his breath, audibly counting his coinpurse, no doubt calculating what Drakensvar–or I–might be worth in a wager or bargain.

My stomach tightened at how clearly the air of greed emanated from them. Invisible but unmistakable.

Skúli arrived moments later, moving with his usual quiet authority. His eyes briefly met mine, sharp and unreadable. No smile. No nod. All distance and control.

And yet, for a moment, I caught something in his glance.

A hesitation.

"Alura," Astrid whispered at my side. "Keep your wits about you. Watch him. And them."

I turned to her, surprised by her intensity. Her hair was down today, carefully arranged to cover her pointed ears. She gestured subtly toward the nobles, her gaze hard.

"They are testing him. All of us. Maybe even you most of all. Be careful what you offer them—even with your silence."

Politics, then.

Not survival of the body, but survival of wit.

I relaxed my face, smoothing my expression, letting my posture stiffen. Harmless. Quiet. Observant. Something threaded through my chest as if my body knew I was being watched. Not just by eyes, but by something much older.

The nobles spoke in clipped voices, trading offers wrapped in courtesy and threat alike. Timber for jewels. Furs for favour. Alliances framed as generosity. I listened carefully, sorting the words that mattered from those that were meant to distract.

There were so many of them.

And behind it all, there was the unspoken expectation that I report back to Skargrim. Observations of Skúli, the city's strengths, weaknesses, alliances and vulnerabilities. I felt the weight of it pressing down on me like an invisible hand. I could not ignore it, but I couldn't act recklessly either.

I couldn't rush this. Every letter would need careful phrasing, every observation filtered and measured. I needed to learn to move between the shadows and words, to balance honesty with deception. That's what would keep me alive.

The nobles' words dripped with calculation, their smiles were veiled threats, waiting to take advantage. One noble hinted at marriage alliances, his tone smooth. Another suggested higher taxes, spoken like it was a necessity. A third seemed almost fixated on me, glancing repeatedly at me, weighing me. As if I could be bartered or used. My throat tightened. In their eyes, I was reduced to a trophy, another item on display.

Skúli, however, remained steadfast. He listened, evaluating each proposal on its merits and on the good of his people, not his own gain.

"Our people do not thrive on burden," he said calmly. "We will trade fairly, or we will not trade at all."

His voice left no room for argument, and even the wealthiest noble could not hide his irritation.

When a marriage was proposed—Astrid named as though she were a piece on a game board—his refusal was colder.

"I do not trade my family for gold or influence. Any arrangement must be chosen by both parties freely, or it will not exist."

My chest tightened with awe.

Here was a man who did not wield authority for greed, but for justice and protection.

Björn moved closer, brushing against my leg, and I caught myself smiling. The wolf, so silent and commanding, felt like a lifeline in a room filled with hidden threats. Yet, there was something else–a challenge in his gaze. He felt like a warning now.

That nothing here was truly safe.

Skúli's attention was divided between the nobles and business at hand, his jaw tight, posture rigid. He did not smile at their flattery, did not nod at their attempts to charm him. The city was strong, its people loyal, and he carried the authority of both.

My presence felt negligible in comparison.

During a pause in the conversation, he passed close to where I stood on the outskirts of the hall. The nobles' attention remained elsewhere, but he leaned in just slightly, brushing his fingers against my clothes as he adjusted the cloak on my shoulder.

It was small, barely there, yet a spark through me. I looked away, but the faint warmth between us lingered.

Astrid noticed, her eyes flicked between us, her lips pressed into a thin line. She leaned in, whispering again, "Do not let his kindness confuse you. He is a man of iron, not silk. He does not play at charms, and he will not take you to his bed on a whim."

"There is nothing between us," I gritted out between clenched teeth.

Astrid's gaze hardened, though her voice stayed low and steady. "See that there never is. Not unless you mean it. He has lost too much already, and I will not see you wound him out of fear or foolishness. Keep your distance, Alura. Men like him do not bend."

I swallowed, nodding again.

The words settled like both a warning and a shield, as if Astrid meant to guard not just him but me as well. I didn't argue, even as the pull between gratitude and fear made my insides twist.

I had no choice but to tread carefully. Every interaction, every gesture...they carried a weight. And if I wasn't careful, they would crush me.

The nobles lingered, sipping from mugs and murmuring about winter provisions, alliances and rumours from distant lands. I made a show of listening politely, of asking the occasional question, and making mental notes of what seemed important. But my mind kept returning to Skúli, to the instructions Astrid had given me.

Here, in a hall that should be displaying wealth, integrity and fairness held far more power than gold or flattery.

At one point, a sharp-eyed noble glanced directly at me. I met his gaze steadily, letting my expression betray nothing. He gave me a curt nod before disappearing back amongst the crowd, leaving me with an uneasy feeling.

When the nobles finally departed, the hall felt emptier than before. Skúli moved closer to the hearth, his eyes scanning the room as though he were expecting the walls themselves to show their true colours. Björn stood beside him, silent but vigilant.

I dared to exhale. The tension in my shoulders easing slightly, though I couldn't shake the feeling of being constantly observed. I glanced toward Skúli, who stood for a moment with his back to me, the firelight outlining the rigid strength of his shoulders. I wondered what he was thinking, whether he suspected me of anything, or if my careful words and smiles had fooled him for now.

Astrid's voice broke the silence, soft but firm. "You did well. But remember, they will keep watching, always. Even when you think you are alone."

I realised that her warning applied not just to the nobles but to Skúli himself. I had to navigate him as well as the politics. Trust was not easily earned here. And I had to learn the rules quickly if I wanted to survive.

Later, when the hall was empty and the evening had faded into darkness, Skúli approached me.

Publicly, he had been curt, formal, careful to maintain appearances. But now, with no eyes upon us, a quieter side showed. Something almost gentle.

"You handled yourself well," he said quietly, the words short but sincere.

He did not offer me his hand, did not touch me, but his gaze lingered for longer than necessary. There was caution there, but also something else.

A hint of acknowledgment.

I murmured my thanks, unsure how to phrase it, my tongue still felt clumsy around the language.

He inclined his head slightly. "Hold fast. Every word, every glance...they will search for your weaknesses. Do not give them once."

I nodded again, my thoughts were spinning. The weight of the information I would eventually have to provide, the impression I would have to make. Politics, lies, the knowledge that much of what I had heard felt meaningless. And yet, I would still be expected to sift through it all.

For the first time, frustration edged past fear.

For a moment, I allowed myself to imagine a world where I could navigate this world without fear, where I could move among the nobles, the wolves, and the shadows without being consumed by them.

CHAPTER ELEVEN
ALURA

I woke up choking on the remnants of ash and sea-salt air. The dream clung to me like cobwebs. It was the voice again, but this time there was a woman to go with it. Her hands outstretched, her lips moving soundlessly, the wind howling too loud for me to hear. She stood on the shoreline with her blonde hair whipping around her face. When she reached for me, her touch burned, and I knew I could not follow her into the waves.

I jolted upright, sweating, the furs tangled around my body.

The house was quiet except for the heavy sigh of the hearth-fire and the faint scratching–always that god's damned scratching. My breath steadied as I pressed a hand to my chest.

She was more than just a dream. I could feel it pressing inside of me, demanding to be remembered. Each time she came to me, her urgency grew sharper, her eyes more wild.

The sound of claws scraped against the wood again, dragged me back into the waking world. A low hiss followed. I squeezed my eyes closed.

I hated that sound—it burrowed under my skin, setting my teeth on edge.

I'd overheard some people claiming it was a blessing, a creature of omens, but it watched me with too much knowing, my skin prickling in a useless attempt at warning.

Before I could shake the unease, a knock came at the chamber door.

"Letters," Astrid's voice was curt.

I pulled a woollen shift over my head and walked barefoot to the door. Astrid stood with her arms folded, eyes sharp. She thrust the wax-sealed parchment into my hand.

The seal was the King's. Two ravens. My stomach churned as I broke it open.

Alura,

I trust you remember the importance of your position. Eastern border, one week. Do not disappoint me.

−S.

My fingers trembled. The parchment may as well have been chains tightening around my throat.

Astrid tilted her head, searching my expression. "Bad news?"

I swallowed. "A reminder."

Her eyes narrowed, but she didn't press. She left me standing in the doorway with my heart pounding too hard for so few words.

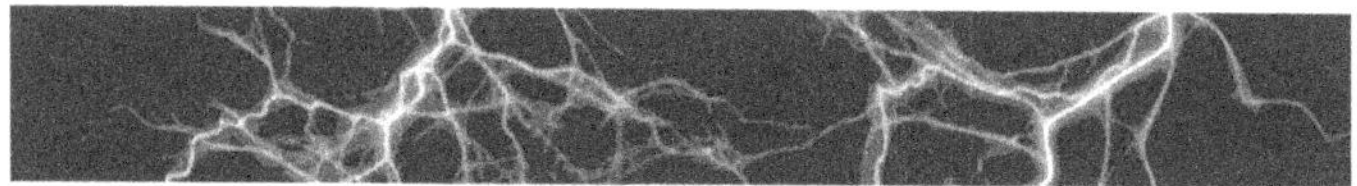

The rest of the morning I forced myself into motion. If I stayed still, I'd suffocate on the weight of the letter. The hall was thick with the smell of smoke and stew, the benches cluttered with crumbs and stains from days of councils that I was not permitted to attend to. Skúli's men tread in and out, leaving muddy boot prints and laughter that turned into wary silence whenever I entered.

They thought I was cursed. I saw it in the way they touched the edges of their charms when I passed, the way they did not quite meet my eyes. Even the women whispered when they thought I could not hear.

I needed to change that.

So I scrubbed. I gathered cloth and hot water from the kitchen and began to clean the long benches, the mud and dirt ground into the floor. The work left my arms aching, my palms raw, but it was something. Something I could control.

By midday, I stoked the fire to life and set a pot of broth to simmer. I chopped root vegetables and herbs, my hands moving in muscle memory. The smell of onion and garlic filling the air, rich and homely.

Astrid passed through once, pausing briefly. "Trying to win his favour?"

"Trying to prove I am not useless," I muttered, though the truth twisted deeper than that.

She leaned against a table, arms folded. "Careful. Some will see eagerness as weakness."

Her words struck. I thought of the letter, of the King's demand. My throat tightened. "And what am I meant to do? What do you see?"

Astrid's face softened, just barely. "I see someone who does not yet know if she is prey or hunter."

She left before I could answer.

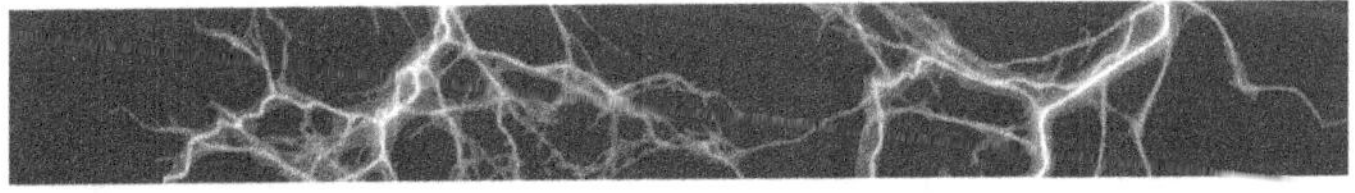

When Skúli finally returned from the training yard, the hall was warm and lit with torches. I had laid the meal out myself. Bread, salted fish, the broth steaming hot in carved bowls.

He stopped in the doorway, his shoulders dusted with raindrops. His eyes swept the room, lingering on the scrubbed floors, the arranged benches, and finally on me. Something unreadable flickered in his gaze.

But when his men followed him inside, the mask dropped back into place. His voice came hard, meant more for his men than for me. "What are you doing here? The hall is not your burden."

Heat flared in my chest, my cheeks burned with his sharp words, but I met his gaze without flinching.

"Then whose is it?" I snapped at him. "Yours? You have more dirt on your hands than time to clean. If I waited for you or your men to care, we would still be walking through filth."

A ripple of laughter echoed out of his men, some hollered that I had the fire of dragons in me, it was quickly stifled when he glared at them.

He sat heavily at the head of the table, Björn beside him. I felt pinned beneath both their gazes. Static prickled under my skin, the kind that appeared before storms.

The men ate noisily, but my food went down like ash in my mouth. Skúli didn't dare speak to me again in front of them. It was only after the hall had emptied, the torches burning low, that he moved closer. I was gathering bowls when his hand brushed mine–briefly, deliberately.

Warmth flared where we touched, as if something unspoken passed between us. My pulse thudded in response, sharper than just nerves.

"You do not need to prove yourself with chores," he said quietly, too low for anyone else to hear. His eyes were softer now, not the hardened shield he wore in front of the others.

The touch startled me more than the words. "Then what am I supposed to do?"

His jaw tightened. "Stay alive."

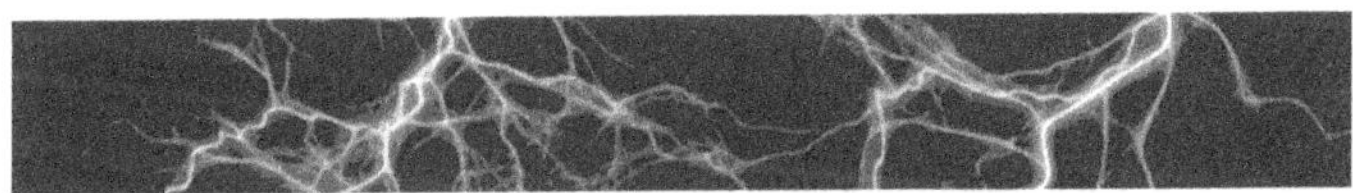

The fire had burned low that evening, throwing long shadows across the hall. The men had all left the hall, leaving only the crackle of embers and the occasional creak of timber.

I lingered, unwilling to retreat back to my chambers. Sleep was a fickle thing lately, and besides, the silence was calming, it wrapped around me like a cloak. I drew my knees up to my chest, warming my hands over the dying flames.

I didn't hear him at first, then he was there. Skúli leant against a table on the other side of the hearth with the ease of a man who belonged in the shadows. His gaze was set on me.

"You keep strange hours," he said at last.

I stiffened. "So do you."

A flicker of amusement ghosted across his face. "I sleep when I need to. You…" He tilted his head, eyes narrowing slightly. "…you do not strike me as someone who lets her guard down easily."

Heat crawled over me but I masked it with a shrug. "I have learned not to."

He stepped closer, the firelight etching his features. Scarred, solemn, dangerous. Yet there was something gentler beneath it all, something he seemed reluctant to show.

"You are hiding something," he said softly—almost gently. But the words were a blade in disguise, he was too close to the truth.

I forced myself to hold his gaze. "Everyone is."

He studied me, as if he could reveal the truth with nothing but silence. Then his mouth curved, not quite a smile. "True. But yours weighs heavier."

I let the words settle, tasting them. It was a truth I could neither confirm nor deny. I wrapped my arms tighter around myself, choosing my response carefully.

"Then perhaps it is best we both keep our burdens."

The fire popped, filling the pause. For a moment, I thought he might come closer, demand more, unravel the threads I'd been working hard to keep knotted.

Instead, he stepped back. His voice was softer now, but laced with warning. "Wise words. Just remember...secrets have teeth."

My pulse thrummed as he left me in the quiet. Every nerve in my body was burning by what had just happened.

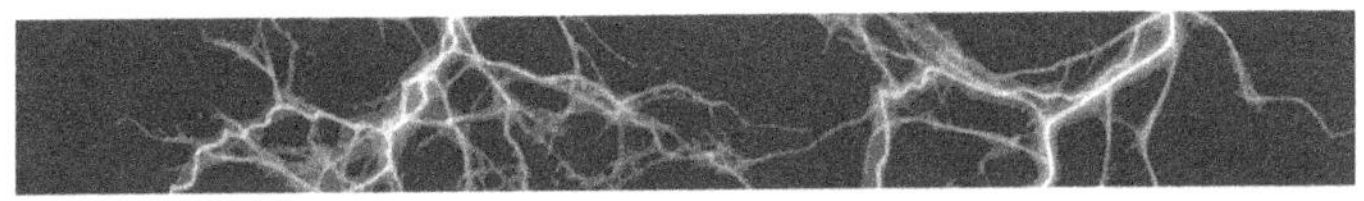

By dawn, my nerves were frayed thin. I cornered Skúli in the yard as he was checking practice weapons.

"You cannot keep me here like a prisoner," I snapped.

His head lifted sharply. "What?"

"You have banned me from leaving the hall, from going to the village. I cannot breathe in here. Do you mean to keep me under lock and key like one of your beasts?"

His eyes flashed. "This land is not Hayhjem, Alura. Beyond these walls are men who would slit your throat. I will not have your blood on my hands."

"I am not helpless!"

"You are not free either," he bit back.

I took a step back as the words cut at me. "So I am a prisoner."

His mouth tightened as he looked away, his jaw flexing. "You are...under my protection."

"Protection feels a lot like chains."

For a moment, something raw crossed his face–regret, maybe. But he only shook his head. "Better chains than a grave."

I turned from him before he could see the tears threatening to rise. Björn followed, shadow-silent, as though he wanted to remind me that I wasn't truly alone.

Not here.

Not anywhere.

CHAPTER TWELVE
ALURA

I awoke to the low thump of boots against stone. Not the heavy march of guards or the soft scurry of servants–but a quiet, measured stride that I had come to recognise.

Skúli.

My pulse leapt as I sat up quickly, gathering the furs around my shoulders, smoothing my hair. He didn't bother knocking and the door creaked open to reveal him, broad shouldered and grim, carrying a wooden tray balanced in one hand.

"Eat," he gently said, setting it on the table by the window.

His tone was curt, but the faint steam rose from the porridge, and the careful slice of cheese beside it spoke louder than his voice did.

"I do not need to be waited on like a child," I muttered, though my stomach betrayed me, growling like a beast.

His gaze flicked to me. "You need strength."

I crossed my arms, waiting for him to leave. But he lingered, standing there like an immoveable wall. Finally, he spoke again, his voice lower, more weighted.

"In two weeks, we will go to Hayhjem. The King expects my report. I cannot afford for anything to happen to you before then."

My breath caught. His words were wrapped in contradictions, like I was something breakable and yet something dangerous if left unwatched.

"What you mean," I said coolly, lifting my chin, "is that you cannot afford for me to make *you* look weak."

The corner of his mouth twitched, but it could have been from irritation or amusement. "Both."

The urge to hurl the tray at him was strong, but so was the urge to eat every bite of porridge he'd brought up.

Instead, I gave him the sharpest glare I could manage. "You cage me here like a bird, and then act surprised when I peck at the bars."

His jaw tightened as I struck a nerve, the faintest flare of his nostrils betraying his temper. But he didn't rise to the bait.

Instead, he turned toward the door, tossing over his shoulder, "Stay inside. It is not a request."

I exhaled, trembling with a mix of hunger and fury. I stared at the porridge until my stomach won the argument. As I ate, a single thought wound itself tighter and tighter in my mind.

I could not stay here, not if I wanted to live.

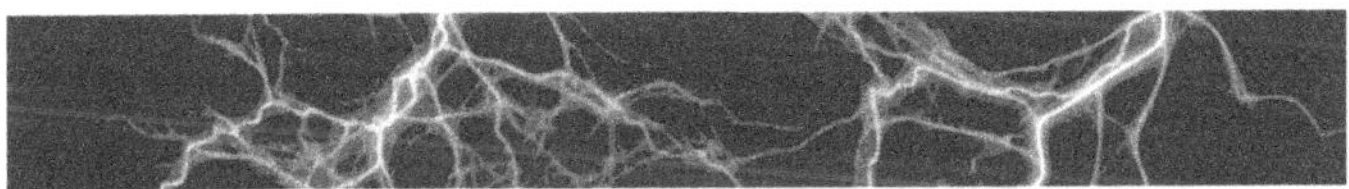

I waited until the great hall grew noisy with training and the shuffling of feet. Then I slipped out through the side door in the front yard, cloak drawn close, heart hammering. Every step felt like I was stealing something.

My instructions had been clear. Follow the ridge east, past the withered oak, until I saw the cairn of stones. Wait there. Someone would find me.

The morning air bit at my cheeks, sharp and clean, and for the first time in weeks I felt a rush of freedom. I hurried across the frosted ground, boots crunching softly.

It wasn't far. The cairn stood like a lone sentinel above the frozen grass, and beyond it the land fell away toward the border. I wrapped my arms tight around myself, scanning the horizon.

A shadow stepped out from the treeline. The man was lean, wrapped in a dark cloak, his face half-hidden. His hand rested casually on the hilt of a blade on his belt, though there was nothing casual about the ways his eyes assessed me. He moved with a confidence that sent a shiver crawling up my spine.

"You are late."

"I came as quickly as I could." I forced my voice to be steady.

"You are supposed to *come* as quickly as you are told." He studied me for a moment, then took a step closer, boots sinking softly into the mud. "And? What have you seen?"

I clenched my fists, my fingers digging into the wool of my cloak. "Nothing. I am not allowed to leave the hall. I see soldiers train, nobles grovel, servants whisper. Nothing that would satisfy a King."

His lips curved into a smile that didn't reach his eyes. "Then you must find another way." He stepped closer, lowering his voice. "Men like Skúli do not guard their tongues with women. He is proud. Win his bed, and you will win his secrets."

My stomach lurched.

Astrid's voice cut through my mind. *He is a man of iron, not silk.*

The thought of using my body as a way to gain knowledge made my skin crawl. Heat flared up my neck, not with desire but revulsion. Shame burned within me at the very suggestion, sickness rose inside me as if the very idea of trying to seduce him for scraps of information would hurt me more than any chain.

"No."

The word rasped out of me before I could stop it, harsher than I intended.

He smiled faintly. "No?"

"I will not seduce him. I was forced into this, but I will not crawl further. I will not whore myself for your King." My voice cracked with anger.

The shift in him was immediate. He moved so quickly that I hardly saw it—his hand in my cloak, yanking me forward, knife flashing just enough for me to feel its cold press under my jaw as his smile disappeared.

My pulse thundered, but a shiver ran through me, hardening me, almost like a shield rising in response to the threat. My breathing faltered.

"You think you have a choice?" His words were a calm whisper, hot against my ear. "You think he will free you if you give him nothing?"

I froze, my pulse roaring. Behind my eyes, the dream-woman's face flickered again, sharp as lightning. Her hand reached. For me? Warning me? I felt a strange stirring, a pull I didn't understand, as if some part of me was trying to push the knife away.

"I will–" My throat bobbed against the edge of the blade. "I will try. But I will not do that."

He clicked his tongue. "Then you risk more than pride, girl. The King grows impatient. He has no use for pretty trinkets that bring him nothing. If, when you arrive in Hayhjem, you cannot give him something of worth–your freedom is finished. Your life forfeit."

The man drew back. A ripple of heat ran through me as he did. "Think carefully. You have two weeks. Either you clip Skúli's wings, or the King will clip yours."

He stepped back, disappearing into the treeline as swiftly as he had come. I stood trembling, my breath clouding in the cold air. My hands ached where my nails had bitten into my palms.

I wanted to scream. To run. To hurl myself at the walls of the great hall of Drakensvar and demand the truth. But all I could do was turn back, cloak drawn tight and the man's words echoing with every step.

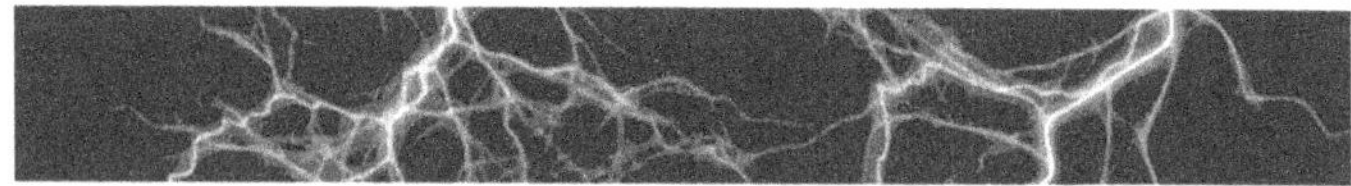

The great hall smelled of smoke and roasted meat. I forced my hands to be steady as I gathered plates left behind by the men at practice. I tried to lose myself in the cleaning, in the scrape of bowls and the hiss of the hearth.

But every sound seemed sharpened. The steady scratching that seemed to echo in this place made my teeth grind. I swore that whatever creature this was mocked me.

I slammed a pot down harder than I'd meant to.

"Careful," Astrid said from the bench, arms crossed. "You do not want to break Skúli's dishes."

I forced a smile. "Then maybe he will let me replace them, with plates that do not weigh as much as a shield."

Astrid laughed, her head thrown back before she rose, moving closer and dropping her voice. "You are funny, and clever. Keep it that way. They are all watching you, waiting for a crack. If you falter, they will tear you open to try and get ahead with my cousin."

"Why tell me this?" I asked with a sigh.

"Becuase you are in our home now. Which means if they strike at you, they strike at us. I like you, but I will not see Drakensvar bleed because of you."

Her words were sharp, but she was loyal. To Skúli. To Drakensvar. And perhaps, in some roundabout way, she was looking out for me.

I nodded, swallowing down the rising pressure in my chest. "I will be careful."

When Skúli returned that evening, the hall quietened with the weight of his presence. His gaze flicked over my briefly, cold as ever.

But later, when the torches dimmed and the hall was empty, I saw his shadow fall beside mine. His hand brushed the cup I carried, steadying it before it slipped from my fingers.

"Careful," he murmured, so low no one else could hear even though we were alone. His eyes lingered for a moment longer than necessary, then he was gone again.

It was nothing. A fleeting kindness. Yet it brewed inside of me like a warmth I had no right to feel.

That night I lay awake staring at the rafters, the spy's words and Skúli's steady gaze twisting together until I could hardly breathe.

Two weeks.

To decide whether I was a prisoner.

A pawn.

Or something else entirely.

CHAPTER THIRTEEN
ALURA

The scratching had been driving me mad for days. Always faint, always just out of reach–like a claw on stone. Patient. Deliberate. I thought at first it was in my head, some cruel joke that my mind was playing on me. But no. When I pressed my ear to the wall near the hearth, the sound grew louder. Something was living inside the great hall with me.

That morning, as pale light spilled through the winter, I finally saw it. A flash of scaled skin darting across the rushes near the hearth. I dropped the cloth I was folding and lunged. It scrambled with surprising speed, claws scratching on the stone before I managed to pin it with a copper pot. The thing hissed, tail lashing against the floor.

Carefully, I lifted the pot, just enough to peek.

It wasn't a rat–though Astrid had been teasing me that Drakensvar's rats could eat through oak. This creature was no rat at all.

It was a lizard.

Slightly larger than my hand, its skin was a mottled blue, with flecks of gold down its spine. A frill flared around its neck, a vivid warning. Its eyes glowed faintly amber, and when it hissed again, a wisp of something that looked like mist rose from between its sharp teeth.

I froze. "Gods..."

The creature cocked its head, as if unimpressed with me. Something tugged between us, drawing me closer to the little creature. Then, before I could snatch it, it darted under the table and vanished from sight.

Skúli found me kneeling on the floor, breathless and red-cheeked.

He raised a brow. "Have you taken to wrestling pots now?"

"There was a lizard," I said, pointing furiously to where it disappeared. "It was glowing. And it hissed... mist at me."

Skúli's expression shifted–not one of disbelief, but something older. Something weighted. He crouched beside me, running his hand along the floors where faint claw marks lay. "A dreki."

I blinked. "A...what?"

"Dreki lizard," he said, voice low. Reverent. "You may call them pests. My people remember them as dragons."

He leant back on his heels, his eyes distant as though he was gazing into centuries I could not see. "Long ago, they say the mountains shook with the beating of their wings. Dreki once harnessed the elements. They breathed fire, carved rivers, guarded treasures of gods and men. But when the magic left, so too did the dragons. They dwindled, until only these remained. Little scaly echoes of what they once were."

The air seemed to shift around his words, as though the hall itself remembered. I thought of the little creature's eyes, burning like embers and shivered.

"And you just...let them run about?"

His mouth twitched, half amused. "They keep the rats away. And some say they bring you fortune, if you catch one."

"Well, I caught one," I scowled. "Does that mean fortune or doom?"

"Depends," he said, rising to his full, towering height. "What did you do with it?"

I bit my lip. "Let it go."

Skúli let out a rumble of laughter, deep and warm. "Then you spared yourself a curse. Come."

"Where?"

He offered his hand, rough and calloused, the skin scarred from battles that I could only imagine. As I took it, the place where our skin joined crackled. He looked at me curiously, but didn't say anything about it.

"Beyond the walls."

My heart stuttered. I hadn't been allowed outside since arriving in Drakensvar. The fortress had become my cage, its gate always closed to me. "Are you joking?"

"I only joke sometimes." His grin was wolfish. "Today, I am serious."

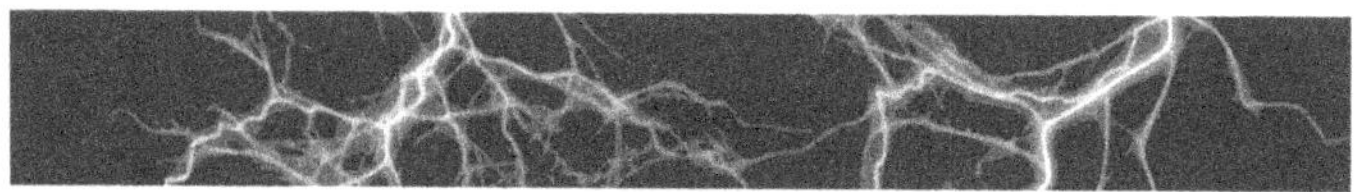

The gate groaned open, and the autumn sun struck my face, warming me. The air outside smelled sharper, freer. Sea-salt mingled with pine smoke and the faint sweetness of baking bread from somewhere beyond. My breath caught.

Drakensvar stretched before me, no longer the bleak stronghold I had been cooped up in. The city clung to the shoreline, its streets alive with colour. Stalls brimmed with dyed cloth, barrels of fish, carved bone charms and steaming bread. Children darted between carts, laughing high and bright, while circles of dancers spun to the beat of drums in the square.

I turned slowly, drinking it all in. For the first time since being dragged to this cold, harsh land, I felt the stirrings of wonder.

Skúli walked at my side, his hand resting lightly at the small of my back as though to guide–or claim–me.

Men bowed their heads when he passed, women whispered, their eyes darting towards me with curiosity. Some smiled. Others stiffened, crossing their arms or turning their backs to me, as if I unsettled them. Children paused mid-laugh, glancing at me before darting away. I straightened and tried to not feel like prey.

A group of dancers whirled past, their dresses flashing with bright embroidery, hair braided in intricate designs. Their joy was infectious, yet I noticed people questioning my place among them, beside him. In their eyes, I was different–foreign. Strange. Perhaps even dangerous.

"Do you want to join them?" Skúli asked, reading the tension in me.

"I would trip over my own feet."

"You would charm them anyway."

The words were tossed lightly, but they hit deep. I shook my head and veered toward a stall of trinkets. Silver pendants gleamed in the light, shapes like wolves, ravens and spirals of storms. My fingers lingered over a pendant etched with a dragon.

Skúli plucked it from my fingers and pressed it into my hand before I could protest. "A dreki for the girl who caught one."

I stared at him. "You do not need to–"

"I know." His eyes softened, just for a breath. "But I would like to."

The weight of the silver in my palm was more than metal. It was acknowledgement. A tether. Dangerous, perhaps, but real. I looked down at the dreki in my hand, its cool surface grounding me, yet the weight in my chest grew heavier.

Each glint seemed to whisper the truth I had tried to bury. I was here to watch him, to report, to betray the kindness he offered so freely. My promise to Skargrim clashed with an instinct I couldn't trust. The one that wanted to protect Skúli, to honour his kindness.

Guilt settled over me like a shadow, and for the first time I wondered if surviving this task would ever feel like anything but a betrayal.

We walked further, through narrow lands and wider courtyards. Merchants hailed Skúli by name, offering spiced mead and roasted chestnuts.

He bought me a scarf dyed a brilliant blue, wrapped it around my neck with a surprising gentleness. I wanted to hate him for the ease with which he bound me closer, but warmth spread through me.

Still, there were wary glances cast in my direction. A fisherman stiffened when I approached, then muttered something under his breath. Children paused mid-chase, whispering, before pointing at me and running in the opposite direction. Even as Skúli greeted his people with ease and authority, I could feel the ripple of unease trailing behind me.

And then–

"Skúli."

Her voice was bright, warm as a midsummer sun.

I turned and an older woman approached, tall and graceful, a walking stick in one hand as she favoured a leg. Her hair was a brilliant silver, her cloak fastened with a brooch of gold. She carried herself like someone used to being obeyed.

Skúli's face lit up with recognition. "Freydis."

He clasped her forearm with the ease of old friendship, his smile genuine. Her gaze slid to mine, lingering with open curiosity. Her eyes were sharp, knowing, as though she could peel me open with a glance.

"And this must be your..." She trailed off, letting the question linger.

"Alura," I finished for her.

She tilted her head, lips curving in something between a welcome and a warning. "I have heard much."

Her words rang with double meanings. I felt suddenly small beneath her gaze, like she knew secrets about me that I wasn't even aware of.

Skúli oblivious, or unwilling, simply grinned. "She is full of surprises."

"Yes," Freydis said, still watching me. "I can see that."

The market noise seemed to gather around us, but her eyes held me pinned. Somewhere inside my cloak, the dreki pendant burned against my skin, as though it recognised her—or was warning me of her.

In this city of dragons and wolves, who was truly the most dangerous?

CHAPTER FOURTEEN
ALURA

Hayhjem rose like a black tooth above us, its jagged edges stabbing through the mist. Wind off the water cut against my cheeks as our horses clattered up the frozen stones. Even Skúli, who never seemed unsettled by anything, held the reins tighter than usual.

"Keep your eyes forward," he murmured.

I obeyed. The guards lining the walls watched in silence, wolf pelts brushing iron, the gazes heavy and measuring. It felt less like an arrival and more like riding into a pit of vipers.

The gates swallowed us whole.

Inside, the keep was colder than the pass—the stone hallway dripping with condensation, air thick with rot—like meat left too long in the dark. I told myself it was only a place.

My skin didn't believe me.

I walked beside Skúli, my soft shoes echoing. He hadn't spoken since the warning at the gate. His silence pressed on me heavier than Drakensvar's walls.

We were led into a hall that reeked of pine tar and sweat. The throne at the far end looked more like a beast's carcass than a seat of power after being in Drakensvar. And there, lounging in it, was King Skargrim.

I had imagined him many times since I left. But nothing could prepare me for what I felt when I came back. His gaze cut across the hall like blades.

"Well," he drawled, rising slowly. "He returns. And he drags my gift with him."

I flinched. He meant me.

Skúli stepped half a pace closer, his hand grazing my arm. Not out of comfort. But command.

Do not speak.

Skargrim rose from his throne, the weight of his crown like iron pressing down around us. Conversations died. Tankards halted midair. Even the fire in the great hearth seemed to shrink.

"Skúli Ulfhednar," he said, his voice filling every shadow. "Last of your kind. You burrow in the north like a rat, but I knew you would crawl back eventually. Especially when called like a dog."

The hall stirred. Whispers darted like knives through the crowd. Then his pale eyes slid to me.

"And you, my pretty trinket."

Heat climbed in my throat. Every instinct begged me to defend myself, to shout that I was no trinket, no man's property. But Skúli's fingers grazed my wrist.

Another silent warning.

Skargrim's smile sharpened. "What are you, girl? A bed-slave for wolves?"

The hall tilted.

Heat crawled under my skin, sharp and wrong. A buzzing started in my ears, my vision swam. Shapes blurred, voices stretched and echoed strangely. My hands prickled, light shivering at my fingertips. Gasps rippled through the room.

"So," he murmured. "You do have teeth."

I tried to steady my breath, tried to push the dog from my mind, but everything was wrong. The echoes of laughter and murmurs twisted together, faces melted together in the corners of my vision.

"Pathetic. She crackles like wet kindling but does not know how to burn."

The insult sliced through me, but what came next was worse. A chill slid along my spine, whispers of something inside me that I could not name, something watching, waiting, and I had no idea whether it was mine–or his.

"Take her."

The command rang like steel on steel. Guards surged forward, spears striking the stone in unison. I twisted, panic flooding me, but hands like iron clamped onto my arms. Skúli shifted, a snarl rising low in his through, but he couldn't stop them. There were too many.

Skargrim descended the dais with a predator's grace, circling us both. His cloak dragged like blood spilling across the floor.

"You bring me no tribute, no oath," he says to Skúli. Then he turns to me, "And you bring me no news. Tell me why should I not slit both your throats here and now?"

The guards wrenched me away, dragging me across the hall. My heels scraped across the floors, the thunder of my heartbeat drowned the horde of voices around us.

I caught one last glimpse of Skúli, his shoulders squared, jaw clenched. Fury simmered in his eyes–but he was not moving.

The doors slammed shut, and the world became iron and shadows.

The chamber I was taken to was cold as stone, barely lit by a sputtering torch. They shoved me into a chair and shackled my wrists to the arms. The iron bit into my skin.

My breath fogged the air, sharp with the scent of damp earth.

Skargrim dismissed his guards with a flick of his hand. Only two remained at the door, silent shadows against the wall. He loomed closer, arms clasped behind his back, his eyes drinking me in.

"My trinket lives. Thrives. I see I underestimated you." He crouched before me, tilting his head. "Not a whore or a slave."

I tried to keep my face blank, but something stirred within me at the word. A whisper at the edge of thought.

"You should have fetched a higher price." His mouth twisted into something between a smile and a sneer as he circled me, slow as a wolf. "Turns out the lamb was not just meat for the table. There is...something in you."

My fingers dug into my palms, nails biting at my skin. "I do not know what you mean."

His laugh was a short, harsh bark. "Do not play dumb, girl. My hall whispers with it. Old power. I should have smelled it sooner."

"When I gave you to him," Skargrim said, circling me. "You were bait. A trinket to catch the wolf who thought himself untouchable. But now..."

He crouched suddenly, bringing his face level with mine. His breath smelled of mead and iron. The torch sputtered, as though stirred by a sudden draft. My pulse jumped, my body hot, though I felt no heat on my skin.

Skargrim's eyes sharpened. He saw it. The faint shimmer at my fingertips before it died.

"There," he hissed, eyes alight with greedy hunger. "There it is. Do you even know what you carry?"

My lips parted but no words came.

He stood, pacing, voice growing colder. "With that trickle of power, I could break the Jarls. Bend the chieftains. Burn Drakensvar to ash if I choose. And yet–he thinks he can keep you away? His prize, his secret?"

He leaned closer, voice soft but venomous. "Tell me, little witch, what secrets does Drakensvar keep? What does the wolf hide in that forsaken hall of his? What schemes brew in his hall? Is he gathering swords? Swearing oaths?"

"I do not–" my voice cracked, and I bit it down. "I do not know anything."

"Liar." The word cracked like a whip. Sparks seared across my skin. "Your fear answers me louder than your words ever could."

He slammed a hand on the table beside me. My skin tingled, a strange electric feeling racing through my veins. Fear made it sharper, hotter.

His hand shot forward, fingers clamping around my jaw, forcing me to meet his gaze. "Do you know what

wolves are without a pack? Weak. Desperate. Starving."
His thumb brushed my lip, almost gentle. "Perhaps he
does keep you because you sate his hunger."

My stomach churned. I tried to jerk back, but the chains
held me tightly.

The King's smile curled. He stood, the weight of his
authority pressing down like a boot on my chest. "If you
were still mine, I would bleed you slowly until the truth
spilled out. But perhaps there are other ways."

My breath caught.

Skargrim tilted his head, his smile cunning like a snake.
"Perhaps you would like a gentler fate. A warm bed,
gold at your wrist, your stormlight serving a King rather
than some brooding bastard clinging to the old ways. You
would like that, would you not? To be useful?"

I forced myself to look at him, though my mind
screamed at me to look away. "I tried to spy for you. I did
as you asked. But I will never bend to you."

Skargrim's smile vanished. He stopped back and nodded to the guards at the door. "Bring her out."

I was unshackled, two men seizing my arms as they
dragged me upright.

Skargrim's voice rose, echoing through the chamber. "If
she does not bend, she will break. Let the wolf watch her
suffer."

They dragged me back into the great hall. Skúli was there, surrounded by warriors. His face was stoic, jaw clenched so hard the vein in his temple jumped out.

"Alura–" His voice was rough, strangled, but the guards shoved him down before he could move.

Skargrim strode into the centre, spreading his arms as though addressing an audience.

"Behold," he barked, "what comes of secrets kept from a King." His eyes fell on me, sharp and cold. "I will have you whipped until your back is nothing but ruin. Let them see what happens to liars."

My knees trembled.

Guards shoved me forward, one already reaching for the lash that hung on the wall. The braided leather glistened like a serpent in a firelight.

"No!" Skúli's roar almost shook the rafters. He ripped free of one guard, but more pressed in, forcing him down again. His teeth bared like a cornered wolf. "Touch her and I will destroy you."

Skargrim's brows lifted, a cruel amusement sparking in his eyes. "Ah. So the wolf shows his teeth."

He listed the whip himself, running the leather through his hands as if he were savouring it. Something inside me heated–bright and raw, spilling like lightning down my veins. Flames leapt along the torches.

"Do you see? The fear? It changes her. Allow me to demonstrate."

The guards moved, dragging me to kneel in front of the King as he lashed his whip at my back. The fire hot sting brought tears to my eyes but I refused to cry out. I refused to give him the satisfaction.

Skúli's eyes met mine, murderous. "I will take her punishment. She does not deserve this."

Skargrim laughed, short and cruel. "You? She is a slave. You are free. You cannot take what belongs to me."

"She is not a slave," Skúli said firmly. "Not in Drakensvar's eyes. And I will not watch you harm her when she stands by my side."

Skargrim leaned in close to my ear, whispering so only I could hear him. "Perhaps I underestimated the advantages of letting you live. You have power, yes. But I still need information, and a live spy is more valuable than a corpse. And besides," he added, voice low. "You are bound to him in ways I do not understand, yet. But I will find out. Bring me back information."

My skin prickled as I was thrown out of the way.

"Very well. If you care so much for you little...thrall." Skargrim tossed the whip to the guard, then pointed at Skúli. "Then you wear her punishment."

The hall erupted in murmurs, half shocked, half eager for blood.

My heart stuttered. "No–"

The guards dragged Skúli forward, tearing his tunic down the back. His skin was bare, the scarred muscles of his shoulders as taut as bowstrings.

My vision blurred, the edges of it sparkling with light. "Stop!" I screamed, thrashing against my captors.

Something inside of me snapped. Heat, raw and bright, spilling like lightning down my veins. Flames leaping higher, shadows writhing across the walls. One of the guard's cursed, flinching back.

Skargrim's head whipped toward me, his expression fierce and greedy. Skúli lifted his head, blood already smeared across his lip from struggling. His gaze locked on mine, fierce and unyielding.

When the whip struck his back, something inside me broke open.

Not rage.

Terror.

The torches flared violently, shadows ripping across the walls. Someone shouted.

The sound of the second lash split the hall.

I screamed.

The lights died all at once.

Skúli staggered forwards but did not fall, much to Skargrim's dismay. His predatory eyes watched us both, flickering between us as he tried to make sense of what was happening.

Another lash struck.

Skargrim raised a hand. "Enough. Let him bleed, but not break. A king must show mercy...sometimes."

Skúli straightened, his back striped with red. He met my eyes, his voice raw but steady. "Do not give him anything."

Skargrim's gaze lingered on me, his hunger plain to see. "You will learn, girl. If you will not bend to me, then I will break them until you do." He straightened. "She goes. For now. Keep her safe, Ulfhednar, or the next time I see sparks, they will burn differently."

Skúli didn't flinch. His jaw remained tight, eyes flickering into mine. Almost like it was an acknowledgement that he would protect me.

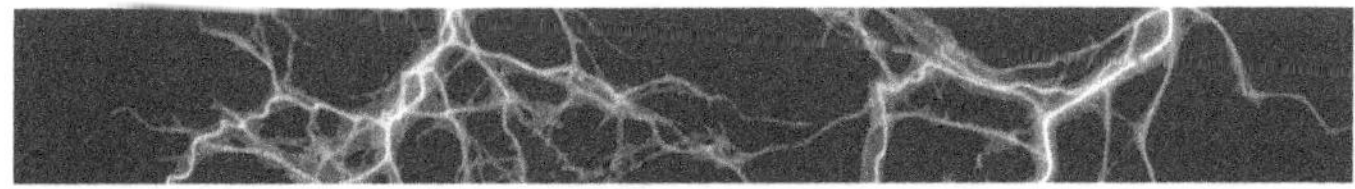

We rode in silence—not because there was nothing to say, but because everything felt dangerous to let out. The hoofbeats of the horses struck the frozen earth in a rhythm too loud, too sharp, each thud sounding like a hammer to my skull.

The King's words clung to me like frostbite. Bed-Whore. Useful. Destroy Drakensvar.

And beneath it all, the hum.

My hands trembled against the reins no matter how tightly I tried to grip them.

Skúli didn't speak, didn't even glance at me. His jaw was set like carved stone, and though I'd seen him annoyed before, I had never seen him angry. This was something cold and sharp. His knuckles were white, his shoulders rigid.

I swallowed, my throat dry like tinder. I hated the silence between us, hated the way the King's shadow still loomed over us even though we'd left his hall far behind. My breath smoked in the air, shallow and uneven. Finally, I tugged my cloak loose from my shoulders.

"You are bleeding." My voice cracked. I didn't know if it was from the cold of the memory of the whip slicing his back, but my chest ached with it. "Take this. At least until we get home."

He didn't even look at me. "Keep it."

"Skúli–"

He urged his horse ahead, cutting the distance between us like he could outrun the words. I bit mine back, staring at the cloak bunched in my hands, useless. My throat burned and so did the strange hum beneath my skin–the power that had flared in the King's presence. The one I still couldn't understand. It wanted out, it wanted to rise, and I was terrified of what would happen if I let it.

By the time Drakensvar came into view three days later, dusk had settled over the mountains. The sky was bruised with violet and ash.

Astrid was waiting.

The moment she saw us, she stormed forward–eyes flashed with anger, hair loose from its braid, her mouth sharp with fury.

"What happened? What did he do?" She shoved past me like I wasn't even there and went straight for Skúli. "If that bastard so much as laid a finger–"

"Astrid."

"No! Do not tell me to calm down." Her hands curled into fists at her sides, her whole body quivering with wrath. "You reek of blood. What did he do? Tell me, and I will slit his throat myself, crown be damned."

I opened my mouth but the words refused to come. The King's threat pressed down on me like an invisible hand at my throat, squeezing. If I spoke it aloud, it would be real, and I couldn't bear it–not yet.

Skúli's voice was steady, too steady. "Astrid."

She froze at the tone, her eyes locking on him.

"He wants us rattled. That is all." His face was unreadable, but I caught the brief look toward me, quick as a blade in the dark. "Do not give him what he wants."

Astird looked between us, her fury praying at her edges. "He hurt you."

Skúli only shrugged, though his back was still stiff, the blood soaked tunic stuck to his skin. "I have had worse."

I clutched my cloak tighter in my lap, the memory of the whip echoing in my ears. I stayed quiet because silence was the only thing I still had control over.

If I spoke, I might scream.

If I screamed, the fire in my veins might answer.

Astrid cursed low and vicious. "One day, Skargrim will choke on his own blood. And when he does, I'll dance on his grave."

I believed her. And for the first time, I prayed she was right.

CHAPTER FIFTEEN
ALURA

A week later, I was sitting in the great hall, tending a fire I'd started myself. The crackle of logs filled the cavernous space, sparks spitting upward into the smokey rafters. I'd grown used to the stillness of the hall when the others were away, but this silence carried a weight of its own.

I'd barely seen Skúli since we returned.

He'd been avoiding me. Avoiding the things we had not spoken of—my power, Hayhjem, the way he had taken my punishment without a second thought.

The door banged open and Astrid swept in, a basket against her hip. Her cheeks were red from the cold, her smile wide enough to fill the room.

"There you are," she said briskly, striding toward me. "Heard you have been pacing about like a hen in a coop." With a grin, she set the basket down beside me and nudged it with the toe of her boot. "So I brought work."

"Work?"

I peered into the basket and groaned. Inside lay an ungodly amount of wool—unwashed, tangled, and clumped together. Waiting to be combed and spun.

My worst nightmare.

I could almost hear the echoes of that long, hot summer at the reconstructed Norse village where I'd learned this lesson the hard way. Hours spent teasing stubborn knots from coarse, scratchy wool, my fingers raw from the constant friction of combs and spindles. How the scent of lanolin clung to my clothes and how I'd cursed the sheep, the sun and my own clumsy fingers.

Staring at this basket, the memory came back sharp and unwelcome. It seemed to sneer at me, daring me to try my luck again.

Astrid's brows rose at my expression. "Do not look at it like it is shit on your shoe. Spinning and weaving is honourable work among our people."

"Oh, I did not mean–" I hurried, cheeks flushing. "I know it is. I just...I hate it."

She squinted, unimpressed, then tapped the wool combs and spindle resting on top. "Hate it or not, you will give it a go. Unless you would rather sit here with idle hands."

"I will try," I muttered, biting my lip. "But I am not very good."

"Did your mother not teach you?" She asked, not un-kindly.

I shook my head. "I do not know my parents." The words came quiet, heavier than I meant.

"Oh." Astrid's voice softened. She settled beside me and laid a warm on hand on my shoulder. I offered her a half-smile in return.

"Well," she said after a moment, her tone bright again, "then I will teach you. My mother taught me, though I was always more interested in wrestling the boys and knocking them on their arses. Still, I was not half bad."

That made me laugh, and the tension eased. "I would like that."

We spent the day together. First combing out the wool until it lay smooth and cloudlike, then coaxing it into thread on the spindle. My hands fumbled constantly, tangling, breaking, twisting too tight. But Astrid corrected me with patience, her laughter quick and generous whenever I made a mistake.

Bit by bit, I managed to spin a length of thread without disaster, and the small victory made me shine with a pride I didn't expect.

By nightfall, the fire had burned low and our basket was lighter. My arms ached pleasantly.

"Can I ask something personal?" I asked, watching the spindle whirl between my fingers.

Astrid shrugged. "Ask."

"Your ears. Is it a family trait? Skúli does not..."

She chuckled. "I thought you would ask something scandalous." With a sigh, she touched the pointed tip of one ear. "They are why I am not supposed to go beyond Dreki Pass. Skúli and I share our father's blood. Our mothers were best friends. I got these from her along with this cursed red hair. Some say we descended from the Alva, elves, back when they still roamed. Stories only, of course. But stories that make some people wish me dead."

"That is awful," I whispered.

Astrid nodded. "It is. That is why Skúli was so mad when I went after the bear. Not because of the bear–but because if the wrong people had seen me, they would cut my ears off and call it a game."

My hands stilled.

For the first time, I understood the way Skúli watched her when she walked out the gates. It was worry disguised as scowls.

We continued our work in silence for a while before I opened my mouth again. "You go out a lot...do you have a boyfriend?"

She laughed. "Gods, no."

"Someone you like then?"

"Yes," Astrid said with a sigh. "But he is away. Brokering peace and probably whoring."

I smirked, teasing her. "Any man who whores instead of being with you is a fool."

Astrid shot me a look, half amused, half exasperated. "Flattery will get you everywhere, you learn quickly."

I shrugged, fingers busy. "I call it the truth."

I managed another neat length of thread and Astrid cheered, clapping me on the back. "See? You are a natural!"

"Good work."

The voice came from the edge of the firelight.

I froze.

Skúli stood at the edge of the firelight, broad shoulders outlined by the glow. Without his heavy cloak, dressed in a black tunic embroidered in gold, he looked every inch of what he was meant to be. His arms were folded across his chest, his mouth curved in something between approval and pride. At his feet, Björn lay with his green eyes fixed on me.

"Thank you," I murmured, forcing my gaze back to my task. My cheeks felt like they were burning hotter than the fire.

If Astrid noticed, she gave no sign. Instead she grinned. "There is a healer in town who will pay for this yarn. For bandages mostly. She is getting old, and I think she is glad for anyone willing to help."

"Perhaps Alura might apprentice with her," Skúli said.

I nearly dropped the spindle. Our eyes met and I saw that he was utterly serious.

Astrid choked on a laugh, turning red when I glared at her. "Sorry," she wheezed.

"Why not?" Skúli pressed.

"She has not left the hall in a week," Astrid countered. "She has not run, has not poisoned us, has not slit our throats. Yet, you keep her locked up."

His fingers stroked his beard as he studied me. The silence stretched long. Finally, he nodded once. "I will speak to Freydis tomorrow."

Astrid left to prepare supper, humming smugly.

Skúli took her place beside me. He said nothing, only watched the careful motions of my hands, close enough that his head brushed against my skin. It took all my concentration to not jumble.

After a while, he asked quietly, "Where is your home?"

"Far away," I sighed. The words felt hollow. I didn't even know how to answer his question.

"But you want to go back."

"Of course I do!" My voice snapped sharper than I meant, and heat prickled under my skin again, that strange energy threatening to surge. I forced myself to breathe slowly. "But I do not think I can."

"All things are possible."

I didn't answer. Because if I did, I might admit that part of me wondered if staying wasn't so bad but that would be betraying the very reason I was here.

"What about your family? A husband?" He pressed, tone casual but eyes too keen.

"No."

"How many winters have you seen?"

"Twenty-six summers," I said. His brow furrowed. I added, "I was found on the summer solstice. A newborn. I never knew my parents.

His expression shifted–shock, pity, something heavier. "And who raised you?"

I bit my lip and set the spindle down in the basket, trying to find the right words. "The King of my people," I said. "Well...his...household."

That earned a flicker of outrage from him. "No clan? No kin to claim you?"

"No," I whispered.

And then, almost without thinking, a memory slipped past my defenses. That memory of Professor Halvard, his laugh echoing. The way he winked at me. I had liked him as a teacher, respected him even, and now I only felt the sting of betrayal when I remembered how he'd tried to turn lessons into something else.

Skúli's jaw tightened. I could see a flash of anger in his eyes, reacting to what I had been thinking about.

"You look scared," he said quietly, his voice low, more of an observation than a question. "What are you thinking of?"

"My teacher."

His jaw tightened. "What did he do?"

I hesitated, swallowing the knot in my throat. The memory was sharp and bitter. "He...tried to make it more than just lessons. Tried to...I do not know, turned his attention to me in ways I did not want. I respected him and he..." My voice faltered, and I shook my head, ashamed of the vulnerability I hadn't meant to expose.

Skúli's hands curled into fists at his side, the anger in his eyes flaring. "A teacher," he said slowly, teeth gritted, "should never touch a student like that. Never. You deserved better."

"I know," I whispered, my fingers tightening on the spindle. "I learned to keep myself safe."

"You should not have had to," he growled under his breath, jaw tight. Then his voice softened slightly. "No one should. You deserved a home, someone to protect you, someone to see you as more than prey or a toy."

I looked at him, the weight of his words settled over me like a shield. For the first time in years, it felt like someone understood. Someone truly saw the fear I had carried silently and refused to let it define me.

"You are strong," he said finally. "Stronger than anyone who tried to break you. You are still standing. Is that why Skargrim scares you so much?"

I nodded slowly.

Astrid returned then, plates in hand, saving me. Supper was quiet, peaceful, until Astrid propped her chin on her fists and asked, "Alura, how many of our stories do you know?"

I froze, like we were caught doing something. "A little."

"Do you know how the world was made?"

"Something about a giant's corpse?" I said lamely, unsure of how to tell them both that I'd spent my entire life studying the sagas.

Astrid gasped in shock. "Skúli, tell it properly. Like when we were kids."

He grumbled, as he got up from the table to go fetch something. I felt bad for him for a moment, he'd only been halfway through his dinner, and I wasn't sure he'd eaten all day. Astrid didn't mind his grumbling though.

"You are going to love this," she told me. I couldn't help but believe her.

When Skúli returned he had a small pouch and a cup of mead. Astrid beckoned me to get up and take a seat around the fire. We took our places on the seats around the fire as Skúli scattered a powder into the flames, they flared green-blue, casting strange shadows across his face.

"In the beginning," he intoned, his voice deep and ancient, "there was only Ginnungagap..."

Astrid wiggled like an excited child. "This is my favourite story."

The tale unfolded–of fire and ice, of Ymir the giant, of Audhumla the cow, of gods born from salt and frost. His words wrapped around us like smoke, each pause deliberate, each image vivid. He sprinkled water on the fire, making it sputter. When he winked at me mid-story, teasing, a shiver coursed through me. The energy under my skin stirred violently, sparkling like lightning trapped in a glass.

He ended with Odin's slaying of Ymir, the world fashioned from bone and blood. The fire sank back to its ordinary glow.

Astrid clapped and whistled. I could only stare.

Skúli's gaze met mine. For an instant it was as though he saw what was burning under my skin, the part of me I was trying to smother. His eyes narrowed, pained. Then he turned on his heel and left the hall without a word.

I didn't see him again for the rest of the night.

CHAPTER SIXTEEN
ALURA

The cold whipped around me as I stood in nothing but my underdress. My bare feet sank into the dark mist swirling beneath me, curling around my ankles like living smoke. Shapes stirred within it—hunched things, faceless and waiting. Watching.

Then the runes came.

Their familiar silver fire burned into the air around me, one by one, cutting through the dark.

ᚦ. Thorn. A threat. ᚺ. Hail. Chaos. ᛉ. Protection—shattered.

The voice followed. No longer soft and ethereal as before but sharp as the wind, cold and commanding.

"Alura."

I spun, but saw no one. Only the runes glowing against the void.

Then, out of the darkness, two white-fire eyes opened.

"The shield sleeps. The blade moves unseen. Wake."

Great. Riddles.

"What do you mean?" I demanded, my voice shaking against the silence.

Memories flashed before my eyes—no, not memories. Images. Not my own.

Something was happening now.

A knife glinting in the dark. A door. A wolf's claws scratching against it. And Skúli—sleeping soundly, chest rising and falling, one hand tucked under his pillow, utterly unaware of the shadow moving toward him, blade in hand.

"*You must go.*"

"Go where?" I shouted into the void. "You brought me here, you spoke in riddles, then vanished for weeks! Now you order me to go?"

"*Wake, Storm-Born. The hearth has been breached.*"

More runes burned into the air before me, but before I could speak, before I could demand answers, the dream shattered.

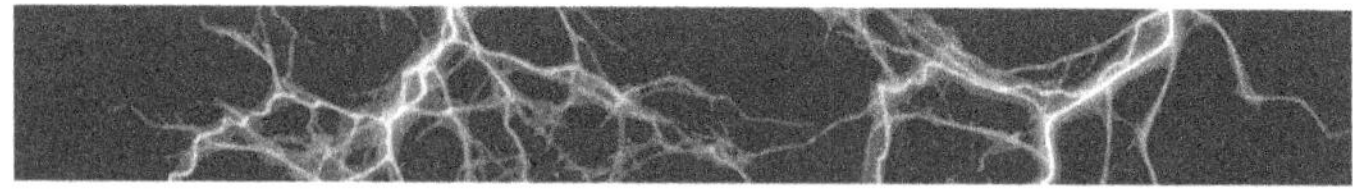

I gasped awake, the dream still lingering fresh within my mind. Darkness cradled me softly, the coals in the hearth glowing soft and red. Frost etched itself onto the window.

Winter was here, and I could feel it in the chill all around me.

A whine came keening under my door, the sound of scratching at my door.

Björn.

I flung the blankets aside and rushed to the door, my bare feet pounding against the cold stone. When I pulled it open, Björn looked up at me, his green eyes bright and urgent.

Help me, they seemed to say.

"What is it?" I asked as he gently licked my hand.

Björn growled, deep and dangerous.

Then came the deliberate scrape of boot on stone.

Someone was inside.

Before I could think, I was moving. Skúli's door was locked. My fists pounded against it, my voice raw from panic. "Skúli! Skúli, wake up!"

No movement. No sound.

Time was running out.

I hurled myself at the door, my bare foot striking at the wood. Something tore through me in a blinding flash–something raw, jagged, mine and not mine. Power exploded outward in a blinding flash.

The door splintered, swinging inward with a crack.

The room was dark. Still. Except for the shadow.

A figure slid along the wall, silent as death, a knife glinting faintly in the heath's glow. His arm rose above Skúli's sleeping outline, oblivious to the danger.

I tried to scream. No sound came.

The intruder's head snapped toward me.

The knife arced down.

I didn't think—I moved.

I raised a hand as heat tore through me, wild and primal. Tearing out of my body as I let out a small gasp of pain. Power burst from my palm in a jagged torrent or purple-blue light. It stuck the wall behind the assassin with a deafening crack, sparks scattering like fireflies.

The man cried out, dropping the blade as he stumbled back.

Skúli surged upright, dagger in hand, already moving. Björn lunged with a snarl, slamming the man to the floor. The sound shook the rafters.

And then my legs gave out.

Power rippled through me, leaving only ash and smoke in its way. My head pounded violently, nausea clawing up my throat. The room tilted.

I wiped my nose, staring in horror at the streak of blood on my hand.

The world was too loud. Too bright.

"Alura!"

Skúli's voice broke through the chaos, sharp with panic.

He was at my side in moments, the dagger forgotten. He dropped to his knees before me, his hand hovering, unsure if I would let him touch me. I tried to shove him away, but my body trembled uncontrollably.

"I did not mean to," I whispered, my voice cracking and raw. "I did not mean to do it."

My palm still glowed faintly, veins lit like rivers of lightning beneath my skin. Energy pulsed—hot and foreign. I stared at my own hands in horror.

I flinched.

Not from him.

But from myself.

"Easy," Skúli said softly, his voice calm and steady, like a tide rolling in. "Breathe. You are alright."

"No. I am not."

Astrid's voice cut through the silence that was building between us. "What is going on?" A pause echoed as she took in the surroundings. "Are you alright?"

"She is fine," Skúli replied stubbornly. "I have her. An intruder tried to come in. Alura alerted me. Go back to bed. We are safe."

Astrid hesitated for a moment but left us alone.

When I dared to look up, I braced for disgust, for fear. But he only looked at me with the same quiet, unreadable look he always had. Not judgment. Not revulsion.

Something else.

"You protected me," he murmured, as if the words were strange in his mouth.

I wanted to argue. To say no, I'd lost control, that I was dangerous. But the words caught in my throat, lost to the pounding in my head.

He must have seen it, because he guided me closer to the fire, settling me against him. His arms wrapped around me, steady, solid, an anchor.

Björn pressed close, laying his bloody muzzle in my lap with a low whine.

The firelight flickered across Skúli's face, throwing his jaw into shadow, his eyes dark and heavy.

"We will talk later," he whispered.

And I was grateful. Because right now, the only thing I could do was breathe.

CHAPTER SEVENTEEN
ALURA

When I began to stir, I had the oddest thought that perhaps I wasn't in my own bed. It smelled different. It felt different. Too quiet—no rustle of wind against the window, no low creak of the rafters as the timber settles. There was a silence that felt unnatural.

I stretched out my stiff joints and rolled over, blinking against the pale morning light. My heart slammed against my ribs as the realization set in.

This definitely wasn't my bed.

The fur blankets were too thick. The pillow, too firm. And the scent—smoke, pine, cold leather. And underneath it all, warmer lingered.

Mead.

Honey wine. The kind *he* favoured.

I was in Skúli's bed.

I sat up too quickly. The room tilted, pain needling behind my eyes, sharp as glass. My stomach lurched. Near the bedside, a faint smear of dried blood caught my gaze. The scent of iron clung to my nostrils.

Gods. I had–

"You are awake."

The voice made me flinch.

Skúli stood near the hearth, sleeves rolled up, stirring something in a small pot over the fire. His axe leaned against the wall within arm's reach. The swords across his back caught the light as he shifted.

Always armed. Always ready.

He didn't look at me, only gave the pot another slow stir.

"You passed out after–" He stopped, jaw tightening. "After everything. I put you to bed." He paused, his voice dipping quieter. "You were cold. Shaking."

I swallowed. "The man–"

"Dead." He turned to me then, face cold and hard. I flinched before he smoothed his expression. "No use coating it in honey. He has been sent back to where he came from. Cowards do not go to Valhalla."

He took a step closer, and this time his eyes met mine. "And...do not worry." His voice softened. "I slept on the floor. I would not share the bed with you unless you were wanting that."

The words made heat rise to my cheeks.

The memory of my professor burned at the edge of my mind, the way his eyes lingered too long, the way he had tried to turn trust into something else. And here was Skúli, blunt and unflinching, offering me safety without taking advantage. Respect without expectation.

I let out a shaky breath.

"Thank you," I whispered.

He crossed the room and placed a wooden cup on the table beside me. "Drink. It will help."

The bitter brew hit the back of my throat like earth and flowers crushed together. I wondered if it was something his mother once brewed for him, or if he'd learned it from someone else, someone long gone.

Either way, it steadied me.

A little.

I had been expecting fear from him, but there was none. Just his presence. Solid and unwavering. His eyes held a quiet intensity, the kind that made you feel like nothing around you could hurt you as long as he stood there. Not angered or impatient, just watchful.

"I did not mean it," I whispered, recalling the events of last night. "It just...came."

He nodded. No judgement. No surprise. "Seidr is like a blade. Better drawn when needed than buried in your back."

The word lodged in me.

Seidr.

I knew it from my studies. Half-whispers and fractures notes in old texts. A magic nearly erased entirely. Most of it had died during the Crusades, stamped out, scattered.

Skúli looked away quickly, as if he regretted saying it aloud.

"I should have stayed awake. Should have noticed him." His jaw tightened. Anger–not at me, but at himself. "It should not have come to that."

"You protected me too," I said softly.

He didn't answer but something in his shoulders eased as he sat on the edge of the bed. Not close, not distant. A careful and comfortable distance.

Still, something in me wanted him nearer.

"You do not have to be afraid of what you are."

I turned the cup in my hands. "I do not even know *what* I am. What if I hurt someone? What if people look too closely and see a monster?"

He looked at me then–truly looked.

"Let them look. You saved my life. All our lives."

The words sank into me, heavy and warm, like armour I hadn't realised that I needed.

When he stood, he spoke so quietly that I almost missed it. "Next time you dream of danger, just wake me."

I wanted to tell him I hadn't known it was a dream. That I *had* tried to wake him.

But he was already gone, Björn at his heels. Only smoke and leather remained, and the slow, steady rhythm of my heartbeat.

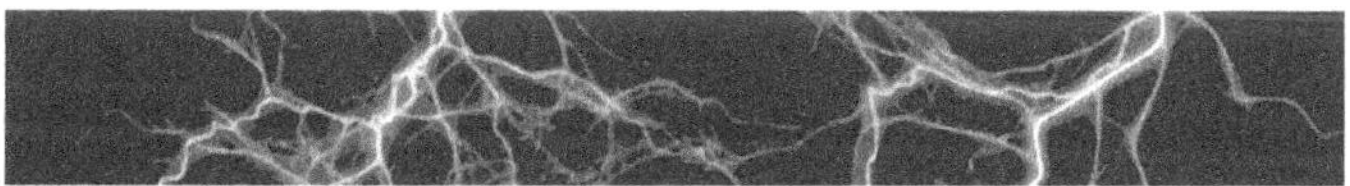

Later, when I dragged myself from bed, I got dressed and tucked the dirty ones under one arm and headed downstairs. I nearly collided with Astrid at the foot of the stairs.

She gave me a knowing, thankful look. Her sharp eyes told me she knew what happened last night before she slipped out the door without a word.

I braced myself for the chores ahead, but when I stepped out into the courtyard, Skúli was already there. Björn bounded over like a large puppy, tail high, and licked my free hand.

Skúli let loose a laugh, a rare, deep sound that echoed off the courtyard.

"So he does like you," he mused. "You are not cleaning today. Your new teacher is waiting."

"I am not really up for healing lessons," I muttered.

He came closer, close enough that his scent curled around me. "I was not asking. And she is not only a healer, Alura."

"I do not understand."

"You will."

He took the laundry from me and dumped it by the door. Then, to my surprise, he took my hand and led me toward the gates. My pulse leapt. The walls loomed until he pushed open the gates.

The cold wind outside whipped around me. It felt so open. Skúli let go of my hand and strode ahead, Björn at his heels.

We passed cottages as whispers trailed behind us. Shutters closed. Doors latched. Some people glared openly while others stepped aside as though I carried disease. Skúli ignored them, head high and shoulders unyielding. I tried to mimic him, even as my insides knotted.

By the water's edge stood a crooked cottage. Waves licked at the doorstep, and the scent of salt and ash rolled from within. The door creaked open.

The woman from the marketplace stepped out.

"You look like you have stepped straight out of a storm cloud, girl."

Her voice was low and wry, cutting through murmurs like a blade. She leaned on a carved walking stick, more ceremonial than practical though she did favour one leg more. Her silver hair was in a braid, and a brooch pinned her cloak closed. Her eyes were pale, nearly colourless, and they pierced me so deeply the hairs on my neck rose.

The crowd that had followed us hushed as she stepped forward.

"Freydis," she said simply. "Of Vardengrim. Or remains of it."

The murmurs vanished. Feet shuffled. People melted away, leaving silence in their wake.

"I-I do not know of Vardengrim," I admitted.

Her head snapped toward Skúli, her gaze sharp enough to cut. "You bring her to me, yet you do not tell her the stories? She's been here for nearly two moons."

He only shrugged. "It was not my story."

Frustration bubbled in me. "What is Vargengrim?"

Freydis's gaze swung back to me, heavy as stone. "Home of the priestesses. Built by elves of old, before they left our realm. Birthplace of the one who will complete the prophecy."

Her eyes narrowed, peering into me as if she could read me.

"You are a priestess."

My breath caught. That was why she had never married, never passed her craft to children.

"Was," Freydis corrected. "Before the gods went silent. Before cowards burned the old halls and the last of the magic was–" she cut herself off, squinting.

Then, without warning, she jabbed her walking stick into my side. "Well...pushed into you."

CHAPTER EIGHTEEN
ALURA

"I do not understand," I said for what must have been the hundredth time.

We sat inside the small cottage, fire crackling in the hearth. I was stiff-backed at the small table, Freydis across from me, her pale eyes sharp as glass. Skúli occupied the chair nearest the fire, his long legs stretched out, his silence deliberate. His mouth twitched as though he was suppressing a laugh at my stubbornness, which only made me scowl harder.

Freydis sighed, rubbing a weathered hand across her brow. "You called the storm," she said slowly, each word crisp, as though she were speaking to a stubborn child. "And lived. That is no small thing."

"I did not mean to–"

Her hand snapped up, silencing me. "Intent belongs to men. Magic cares nothing for what you meant." She leaned closer, her voice dropping to a low rasp meant for me alone. "The threads have begun to weave themselves.

You have tugged on something older than the realms. You need a teacher."

My stomach flipped. I glanced at Skúli who hadn't looked away from the fire, as if this was all perfectly ordinary. Perhaps, for him, it was.

"And you would be that teacher?" My voice was sharper than I intended, a defense against the panic twisting inside me.

Her smile was humourless, thin as a knife's edge. "I would be the fire to keep you from freezing. But *him–*" she jerked her thumb at Skúli, "He is the shield that keeps you from burning the world."

"I still do not see what he has to do with this."

A beat passed .Freydis turned to glare at him. "You really told her nothing?"

Skúli grunted. "I had to be sure. No sense dragging people into prophecy if it does not concern them. I did not want to endanger her."

"You endangered us all by letting her run blind," Freydis snapped. "We have little time. A year, perhaps less. Perhaps more. Fate is fickle."

She rubbed her calloused palms together, muttering under her breath before she fixed her gaze back on me. "How did you come here?"

"Here?" I frowned. "This is Earth."

Freydis tilted her head, considering my words. "Earth. That is not what we call this realm. You came from Midgard."

"You mean...I have crossed realms?" My laugh was brittle. "That is impossible."

"Yes, child. That is what I am saying."

"I am not a child," I bit back.

"Child, when you have lived as long as I have," Freydis replied calmly, "all are children."

I turned to Skúli, hoping for some ground to stand on. "How old is she?"

He shrugged, a flicker of amusement tugging his mouth. "No one knows. She does not speak of life before she came here."

Freydis smirked, unbothered.

"Why help me at all?" I asked, gnawing on my nail.

Her eyes softened, barely. "Because I know what it means to be feared before you even understand yourself. And because what is coming will either forge you or shatter you." She leaned forward. "You did not come here by chance. You were brought. The gods will not say how, but they did. Now, listen."

Before I could protest, she reached across the table. Her palms were warm, rough. Against instinct, I placed mine into hers.

The world shifted.

I wasn't in the cottage anymore.

I was in Freydis's skin, heart hammering as a storm ripped the roof from a temple. Wind howled through the halls, shaking ancient stones. Panic clawed up my throat.

I–*she*–ran into a chamber where a woman with pale hair screamed, sweat dripping from her brow. Three priestesses surrounded her, hoods pushed back, their chants weaving through the roar of the storm.

The air tasted of lightning. Power.

The bulge of the woman's belly glowed with threads of silver, violet and blue, weaving into the unborn child.

"No," the woman gasped, desperation cracking her voice. "Not her. Please. Not my daughter."

Her pleas went unanswered.

"She is coming whether you will it or not," Freydis's voice rasped, my lips moving with hers. "Push or we lose her. And we lose this war."

The woman sobbed, clutching her swollen belly. "How do I say goodbye to someone I have never met?"

"You know her," Freydis soothed. "Every kick, every flutter. She is yours. And when we survive this...you will see her again."

The storm's fury swelled, then blurred, spinning me back through shadows and lightning until I slammed into myself once more.

I gasped, wrenching my hands free from Freydis's grasp. "What was that?"

"The night of your birth." Her tone was heavy with sorrow. "I tried to save them all."

"Was it you who took me?"

She shook her head. "No. That was Ingrid. A priestess braver than most men. She carried you into your world."

"Why me?" My voice cracked. "Why now?"

"There is a prophecy–"

"What *prophecy*?" My voice rose, hot as the sparks under my skin.

"Girl, control yourself," Freydis snapped.

A hand landed on my shoulder.

Skúli.

Solid. Grounding.

His touch steadied the fire simmering inside me until it dulled to embers. He didn't speak, but I felt the tether between us.

I turned to him, putting the pieces together. "You have magic too."

"Of a sort. I am Ulfhednar. Bound to Björn. Rare since the gods abandoned us."

Ulfhednar.

The voice echoed in my memory. *The answers you seek lie with the Ulfhednar.*

"I was stupid," I whispered.

A shadow passed over his features. His jaw tightened. "I am the last."

The sadness in his voice lodged deep in my chest.

"Bound to Björn?" I asked, hesitantly. "What does that mean?"

He met my gaze. "An Ulfhednar shares his life with his wolf. Björn and I are entwined. Our breath, our heartbeat, our strength...we draw it from one another. When he hunts, I feel it. When I fight, he is beside me. Injure him, and I know. Starve him, and my body wanes. He is my shadow and my strength. It is not a bond of choice–it is survival. And it is sacred."

I swallowed, trying to picture a connection so deep that it was almost impossible to separate the two.

"If...if he was to die?"

Skúli's gaze darkened. "I would not die. But I would lose a part of myself I could not get back. But if I was to die...then Björn would die too."

Freydis cleared her throat, dragging us back. "Listen."

Her tone dropped into something more ceremonial. Her voice carried the weight older than the room itself.

"From the shadowed edge where the sea swallows the sun, Shall she be torn—child of stars and storm begun. Bloodline forgotten, yet older than flame, Hair like frost-wrought silver, eyes none dare name.

She shall tread where no mortal dares, Drawn by whispers and warrior's stares. A son of the North, of blade and blood, Bound by wyrd, yet born from scud.

Together they summon the wrathful sky, Ravens shall scream and gods shall die. Through ash-choked woods and iron-clad stone, They shall walk where night has grown.

For the Serpent's jest, forged in spite, Shall unravel in the last god's light. The blood of kings shall stain the land, And fire shall rise from a lover's hand.

When the sky weeps flame and the world is bled, Shall fate be fulfilled—and the old gods dead."

The words hung between us, thick like smoke.

I opened my mouth, then stopped myself. Freydis narrowed her eyes on me. "If you say you do not understand again, I will throw my stick at you."

I clamped my jaw shut, then looked at Skúli. He offered nothing, only retreated back to the fire, letting the shadows flicker across his face.

When he finally spoke, it was quiet. "I have never heard the prophecy in full. Only fragments."

"The priestesses kept it that way," Freydis said. "To keep the chosen hidden until the time came."

Freydis's gaze softened, tinged with pity and awe. "You were taken to Midgard at birth, so that no king, no mortal–or god could claim you or use you. We hid you there to protect you until fate brought you back to us."

"Hidden?" I pressed my palms to the table. "You sent me away. I grew up with no family, no love! I had to fight to make my place in the world *you* sent me."

"You grew up *alive*," Freydis said. "And unclaimed."

"This realm," she said, voice low. "It is called Aelfrheim. It is older than kings, older than mortal memory. The lines between gods and men have always been thin here, but now, they fray."

I pressed my hands to my face, hot tears spilling. "So all of this...all of me...I am just a tool?"

"No," Freydis said sharply, though her eyes glimmered with sorrow. "You are the child of mortal and divine. You are the storm's fury, blood and magic intertwined. You are the one who can face what no mere mortal could endure. You are who can stand against the gods themselves if they rise in wrath. But you are not alone."

Freydis's hands rested lightly on mine, surprisingly gentle. "You were hidden to survive, yes. But also to prepare. The storm in your blood is tied to Aelfrheim, to its wyrd.

You carry power the world has not seen in centuries. Power that will either save it...or destroy it."

My power hummed, skittering across the wood. "I didn't ask for this!"

"No," Freydis agreed. "But you were made to endure it."

She turned to Skúli. "Together."

I could hardly breathe. "Together?"

"Yes," Freydis whispered, the weight of destiny pressing down with every word. "He is your tether, your shield and your equal. You share more than fate. The prophecy does not speak of one alone. It speaks of both of you. The child of stars and storm, the last wolf-warrior. Together you will walk into darkness where gods themselves will test your courage. Where fire and wrath will rise, and death will follow. You are meant to survive it, to endure, to shape the world that comes after."

I shook, a tremor running through me, the heat of power in my veins humming and coiling. "And if I fail?" I whispered. "If I...cannot?"

Freydis's gaze was steel. "Then the world will burn without mercy. But you will not fail. Your blood is tempered in both worlds—mortal and divine. You can survive where others would break. Because you are Alura Storm-Born, and no god, no king, no mortal will bend you without a fight."

I let out a shuddering breath, the enormity of it pressing down on me, and for the first time I felt the weight of Skúli's presence not just behind me, but beside me. An anchor, a bond, a shared burden.

Skúli broke the silence. "We ride to meet Skargrim in four days."

I turned to face him. "He said we had two moons."

He shrugged. "The raven came early this morning."

"She stays with me until then," Freydis declared. "She needs control before she faces that snake again. Now it has been unleashed it will be easier for her to lose control. If she loses herself near him, we all pay the price."

Pain flickered in Skúli's eyes.

He turned to me, a question in his eyes. *Do you want this?*

I nodded. "It is okay, I will be okay."

His jaw worked, but he gave the smallest nod.

Freydis groaned, standing with her stick. "Good. Now say your farewells. I will be outside with the overgrown dog."

Once she was gone, Skúli came closer, resting one hand on the table. His eyes burned into mine. "Are you certain? I cannot shield you if I am not here."

I forced a shaky smile. "Did you not say this morning I was the one protecting you."

It didn't land as lightly as I'd hoped, but his mouth twisted up at the ends slightly.

"I will be fine," I say, trying to reassure him. "We are in the middle of the village. It is safe."

"If anything feels wrong," he said, his voice rough. "I will come for you."

For reasons I couldn't name, the words sent a shiver racing through me. A fire awoke in me again as he looked into my eyes–my soul.

"You are..." he hesitated, then said, "remarkable. To be protected at all costs, so you do not fall into the wrong hands. Because what man could resist what you carry?"

He turned to leave, but paused at the door. "I will return in four days."

And then he was gone, leaving only the scent of smoke and steel, and the weight of prophecy pressing against my ribs.

CHAPTER NINETEEN
ALURA

Freydis wasted no time with me. The moment Skúli left, she had me hauling wood until my arms shook, and dragging buckets of water so heavy that I thought my shoulders would split. By the time I collapsed inside her cottage, sweat-soaked and aching, I felt less like a student of magic and more like her lackey.

But I slept well. Too well even. Wrapped in blankets on the floor of the common room, I dreamt of nothing. Not even nightmares.

The next morning, Feydis sat me down before breakfast, her eyes sharp as flint.

"There are five main paths of magic," she began, speaking with the cadence of someone who had said these words countless times before. "Seidr–healing, visions, communing with gods, weaving fate itself. Berserker magic–the kind your Ulfhednar friend carries."

"He is not my friend," I interrupted.

She clicked her tongue in disapproval but pressed on. "Runes. Galdr. And Val-Galdr—the last being death magic. My sisters considered it forbidden."

My skin prickled. "Death magic?"

"Yes. Incantations to call on the dead. The price is steep. Most who try lose their voice. Some lose their mind."

I swallowed, but Freydis only clapped her hands sharply, startling me. "First things first. We tame your stormlight."

"I am not sure how," I admit. "I do not know how it starts."

"That is what I need to know. Think. When does it strike?"

I forced myself to go back over every moment. The storm, the flare of power in Skargrim's hall, even small bursts that I'd shook off. My face burned when I whispered, "When I feel too much. Anger. Fear. Lust."

Her eyes narrowed. "Lust. With *him*?"

Heat flared across my cheeks. I nodded once.

"Have you fucked?"

The bluntness made me choke. "No!"

"Good. Stay away."

"Why?"

Her stare pinned me in place. "Because you could burn the realms to ash before he could get his trousers off. You are unstable. That is not your fault–but it is your danger. We are working on stability."

The word rang hollow in my chest, foreign and uncomfortable. *Stability.* I almost scoffed at it–until the familiar prickle ignited under my skin. My veins lit up in a glowing thread of silver-blue.

Freydis inhaled sharply. "By the Norns…Alura, you are alight."

The glow crawled up my arms, humming under my flesh. The stormlight throbbed with raw, wild energy.

"Your eyes," she whispered. "They change. Has Skúli told you this?"

I shook my head.

"Stupid boy," she muttered. "He should have dragged you here the moment he saw it."

We trained until my body screamed. She forced me to summon, bury, summon again. Until my skin stopped glowing and the stormlight obeyed. By nightfall, I collapsed into a dreamless oblivion.

The next day was worse. She pushed me harder, like she sensed Skúli's return and wanted me wrung dry before he came.

"Unnatural," she repeated, every time I faltered. "You feel it because it is. But unnatural does not mean unworthy. You were given this gift for a reason. Use it wisely."

Freydis told me variants of this throughout the day. Pushing me harder and scolding me when I let myself lose control. By evening, my veins obeyed my will. I fell asleep before supper.

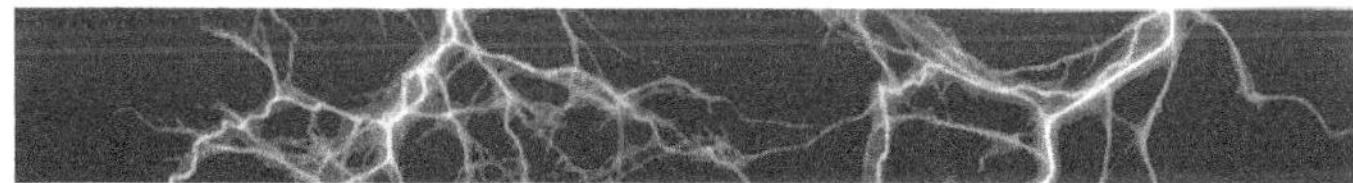

The dream came again.

"Storm-Born."

Shadows curled around me like old friends. The voice slid into my mind, soft and consuming.

"What is this?" I demanded.

"What your power will become if you do not tame it. If you do not tame yourself."

"You cannot tame a storm."

Light burned through the dark, and white-fire eyes flared before me.

"No." The voice agreed. *"But you are not just the storm. You are my wrath."*

"Who are you?" I snapped.

"I am no one. I am everyone. I am you. I am me."

I clenched my fists. "Are you...my mother?"

A silence, heavy as stone, stretched between us.

"No," The voice said at last. *"She cannot return."*

"Where is she? What did you do to her?"

"I welcomed her. As I will welcome you, one day. My hall is filled with the sisters who came before. They wait for you."

My stomach dropped. "You mean I'm going to die?"

"Everything dies, child."

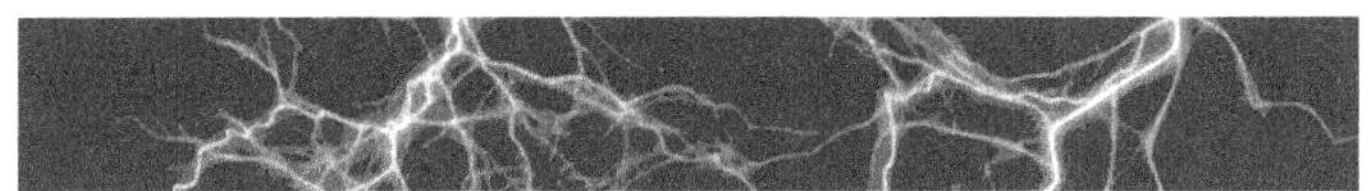

I woke up gasping, drenched in sweat.

"Bad dream?"

My head snapped up. Skúli sat by the fire, his axe at his side. His eyes were shadowed, weary, like he hadn't slept in days.

"You are early," I whispered.

He only nodded.

Something tugged low in my chest. I hated to admit it, but part of me had missed him. Even the fortress. And Björn.

"Are you alright?" I asked carefully.

"Just eager to get this over with." His voice was flat, clipped.

Before I could answer, a frantic pounding rattled the door. Skúli's hand instantly went to his axe.

"Open it," Freydis barked from her bedchamber. "We have a patient."

I swung the door wide. A young woman stumbled in, clutching a limp child. His breathing was ragged, his chest rattled wetly. She was sobbing, begging for help.

Freydis swept forward, but I froze in the doorway, every part of me screaming. And then–I felt it. The stormlight rose, eager and dangerous.

"Rein it in!" Freydis snapped.

I shoved it down, teeth gritted, then said firmly, "Where do you need me?"

"Out of the way."

"I can help." Freydis shot me a look, but I stood my ground. "I have seen this before, when I was a child. I know what he needs."

She paused for only a moment–then gave a single nod. "Then do it. Quickly."

I ran outside, barefoot and wild-haired, filling buckets, boiling water, shoving pots into Skúli's hands. The fire roared as he worked beside me, silent but efficient. Steam filled the air and the boy dragged in shuddering breaths.

"Did he have a fever? Chills? Nausea?"

"Yes–all of it. The rest of us recovered in days. But he–he only grew worse."

I pressed my hands into hers. "Keep everyone away from your house. We will care for him."

She nodded and fled, leaving her son in our care.

Freydis studied me as I wrung out a cloth and laid on the boy's brow. "What do you think it is?"

"An infection in his lungs," I answered. "The steam will help him cough it up. Fluids, herbs for the fever."

Freydis's lips curved, a rare approval glimmering in her eyes. "You will make a fine healer. When you return from Hayhjem, I will take you as my apprentice."

Before I could answer, Skúli growled low from his post at the fire.

"As long as she comes home every night." He glanced up, his eyes hard, voice quiet but iron. "Every. Night."

CHAPTER TWENTY
SKÚLI

The road bent long and winding through the woods. The sky was low and iron-gray, the kind of brooding light that pressed shadows close against the ground. Snow had fallen during the night—not enough to bury the path, but enough that each hoofbeat pressed clean marks into the white. Behind us, Drakensvar had grown small, a dark smudge against the mountainside. Ahead, the mountain mist curled in faint threads.

Alura rode beside me, her cloak pulled tight against the cold. Her mare's breath steamed into the air, the strands of her pale hair had escaped its tie, whipping against her cheeks. She looked tired–she often did now–but there was still a fire in her eyes, restless and unyielding.

For a time, neither of us spoke. The silence between us was strange, heavy, but not unwelcome. Not quite peaceful, not quite hostile. Just there, the way winter always was–something to be endured.

It was Alura who broke it first.

"Where is he?"

I did not need to ask who she meant. "Björn?"

She nodded, her gaze fixed on the road.

I tightened my grip on the reins. "Not here."

"That much I gathered," she said dryly, a faint twist of humour ghosting her lips. "You have hidden him well. Too well."

"That is because it is not safe," I said, sharper than I intended. Her head turned toward me, her brows lifting. The look in her eyes–questioning, accusing–forced me to add, "He cannot leave Drakensvar. Not now."

"Because of what he is?"

The words hung between us, sharp as the bite of frost.

I exhaled, slowly. "Yes."

She studied me. There was hurt in her face but she was unsurprised. "Like Astrid," she mused. "You think they will come for him."

"I do not *think*. They will. As the last Ulfhednar, I am at risk. Björn even more so. They will hurt him to get to me." My throat burned with the words. "You know this."

Her hands tightened on the reins. "He is a wolf, Skúli. Your wolf. He deserves to be–"

"Safe," I cut her off. "And that is why he remains where he is. In Drakensvar."

She fell silent, though I saw her jaw clench, her breath quicken. We rode on, the crunch of the snow beneath hooves echoing out. I could feel Alura's tension, the way her fingers flexed around the reins and it made the cold in my chest spread. I hated that she had to understand.

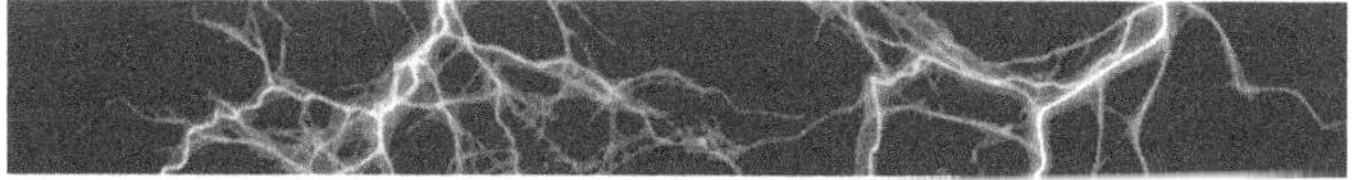

The second day on the road, I noticed the way her thighs pressed against the saddle, how she shifted with each bump and jolt. I tried not to stare, but still caught myself stealing glances out of the corner of my eye, hiding smirks when she thought I was not watching. She was tired, yes, but stubborn. She carried herself with a fire that didn't ask for permission, and I could not help but respect it...and fear it in equal measure.

She shot me secret grins too, small curves of her lips that hinted at amusement, teasing, or challenge. I knew when she thought I was asleep or too focused on the trail to notice, and I savoured those moments—the quiet game between us.

I was quieter this trip, a whole day of it so far, punctuated only by grunts or clipped observations. The road demanded focus, and the company–though familiar–was enough without constant conversation.

By the third day, around a small campfire, I felt the pull of conversation. Or maybe the pull of her presence. I could not sit and let her fade into quiet isolation beside me any longer. The fire crackled between us, a fragile circle of warmth against the dark forest.

I watched her hug her knees to her chest, the wool cloak over her shoulders, furs draped over her lap. The way the flames painted her features, sharp and pale against the darkness, made me ache with a strange, protective longing. I wanted to reach across the fire and hold her, shield her, warn her of every danger I knew waited ahead, but the words lodged in my throat.

"You have been quiet," she said finally.

"I often am," I muttered, shrugging. Then, faintly, almost teasing, I added, "You just notice it more when it is just us."

She rolled her eyes, but I could feel her warmth even in that small gesture. It steadied me.

For a long while, we let the silence settle again. The wind whispered through the pines, carrying the scent of burning pine and snow. It felt like protection, or maybe a reminder that the forest saw all and judged none.

Then I said it, softly, more to the fire than her. "I have seen her too."

Her head snapped up. Confusions, curiosity, a flicker of fear in her eyes. "Who?"

"The eyes," I said. "The voice. In dreams."

Her breath caught. "You have seen her?"

I nodded once, thumb rubbing nervously over my forefinger. "The first time was the night before I met you. She said... *'you are the shield against the storm.'*"

I felt her chest tighten, though I could not see it fully. I knew, somehow, that she understood what that meant—becuase it mirrored what I had sensed in her. A storm that was not just weather. Something alive. Dangerous.

"Why did you not say anything?"

Because I had hoped the vision was wrong. That fate could be avoided. That the girl beside me, bright and burning, could remain...just her, and not the weapon the gods had wrapped in flesh.

"Because," I said finally, each word deliberate and heavy with confession. "When I first saw you, I knew exactly who you were. I wanted...to hate you. To kill you those first nights together."

Alura's eyes widened. Tension twisted through her, but I pushed on as she took a sharp breath. "But I could not.

I could not hate what fate had given me. Could not kill what the gods had marked. And now…" I let the words hang, heavy and unsaid. I did not want to admit it, but I could not lie either. "…I cannot run from what is coming. No matter how badly I want to."

I rubbed my eyes with the heels of my hands, thinking of the nightmares that haunted me. The voice, the lady, yes. But my own ghosts too. My family. The people who had taken them from me, leaving me alone in a world that demanded I survive. That demanded I carry a burden I did not choose.

"They haunt me," I admitted quietly, finally, as if speaking aloud might lessen the weight. "The voice knows things…things I try to forget. Things I buried with fire and stone."

"Who?" Alura asked softly, almost tenderly.

"My father. My brother," I whispered. And then, because it burned to say it, "And my wife and son."

Her gaze softened, but I turned away. I had no right to expect comfort. I had survived on blood and solitude. I had no claim to anything else.

"Do you think it is the gods speaking to us?" She asked, her voice hushed, wary of the dark that surrounds us.

I met her eyes at last. No masks, no defenses. Only the faint flicker of something shared between us, as if the same storm hummed beneath both our skins. "I think whatever it is, it is waking up. And it wants everything from us."

A spark from the fire leapt into the night. I caught it with my vision, tracing its arc, and thought of the storm within her. The storms within me. Fate, wyrd, whatever the gods called it–this was not something we could refuse. Not now. Not ever.

"You are not alone in this, Alura," I said, the words rough but sincere.

Her lips curved faintly, a quiet reassurance that mirrored mine. "And you do not have to be either."

I wanted to move closer, to close the distance the firelight kept between us. I wanted to tell her everything and nothing all at once, to let her see the man behind the wolf, behind the scars, behind the prophecy.

But I did not. I could not. Not yet.

So I settled back, letting the warmth of the fire draw me, the quiet companionship of her presence, and the knowledge that the road ahead would demand everything we had.

"Get some rest," I muttered finally, hoarse. "We have a long road tomorrow."

But still, I did not move. My eyes lingered on her, tracing the shape of her hands, the line of her jaw, the strength she carried like armour.

Tomorrow would come.

The storm would not wait.

And neither could I.

CHAPTER TWENTY-ONE

ALURA

The last leg of the journey to Hayhjem was slow and biting, the frost still clinging stubbornly to the earth. Even the horses seemed reluctant to press on, their hooves slipping on the ice-patched road.

Skúli rode beside me, his shoulders broad, jaw set like stone. He hadn't spoken much since dawn, though I could feel the tension radiating off him. It wasn't only the winter frost that made me draw my cloak tighter—it was the knowing.

Skargrim was waiting. And whatever he demanded of us, Skúli would not bend.

I had already made the decision that I would not be a piece on Skargrim's board any longer. I'd learned to love Drakensvar, and its people.

I stole a glance at Skúli. His scar caught the pale light like a silver strike across his brow, the rest of his face grim. It was always like this when he neared Hayhjem—or at least it was last time. I wondered, not for the first time, if the scars he wore were as much a reminder of the men who gave them as of the battles he had fought since.

The town came into view, smoke rising from hearths, the bitter tang of fish and the salt heavy on the air. I turned to Skúli as the gates loomed ahead.

"If he asks me what you are up to..."

Skúli gave me a quick grin, half mischief, half steel. "Tell him the truth. We are living. That is all. You are training to be a healer."

My voice dropped to a whisper. "And what about...you know?"

"Your powers?" He slowed his horse and I slowed mine, his eyes narrowed. "Keep them under control and maybe he will think it was a trick last time."

I bit my lip. "Are you sure?"

His gaze flicked to me, sharp and unyielding. "Are you putting your faith in Skargrim to keep you safe or me?"

The words stung even though I knew he hadn't meant them to. I swallowed the lump in my throat and forced myself to answer.

"You. Always."

That seemed to settle him, and we pressed on.

Hayhjem was louder than Drakensvar, rougher too. People stopped to watch as we rode through. The whispers weren't subtle, nor the laughter that followed when eyes fell on me.

"His thrall rides at his side now."

"She even wears his cloak–what man parades shame so openly?"

I forced myself to keep my chin high, though the sting of their mockery burned in my chest. Every word was a reminder that I did not belong here, that no matter what Skúli said, I was not one of them.

Skúli heard them too–I saw it in the way his shoulders tightened, the muscle ticking in his jaw. But he did not flinch, not turn to silence them. He only reached down once, brushing a gloved hand against mine where they gripped the reigns. A small touch, brief, yet enough to steady me.

Inside the King's hall, the warmth struck like a hammer. Smoke stung my eyes, laughter and voices crowding close. Skargrim sat in his high seat, a bear of a man with eyes too sharp for his hulking frame. He smiled when he saw us but it was not out of kindness.

"Ah, the wolf returns," he said, spreading his arms. "And with his little *witch* too." His gaze cut to me, lingering.

We approached and his voice cut through the hush. "You do not kneel," he sneered. "Where is the respect? Where is the honour?"

"Is it out of honour and respect that I do not kneel," Skúli answered, his voice low and dangerous. "I kneel for no man. Least of all a usurper."

The room bristled. Men shifted toward their weapons but no one moved.

Skargrim's gaze slid to me. "And her? What is her excuse?"

"You gifted her to me. She is mine," Skúli said evenly. "She does as I do."

"Tell me, Skúli," Skargrim purred, "how do you make use of her?"

The room went quiet. Men leaned forward on benches, women whispered—every one of them hungry for humiliation.

Skúli's voice was as strong as iron. "She trains as a healer."

A roar of laughter broke out, Skargrim's deep voice leading it. "A healer? A slave cannot be a healer. You have been away too long if you think to change such truths."

"She is no slave," Skúli said, loudly, rising to stand at the edge of the dais. "Not to me, and not to Drakensvar."

The words landed heavy, ringing out into silence. Skargrim's smile did not falter but his eyes hardened. I felt all the weight of the hall upon me, eyes pressing, mocking.

My pulse pounded but before I could think better of it, I stepped forward, lifting my chin.

"I am training to be a healer," I said, voice carrying more firmly than I felt. "Call me what you will, mock me as you like, but it does not change the truth. Our healer is growing old and-"

Skargrim cut me off with a bark of laughter.

A ripple went through the hall. Some laughed, some muttered. Skargrim only leaned forward, resting his hands on his knees, studying me like a wolf who's found an amusing prey.

"You have found your tongue at least," he said. "Perhaps that will keep you alive, girl. Or perhaps it will be the thing that breaks you. Tell me, what is he doing up in those mountains?"

The King's teeth ground together as he gripped the arms of his chair. It was only then that I realised his wife was not beside him. She hadn't been last time either.

"We are living," I said.

The laughter spread, spilling through the benches. Too loud, too forced.

Skargrim leaned back, his face darkening. "And is he building an army against me while you patch wounds and stir herbs?" His hand clenched white-knuckled on the arms of his chair.

"No," I said.

Beside me, Skúli went rigid.

"No," Skargrim echoed, almost mocking. "Well. There you have it." He flung his arms wide, and the hall answered with another round of uneasy laughter.

His gaze cut back to me sharply. "And what about your power?"

The word hung in the air like a curse.

I stiffened. A hundred pairs of eyes turned on me, the weight of their suspicion pressing down until my hands trembled. I clenched them together to still the shaking.

Skúli shifted at my side, the movement subtle and protective, but his silence was louder than any shout. I knew he would not speak for me this time. If I wanted them to hear the truth, it had to come from me.

"My power," I said carefully, lifting my chin so I could look him in the eye, "is not yours to command."

The words dropped like stones into the silence that followed, and the laughter faltered. I could feel the weight of every gaze shift to Skúli, waiting to see if he would flinch, if he would drag me back into silence.

But I went on before he could speak. "I am learning to use it so that I can heal. Not for war. Not for show. And not for you." My voice trembled, but it did not break.

A ripple of shock passed through the hall, and then came the sneers, the mutters, the ugly bark of someone's laughter.

"I have had enough of waiting," Skargrim growled, his voice cutting through the noise. "Enough of silence. Enough of your games. After the worst of the frosts, you will raid."

The word hit like a hammer. My throat went dry.

Skúli's growl was low. Still, he forced out, "Thank you."

Skargrim's grin widened. "Do not thank me yet. You are going across the sea–to Eyrie."

My stomach dropped. Eyrie. Foreign land. Foreign war.

Skúli's hand clamped around my arm, not rough, but tight enough to keep him from stepping forward, from tearing the hall apart here and now. His restraint burned hotter than rage.

We turned to leave, the air buzzing behind us with whispers and cruel laughter.

"'Take your thrall with you, wolf!" Skargrim's final jeer followed us down the hall. "Let the gods decide if she is fit to be a healer or a corpse."

The laughter roared again, crueler than before.

I kept my head high, though the weight of a hundred eyes pressed against me. My heart thundered, but my voice was steady when I leaned close enough for Skúli to hear.

"I trust you."

He looked at me, startled, then his expression softened just enough for me to see the truth in his eyes.

And that was enough. Even as the hall mocked, even as Skargrim tried to break us, I knew where my faith lay. Not in a King. Not in a hall full of serpents. In him.

Always.

CHAPTER TWENTY-TWO
ALURA

The great hall's doors slammed shut behind us, the laughter inside echoing like hawks circling carrion. My heart hammered so hard I could hear it in my ears. For a moment, I had truly thought Skargrim might kill us both there, in front of his lapdogs.

Skúli's hand still gripped my arm. Not hard, but tight, like he needed to anchor himself before something inside him broke loose.

"You can let go now," I murmured, tilting my chin toward him.

He blinked as if only just realizing, then dropped his hand with a grunt. "Sorry."

I rubbed the spot absently, mourning the loss of contact even as relief fluttered in my chest. "You were going to tear the King's head off."

"I should have," he muttered, jaw clenched. "But I would rather do it clean. Not in the middle of his court, with a hundred blades ready to gut us." His gaze flicked to me, quick and sharp. "Besides...I would not put you in danger like that."

Something warm and stupid rose in my chest. I scolded myself.

We crossed the frozen courtyard, snow crunching beneath our shoes. I pulled my cloak tight around me.

"Eyrie," I said at last, the foreign name heavy in my mouth. "We are really going?"

"Yes." His voice was low and flat. "The moment the frost gives us passage."

"Is that bad?"

He finally looked at me—not as a burden, not as a thrall—but as if I deserved the truth. "Depends," he said. "On how many swords we bring back. And how many we do not."

I was quiet for a moment, letting the weight of his words sink in. The sea. Blood. Fire. All of it felt impossibly far and yet terrifyingly close. I could almost smell the salt of the open sea, feel the cold breeze whip around my face. I could practically smell death. My skin prickled with a sense of foreboding. It was as if the seeress was issuing a warning.

"I have never been on a ship," I admitted.

Skúli huffed a laugh, humourless but real. "You will hate it. Salt gets into everything."

"Sounds delightful."

Another silence, the snow falling soft around us. Then, out of nowhere, he says quietly, "I will keep you safe."

I turned. "You do not have to–"

"I know." His jaw flexed, eyes on the horizon. "But I will." He glanced at me, briefly. "You did well there. With him. You kept control."

"I did not want to." My breath fogged between us. "I wanted to unleash it on all of them. But I remembered what you said."

For a heartbeat, pride flickered across his face. Then it shuttered, leaving him hard again. "You did more than what I said. You did not let him see you shake. That takes strength that most men three times your size would not have."

Warmth bloomed in my chest where fear had been. "So, I am going with you then?"

He snorted. "Apparently."

"I should learn to swing an axe."

That earned me the ghost of a smile. "I will teach you to defend yourself. We will start tomorrow."

"And maybe how not to be sick on the boat?"

"No promises."

The moment stretched, a little bubble that was all ours, fragile and strange. The King's orders weighed heavy, but for the first time, it felt like Skúli bore them beside me, not above me.

"Thank you," I whispered.

"For what?"

"For saying I was yours. Even if it was just for show."

His gaze found mine, soft and kind.

"It was the truth."

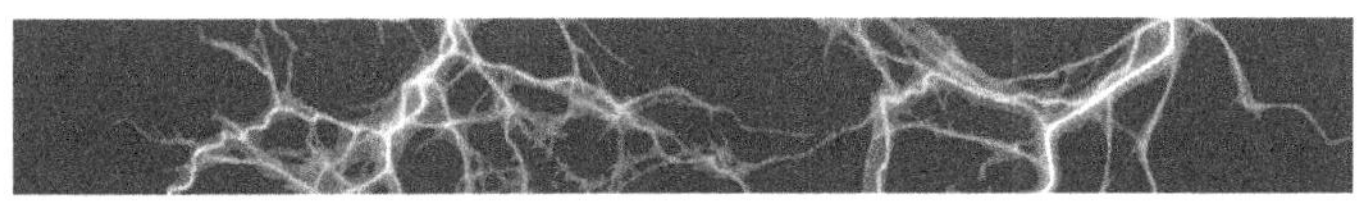

The journey back to Drakensvar took five days. Snow deepened, wind howled through the mountains, slowing us until the horses' breaths steamed thick in the air. Skúli barely spoke a word. He rode ahead, wrapped in silence, eyes on a horizon I couldn't see.

I couldn't blame him. My own thoughts churned with dread. A raid. Eyrie. Across the sea. I didn't know the place, but I knew enough.

Raiding meant fire. Blood. Death.

By the time we reached the pass that opened into the valley, the wind had teeth. Drakensvar loomed below, its stone walls wreathed in smoke and drifting snow. It should have felt like home compared to Skargrim's suffocating hall. Instead, it felt colder.

As we crossed the gates, Skúli's silence became a wall. I trailed a pace behind—not out of respect but because he walked too fast, as though distance itself might save him.

Astrid met us on the steps, her cloak snapping in the wind like raven wings. Her smile soured the instant she saw his face.

"You are back," she said briskly, eyes scanning us for wounds. "What did the usurper want?"

"Later," Skúli muttered, not meeting her gaze. And then he was gone, leaving only frost in his wake.

Astrid's brows rose as she turned to me. "He was bad when you left to be with Freydis."

"He has been worse since we headed back," I muttered, tugging my cloak tighter.

That night I found him in the practice yard—bare-chested despite the biting cold, sweat steaming off his skin. He swung his axe again and again, each strike as though he meant to split the world in two.

"Skúli," I called.

He didn't answer.

"Skúli."

Nothing.

Frustrated, I grabbed a wooden practice sword from the rack, nearly dropping it from the weight. Still, I marched into the ring.

"If you will not talk to me," I said, planting my feet, "then fight me."

He paused, brow furrowing. "You want to spar now?"

"You have barely spoken to me since Hayhjem. You act like I do not exist. So either hit me or talk to me."

Heat flared in his eyes. Then he dropped his axe and picked up a training sword.

We circled, snow crunching beneath our boots. I lunged first, sloppy but quick. He blocked easily, turning my strike aside.

"Why are you shutting me out?" I demanded, striking again.

"Because I am trying not to feel anything," he gritted, parrying with ease. "Because if I start–"

He broke off as I clipped his shoulder with a wild blow. His mouth twitched in reluctant pride.

"If you start what?" I pressed.

He caught my wrist, his grip firm but not cruel. My breath hitched.

"If I start letting you in," he said, voice low, "I will lose what little control I have left."

My heart slammed against my ribs. "Control of what?"

"Of my rage. Of my fear. Of everything." His eyes burned into mine. "I cannot even protect myself from the gods' damned dreams. From the voice–" He stopped abruptly.

"The same voice I hear."

He nodded.

I let the practice sword fall into the snow. Stepping closer, I said, "Then stop pushing me away. We are in this together. You do not carry it alone anymore. I am with you."

For a long moment, he only stared at me, face shadowed and unreadable.

Finally, he whispered, "I knew."

My chest tightened. "Knew what?"

"That you were sent as a spy." His grip tightened just enough to sting. "The moment I saw you, I knew. Spy. Fate. Prophecies. You did what it took to survive but I wanted to hate you. Wanted to kill you. But I could not do it."

The truth hung between us like an axe ready to strike. His sword dipped toward the ground.

I stepped closer, my breath mingling with his in the cold air. "Then do not shut me out. Not now. Not when everything is about to change."

Something broke loose in his expression–pride, pain, need. He leaned closer, his voice rough in my ear.

"Rule number one of sparring," he murmured. "Never drop your guard."

In a blur, he spun me, pressing my back against his chest, his hand still around my wrist, the training sword angled against my throat. His breath seared hot across my skin.

And instead of fear, heat coiled low in my belly—fierce and dangerous. But I wasn't about to let him win so easily.

I let my body go slack for the briefest heartbeat, then twisted sharply, stamping down hard on his boot. He hissed, grip loosening just enough for me to wrench free. I spun, picking up my blade and snapping it up to rest against his throat.

Our eyes locked, both of us panting. His chest heaved, sweat glinting across the hard lines of his jaw.

"Rule number two," I said, my voice low and steady. "Never assume I will yield."

For a long moment, he only stared at me. Then a slow, dangerous smile curved on his lips. Not anger, not mockery. Something darker, hungrier.

The air between us thrummed, blade to throat, pulse to pulse, until it was no longer clear who held the advantage.

And maybe that was the truth neither of us wanted to name.

We were both just as likely to burn each other alive as we were to keep each other standing.

CHAPTER TWENTY-THREE

ALURA

The next few weeks I spent mostly with Freydis. My days were a blur of herbs and stitching, of bloodied linen and the sharp, bitter scents of tinctures. I grew familiar with cherry gourd for bleeding, marsh mallow for swelling, and henbane—deadly henbane—which could soothe pain into sleep, or silence a man forever if misused.

When Freydis learned that Skargrim had ordered us across the sea to raid, her face had gone pale, the creases around her eyes deepened.

"Too little time," she muttered, before setting me to work. Bandages, knots, stitching torn flesh closed—it became all I knew for days at a time.

Skúli had promised I wouldn't see the worst of it. He said I would stay with the camp while he fought—much to my irritation. Still, he made me train with him every night until my arms ached.

"Just in case," he'd say when I dropped the practice blade for the third time.

And though I hated the bruises, a part of me was grateful.

But today was different.

Today, Freydis pressed something heavier into my hand than a bandage or a blade.

"This is smoke-sight," she said, her fingers scattering herbs into the fire. The flames hissed and spat green. "It is an ancient art. Only the priestesses practiced it. But they are gone now, so I will teach you."

"You are not gone," I told her, too quickly.

She gave me a faint smile. "Not yet. But one day, girl, you will be all that remains of our legacy. Better that you be ready when that day comes."

The word girl no longer carried sharpness from her lips. It was fond now, softened with the weight of the long days we spent together.

"The smoke will guide you. Open your mind to the gods, to Yggdrasil. But remember–true Seidr has a cost. Always. The world takes something for every miracle."

Her words echoed in my head as the smoke curled around me, slithering up my arms and across my face, pricking tears in my eyes. I closed them, inhaling deeply, until Freydis and the fire were gone.

Darkness.

Then a flicker, blue light like lightning.

A vast tree rose before me, roots like mountains, branches like an endless sky. Its bark shone with pulsing runes, white-hot and alive.

I reached for one.

And a voice cut through the vision.

The seeress.

"You sleep beneath a roof of shadows. Wake. Wake, and protect the shield."

The runes twisted. Fire seared across the bark, then frost. A door opened where none had been.

I turned–and saw him. Skúli standing in shadow, his axe drawn, a rune burning faintly at his feet.

The ground split beneath him.

"He is your shelter, he is your shield," the voice whispered. *"But shelters crumble. Shields buckle."*

I lunged forward, desperate to reach him, but the earth swallowed him whole. His roar of rage echoed as he fell.

Tears stung my eyes. I went to leap in after him and the smoke tore me away.

I slammed back into my body with a gasp. My skin was slick with sweat, my heart hammering. Freydis was there, a cool cloth at my brow.

"You saw something."

I nodded, still shaking. "Something is coming. Something dangerous. I have to protect him."

Her gaze flicked toward the fire, unreadable. "Then we have less time than I thought."

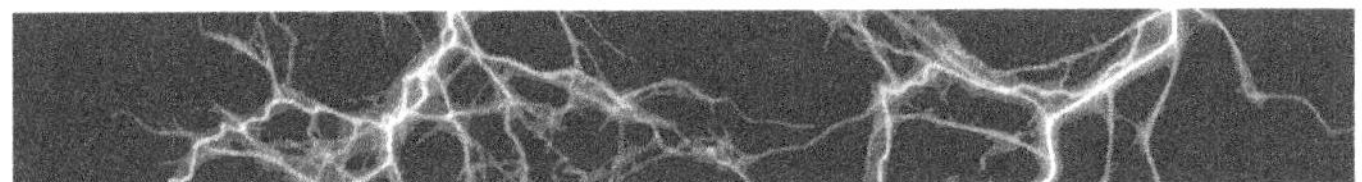

Later, the snow crunched beneath my boots as I stepped into the training yard. Skúli stood waiting, wooden sword in hand, his breath steaming in the night air.

"You are late," he said, not unkindly but with a sternness that made my heart flutter.

"I was with Freydis." I tried to be casual, but my voice betrayed me.

He grunted, tossing me my sword. I nearly fumbled it—my hands still trembled from the vision.

"You look like you have seen a draugr," he said as we began to circle. "What did she make you do? Stitch another broken arm?"

I forced a weak smile. "Not this time."

We sparred. Block, parry, retreat. My arms burned, my footwork faltered. He didn't let up. He never did.

"Focus. Your feet are slow."

But the vision lingered—the whisper, the runes, the ground yawning beneath him. My grip faltered. He knocked the blade from my hands, and it clattered into the snow.

He stepped back, breathing steady while I gasped like a plough horse. His eyes narrowed. "You are somewhere else."

"I am just tired," I lied.

He retrieved the blade and offered it back, hilt-first. His voice softened. "I know what it looks like when someone is haunted."

Our fingers brushed as I took it, and my chest clenched, the pull between us growing.

"Is Freydis pushing you too hard?"

"She is...helping. I want to learn. It is just—" I lowered the sword, the weight too much all of a sudden. "Some things are not easy."

I was dangerous.

To him. To everyone.

He studied me, then turned to fetch his water skin, tossing it over his shoulder without looking. I caught it awkwardly.

"You do not have to tell me what it is," he said. "But if something is wrong, I need to know. I cannot protect you if I do not."

"I am not helpless," I snapped.

"I never said you were." His eyes softened again. "But silence can be a warning. Remember your words, Alura. You do not have to carry this alone anymore."

The seeress's whisper coiled through me.

He is your shelter. But shelters crumble.

I lowered my gaze to the sword in my hands. My voice was barely a whisper. "I will tell you when I am ready."

He held my stare for a long moment, then gave a single nod. "I will wait."

We said nothing else.

But that night, for the first time in months, the silence between us didn't feel like a wall.

CHAPTER TWENTY-FOUR
ALURA

The scent of woodsmoke and something warm pulled me from sleep. Pale light filtered through the shutters, and for a moment I was disoriented, tangled in heavy furs. Then it came back—training last night, Freydis, the sparring yard, Skúli...

And the way his voice had softened when he said, *I will wait.*

I sat up slowly, rubbing my eyes. The great hall was nearly empty except for the low fire still crackling in the hearth—and Skúli, standing with his back to me.

He held a pan.

A battered, slightly blackened pan.

"You are up," he said without turning.

"I...am." I pulled the furs around my shoulders as the room came into focus. I must have passed out at the table after dinner. "Are you cooking?"

He grunted. "Trying."

On the table lay something vaguely egg-like, thick slices of buttered bread, and a small jar of honey. I blinked at it.

"I thought you hated cooking."

"I do," he muttered. "But you did not eat much last night."

"Oh." My chest fluttered. I inwardly told it to shut up before taking the plate.

He poured two cups of steaming tea, placing one in front of me without a word, then sat across from me, arms crossed, watching. I took a bite. The eggs were overdone, but warm. Comforting, in a quiet, unassuming way.

"It is good."

He made a dismissive snort, but the corner of his mouth twitched.

Then, suddenly, he cleared his throat.

"I have been meaning to ask—before we went to Hay-hjem."

My stomach sank. The memory of that place, of everything we'd faced...

He scratched his beard, visibly uncomfortable. "The winter Solstice is coming. Feasting, fire, music, mead...nonsense, all of it." He glanced up quickly. "I thought maybe...you would come. As my guest."

"Your guest?"

"Yes," he muttered, gaze dropping again. "You do not have to, obviously. But people will ask where you are. Where you stand. And...well, I thought it would be...nice."

My heart tripped over itself.

Was this his idea of asking me out?

"I would like that," I said softly.

The relief on his face was immediate. "Good. Then it is settled."

I sipped tea to hide my smile.

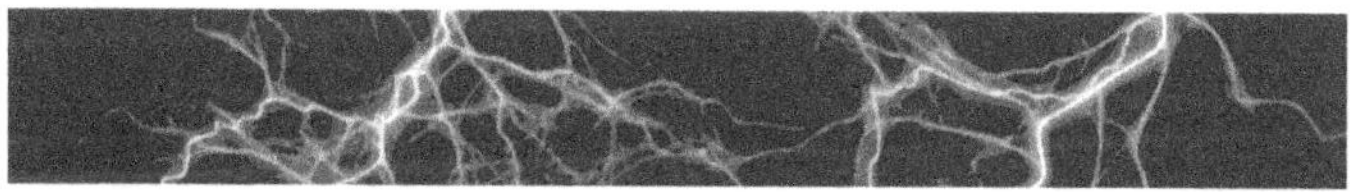

The next week was devoted to preparations for the feast and a lighter training schedule. When Skúli mentioned the gathering, he forgot to mention the sheer size of the attendance list.

It seemed the entire city was coming.

The rhythmic clatter of hooves and shouted greetings broke my thoughts one morning as I sliced root vegetables. The door banged open, and a gust of cold air swept through the room.

"Where is my favourite bitter old man?" A loud voice called.

Skúli didn't look up. "Still here, unfortunately."

The man who strode in had wind-tousled wheat-colored hair, blue eyes brimming with mischief, and the swagger of someone who'd never lost a fight—or been on time. He grinned like the realm owed him a drink.

"Gods, it is cold out there. You would think the mountain would have warmed with all that hot air pouring out of your mouth."

I stifled a laugh. Astrid ran from the back room, her eyes lighting up.

"Eirik!"

"Little Astrid," he said warmly, catching her in a bear hug. "You are almost taller than me now. Still terrifying."

"I *am* taller than you," she said, blushing but grinning. She swatted at him, and he ruffled her hair.

His gaze slid toward me. "And you," he said, stepping closer, voice teasing. "You must be the new thrall."

"I have a name," I said firmly.

"Oh, I like her," Eirik said to his friends. "Fierce. Pretty eyes too… Skúli, if you are not careful, I might steal her right out from under that brooding gaze."

Skúli's jaw tightened. "Try it and you will be picking your teeth out of the snow."

Eirik laughed. "So, it *is* like that, huh?"

"No," I said quickly. "We are just—"

"She is mine," Skúli cut in.

Eirik raised his eyebrows, grinning wider. "Well then. Consider me warned. But someone ought to make sure you do not freeze to death before the feast. I suggest strategic warming in his bed. Purely survival, of course."

I blinked. "Excuse me?"

"Oh, I am teasing," he said immediately, hands raised. "Sort of. But truly—northern winters bite. Someone needs to keep you alive, and apparently, it is him. I am just... offering suggestions."

Skúli growled and brushed past, muttering under his breath. "One of these days, I am going to teach you what real concern looks like."

I couldn't help the smile that spread across my face. I liked him already. Mischievous, protective, funny...and somehow, sincerely caring.

"Exactly," Eirik continued, grinning. "Which is why I take pride in my craft while I still can."

I raised an eyebrow. "Your craft?"

"Managing chaos," he said simply. "And keeping a certain brooding axe-wielder from accidentally freezing his guests to death. Noble work."

Skúli snorted. "You talk too much."

"And you do not talk enough," Eirik shot back. "We balance each other. Like two sides of a blade, brother."

I shook my head, trying to hide my laugh. Across the hall, Astrid crossed her arms, glaring. Skúli's hand brushed against hers, grounding and steady.

"I know he is trouble," she said quietly.

"And so are you," Skúli replied, voice low.

The kitchen bustled with preparations for the feast. Barrels of ale were hauled in, tables set, meats roasted. Eirik danced between tasks, teasing both of us at every opportunity, keeping spirits high, while I felt the subtle undercurrent of care in every glance he threw my way. Astrid glared daggers at me in between jests.

"I am not interested," I murmured, so only she could hear.

"In Eirik?" she asked, startled.

"Yes. You are terrible at hiding it," I said, softer this time. "You deserve someone who sees you."

She huffed, turning away. "He still calls me Little Astrid. He does not even see me as a woman."

"Then we will have to make him see you," I said, handing her a cup of cider with a smile. "But maybe not while you are trying to murder me with your eyes."

She laughed reluctantly.

Even with the cold, the chaos, and the impending storm of war, I realized something important.

There were people here who would fight for me. Protect me. Laugh with me.

And for the first time in a long while, that made the world feel less like it was going to end.

And I was going to hold on to that.

CHAPTER TWENTY-FIVE

ALURA

I stood before the polished copper plate I was using as a mirror, holding up a fur-line cloak.

"Is this too much?"

Astrid looked up from the bench where she was lacing her boots. "For what? The feast? Or for Skúli?"

I shot her a playful glare. "The feast."

Astrid's mouth curved slyly, standing up with a swish of her dark green dress. "It is perfect. You look...radiant. A little terrifying, honestly."

I wasn't sure that was the answer I was looking for. But it was Astrid. No sugarcoating. I liked that about her, even when I didn't.

"I have never been to a feast like this," I admitted, fussing with the braid circling my head.

We'd spent most of the day preparing, Astrid and I. Now, staring at my reflection, I felt the dress might swallow me whole. It was beautiful. White as fresh snow, trailing long, fitted in the bodice and flaring at the hips slightly.

Intricate beading caught the firelight at my neckline and cuffs, embroidery twined down the sleeves, and a woven belt cinched my waist. Astrid had braided my hair and pinned it.

Too much. I knew it was too much.

I lifted the cloak, heavy with its fur-lined hood. Astrid shot me a look sharp enough to slice. *Don't you dare,* she seemed to say. I sighed, fastening it around my shoulders.

"You will be fine," Astrid said, too cheerfully. "People are already calling you the Storm-Witch behind your back. May as well dress the part."

I groaned. "Not comforting, Astrid."

She ignored me, holding out a pair of carved bone earrings. "Here. My mother's. Wear them."

"I cannot take those–"

"You are not taking them. You are borrowing. Do not argue." She leaned close, hooking them in my ears herself. "Besides, you are his guest."

"We are all his guests," I muttered.

She arched her brow. "No. We are attending because it is tradition. He invited *you*. First outsider ever."

"Ever?" My stomach twisted.

Astrid grinned wickedly. "So everyone will be watching. Looking at how beautiful you look."

Heat rushed to my cheeks. "Not everyone."

"Maybe not," she said. "But someone will." A pause, casually as she flipped her braid over a shoulder. "Do you think Eirik will be there yet?"

I gave her a pointed look. "That is the fourth time you have asked."

Her cheeks reddened. "Shut up."

"He will be there," I said, smiling. "And he will notice you. You look beautiful."

Astrid glanced down at herself, smoothing the embroidery on her green dress. "I still look like a girl."

"No." My voice softened. "You look like a woman ready to mark her place in the world."

Her throat worked. "You are better at this than I thought you would."

"At what?"

"Belonging."

Something knotted in my chest at that. I reached for her hand, squeezing. "You have made it easier."

The door creaked. Eirik's voice rumbled from outside. "Are you two done yet? Skúli is starting to growl."

"We are coming!" We chorused.

Astrid rolled her eyes. "Men. No patience."

I laughed, looping my arm through hers. "Then let us give them something worth losing their patience over."

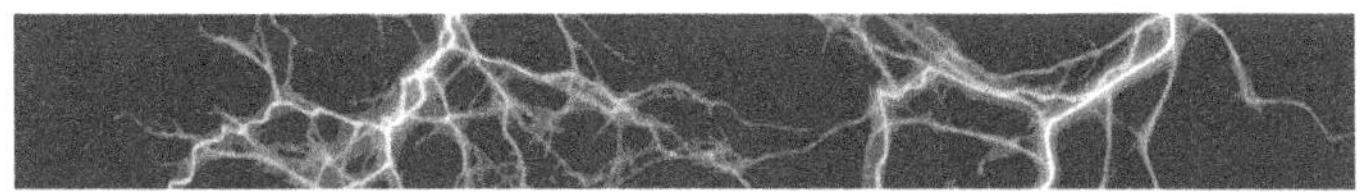

The great hall of Drakensvar had never looked so alive. Pine boughs draped the beams, their scent mingling with roasted meat, honey-wine, and woodsmoke. Laughter rang like hammers on steel.

But my eyes caught only him.

Skúli stood near the central table, arms crossed, Björn sprawled at his feet like a shadow. He wore white like me—his tunic embroidered to match mine, black trousers stark against it. The firelight caught on his tattoos, making them stand out sharply against his skin.

And he was glaring at the door.

Waiting.

For me.

Astrid trailed me through the crowd, scanning for Eirik. I spotted him first, weaving through the crowd toward Skúli with a grin.

"You are going to wear holes in the floor with all that glaring," Eirik said, elbowing him.

"I am not glaring," Skúli grunted.

"You are. It is terrifying." Eirik took a drink. "She is not late. She has not decided to avoid the broody axe-wielder. You are impatient, old friend."

We slipped up behind them. Skúli turned, and for one breath, the whole hall seemed to turn too. His gaze pinned me where I stood, dark and unreadable. I bit my lip, suddenly convinced that it was too much. The dress, the hair, the jewelry.

Eirik whistled low. "Well. She is not the thrall anymore, is she?" he swept into an absurd bow. "Lady Alura, may I claim the first dance? Let us show the broody axe-wielder how it is done."

My cheeks grew hot. I opened my mouth to protest, but Skúli's hand shoved Eirik lightly aside. "She dances with me."

Eirik winked, stage-whispering, "Who am I to stand in the way of fate?"

Skúli closed the distance between us, unfastening my cloak without a word and tossing it at Eirik. His arm bent toward me. "You are late," he said, voice low. "And that dress is far too beautiful to hide."

"I was helping Astrid with her hair," I replied quickly.

"She is lying!" Astrid groaned. "It was hers that took–"

"Ah," Eirik swooped in, cloak already discarded, grinning at Astrid. "You survived your hair, I see."

Astrid flushed a dark crimson. "Eirik…"

"You look like a Jarl's daughter," he said warmly, eyes glittering.

"You say that to all the girls," she muttered.

"Only the brave ones."

Skúli bent close, his voice a rough whisper only I heard. "You look…well." His gaze lingered, softer than his tone.

I smiled up at him. "So do you."

The hall stirred back to life. Astrid stalked off with Eirik, red-faced and feigning annoyance. Musicians struck up a tune, and Skúli led me into the open.

His hand was warm, steady at my waist. His presence swallowed the crowd until it felt like only us.

We danced. Not polished or rehearsed. Just steps and turns and breath, the rhythm easy as falling into the tide. People stared–I felt it–but for once I didn't care.

We stayed like that, entranced with each other and reluctant to part. Though neither of us spoke, we did not need to. This was all we needed.

When the music paused, we stopped with it. We faced each other, breathing in each other. He didn't let go right away.

"Thank you," Skúli said, his voice raw. "For trusting me."

I swallowed. "You asked. I wanted to say yes."

Later, I slipped to the edge of the hall, mead warming my throat. Fires glowed in every hearth. That was when I saw him– a boy crouched near a table, a dreki lizard perched on his shoulder.

It wasn't copper like the one I caught. This one shimmered a pale red, eyes like garnet.

I bent to his level. "Where did you find that one?"

The boy grinned, brushing flour from his hands. "Found him in the woods. He roasts chestnuts for me."

I blinked. "Chestnuts?"

The dreki chirped, a flicker of flame curling from its nostrils. The boy laughed. "He likes the smoke. Keeps him warm."

"Can they all do that?"

He shook his head, seriousness crossing his face. "No. Each dreki's got its own element. Fire, water, earth...rare ones have air.. Mine just likes chestnuts."

I stared, transfixed. "So...they bond?"

"Sort of." The boy shrugged. "You treat them well, they treat you well."

The little creature curled around his neck like a scarf.

"Does he have a name?"

"Bál."

Blaze.

"That is a good name for a dreki."

I smiled, a warmth unfurling inside me. Magic was not just mine. It lived everywhere, in small, surprising ways.

Astrid appeared suddenly, seizing my arm and tugging me toward a long table. "He is brooding too hard again," she muttered. "Which means he is thinking about you. Sit. Drink. Before he scowls holes in the walls."

I let her drag me down. The benches creaked as I joined her and a cluster of others from the hold. Platters were passed, cups refilled. Stories unfurled into boasts, laughter grew rowdy, songs rose rough and strong.

Eirik–predictably–made a great show of flirting with every woman at the table. Yet no matter how dramatically he bowed or winked, his eyes always circled back to Astrid. She blushed scarlet and punched him in the arm every time, which only made him grin wider.

I laughed along with them, but my gaze kept straying. Skúli sat apart in the shadows of the hall, wolf at his side, eyes tracking the crowd. Always watching. Always guarded.

When the mead had loosened the room into warmth and noise, I found myself drifting back to him as though pulled by a string I couldn't sever. I sat beside him without asking.

He didn't speak. Just pushed a plate toward me with a slice of honey cake.

I looked down at it. "You saved one for me?"

He shrugged, looking away, as if it was nothing. "You like honey."

It was such a small thing. Ridiculously small. But it knocked something loose inside me, softening the front that had clung since the smoke vision.

A hush fell as Freydis rose at the head of the hall, raising her hands. Her voice carried clear, steady like a bell.

"As the sun turns low and the night grows long.

We keep the fire, hold the song.

May gods remember, may light return.

May hearts endure and embers burn."

The hall echoed her words, voices rising together. Even Skúli spoke them, low and sure, the cadence of ritual etched into his bones.

I didn't know the prayer. But I watched him speak it, and in that moment I saw him differently–not just the scarred warrior who scowled and guarded and growled–but a man who remembered. Who carried old vows like weapons in his chest. Who needed no magic to keep something sacred alive.

When the final line faded and the fire crackled back into dominance, he turned to me. His voice was rough, his eyes unexpectedly soft.

"Next year," he said, low enough so only I could hear. "If we are still alive, I will teach you the words. So you can speak them with us."

CHAPTER TWENTY-SIX
ALURA

Most of the hall had emptied as the night grew late. Voices faded down the stone corridors, laughter and footsteps dissolved into the long winter night. The hearths had burned low, save for one last fire at the centre. Its flames guttered but steadily painted the room in copper and shadow.

Only the four of us remained. Skúli and I on one side of the blaze, Astrid and Eirik on the other, cups in hand and cheeks flushed with mead.

Astrid was slurring, though she tried valiantly to hide it. "Y-you-you are so infuriating."

Eirik laughed, head tipping back, grin wide as a wolf's. "And you are drunk, little Astrid."

He downed the rest of his cup to prove his point.

Astrid squinted at him, swaying slightly. "I can still beat you. A-any day. A-any time." She jabbed a finger at his chest, missed, and poked his shoulder instead.

He clutched the spot dramatically. "Oh no, struck down by the mighty Astrid. Someone fetch a healer."

I couldn't help the snort that escaped me.

Beside me, Skúli shook his head, though there was a half-hidden smile tugging at his mouth. "They are insufferable," he muttered. "Children, both of them."

"Are they always like this?" I asked quietly, watching the two of them attempt–badly–to shove one another off the bench.

"For years." His eyes softened as they lingered on Astrid. "She has always been in love with him. He only just realised he loved her back about...two winters ago."

I turned to them, eyebrows rising. "You knew? All this time?"

Skúli gave a short, amused chuckle. "Of course. But it was not my place to interfere. They will figure it out eventually."

I frowned. "If you knew, and they both feel the same, why has he not acted on it?"

"Because he is a fool," Skúli said simply, though his mouth twitched. "And because he thinks I would object."

"Would you?"

He shook his head as a pained look crossed his face. "No. Fate brings people together whether I agree or not. I just want them both safe. Happy. The same I want for all my people."

That lodged something inside of me. His world was all duty, all weight and yet, even here, he thought of others before himself.

"She had better make him work for it," I muttered.

That earned a laugh from him, low and warm, like gravel under flames. "That she will."

Across the fire, Astrid and Eirik were still bickering. Eirik was half out of his seat now, smirking.

"I am stronger than you, faster than you, cleverer than you–"

Astrid interrupted with a loud scoff. "Oh please, you are only l-louder than me."

"Louder and better looking."

"Better–" Astrid's face went crimson. She launched herself across the bench at him, trying to knock him backward. He caught her easily, laughing as though it was all a game.

"See?" He crowed. "She cannot resist throwing herself into my arms. Must be love."

"Must be death," Astrid hissed, though her cheeks were still red, her fists pounding weakly against his chest.

I leaned toward Skúli. "How do they drink this much and survive it?"

"Years of practice," he said dryly.

Before I could reply, Eirik slapped his knee. "Tell her, Skúli. Tell her the story. She does not believe me!"

Skúli groaned, dragging a hand down his face. "Not the bear story."

"The bear story!" Eirik roared. "Alura needs to know."

Astrid snorted into her cup. "If you mean the story where you nearly shat yourself at fourteen–"

"I did not!" Eirik looked scandalised. "I fought a bear. With my bare hands. A beast taller than this hall, with claws like scythes." He spread his arms as wide as they would go, nearly tipping himself off the bench.

Astrid rolled her eyes. "It was barely bigger than a dog."

"It was a bear," Eirik insisted, turning to me, eyes shining. "Huge. Mean. Ravenous. I saved us both at that summer cabin."

"You were at a summer cabin?" I asked.

Skúli gave a long, suffering sigh. "We were. He is not lying. He really did fight a bear."

Eirik slapped his knee triumphantly. "HA! Told you!"

"But," Skúli added, deadpan, "it was smaller than he claims. Half starved. Probably lost."

Eirik looked personally wounded. "Half starved? It tried to eat you while you were pissing!"

I blinked. "Wait–you were–?"

"Do not," Skúli growled, glaring at him.

"Oh I will," Eirik grinned wickedly. "Skúli was relieving himself when the bear charged. I tackled it, bare handed, while he–"

"That is enough."

Eirik held up his hands in mock surrender, though his grin didn't fade. "Point is, Alura, I saved his life. He owes me eternally."

Astrid sniggered into her drink. "And you have been insufferable about it ever since."

The laughter that followed warmed the hall more than the fire. For a moment, it felt like family.

But the warmth made me restless. My head was crowded, my chest tight. I rose, murmuring, "I am going to get some air."

Skúli rose instantly, as if it were decided for both of us. "I will come too. It is not safe after dark."

I wanted to argue–but I didn't.

Björn padded after us, a silent shadow on four paws.

The cold outside struck like a blade making me brace after the heat of the feast. Frost clung to stone, glittering under torchlight. Our boots crunched as we crossed the courtyard.

Above us, the sky was dark as ink, stars scattered like rune. My breath curled white in the air.

Neither of us spoke for a while. The silence between us felt sacred, heavy in its own way.

At last, Skúli broke it. "I used to come out here as a boy. After solstice parties. After fights. When I could not sleep."

I looked at him. "To think?"

A faint smile touched his mouth. "To breathe."

We reached the old wall, overlooking the valley stretched in darkness below. Torches flickered in the wind behind us, the shadows stretching long.

My heart thundered. My thoughts clawed at me until I let it out. "I did not know you were a king."

He didn't flinch. "I was not a king. I was the prince." He scoffed. "Prince of Drakensvar. Did Astrid tell you?"

"No. I pieced it together. The way the others look at you. The way the King spoke to you. The finality in your voice."

He leaned both hands on the stone. For a long moment, he said nothing. Then, softly, "It does not matter now."

"It matters to me."

I brushed my fingers against his hand. He stilled.

"My father wanted a dynasty. My mother wanted peace. I gave them neither." Skúli's voice was quiet, stripped bare before me. "She died before the invasion. He died screaming my name on the shield wall with my brother." His jaw tightened, but his voice cracked. "And my wife...she thought I could be more than a weapon."

The world tilted slightly beneath me. "What happened to her?"

He swallowed hard. "She died because I was not fast enough. Strong enough. And I swore I would not let anyone close again."

The silence stretched. My chest ached with the weight he carried, armour built from grief and guilt. But there were cracks, I had seen them tonight.

I placed my hand over his. "You do not need to prove anything to me."

Slowly, he turned his palm, letting our fingers slide between each other. My pulse leapt, wild.

"I think that is what scares me most," he murmured.

The cold bit into my bones, but I didn't move. Not when he looked at me like that–like I was dangerous, precious, inevitable.

Skúli leaned closer, his shoulder brushing mine, his breath warm in the frost. "When the worst of the ice is over," he said, voice low, "everything changes."

I tilted my head toward him, breath catching for a moment. "I know."

The silence stretched between us, not heavy, but taut with something unspoken. I let myself lean, just enough for my temple to rest against the solid warmth of his side. His fur-lined cloak shifted with my weight, carrying the scent of smoke, steel and pine. For the first time in what felt like forever, the world stopped spinning.

His hand tightened around mine, grounding me. Then, gently, he lifted our joined hands to his mouth. The brush of his lips against my knuckles were feather-light, reverent, as though he feared breaking me by pressing too hard. My chest ached with the force of it–how something so small could feel like a vow.

"Alura…" My name, hushed, lingering in the air like a prayer he didn't know he'd spoken. "You will be my undoing, Alura."

I swallowed, words lodging like a spark inside my chest. My heart thundered, but I didn't pull away. Instead, I closed my eyes, letting the silence stretch, letting myself simply be held in the warmth of him.

CHAPTER TWENTY-SEVEN
ALURA

The fire had burned low in the hearth, casting a dim orange glow across the walls of my room. My cloak smelled faintly of pine and smoke.

I couldn't sleep.

Heaviness pressed against my chest, dragging me into restless spirals. Tonight has been one of the best nights of my life. I had danced, I had laughed, I had felt almost normal. And yet, I laid awake.

The conversation with Skúli gnawed at me. His grief, his losses, the words he had spoken.

I swore I would not let anyone close again.

They sat heavy in my chest, tangling with something I wasn't ready to name. It was ridiculous. I had no reason to feel this way about him. A man who had seen me as an inconvenience. And yet...sometimes he was almost gentle.

Before I could stop myself, I slipped from bed, wrapping furs around my shoulders. The cold stone bit into my bare feet as I padded toward the door. My room was too small, too close. I needed air. Distance.

Downstairs, the hall was hushed and nearly empty. The long tables had been cleared, though the scents of honey and smoke lingered. I sat by the dying fire, drawing my furs tighter. The embers whispered, crackling softly.

It had been hours since Skúli and I had stood in the courtyard. He was surely asleep by now. My thoughts circled anyway, chasing themselves in useless patterns. Skargrim, the Seeress, fate. The pull between Skúli and me. And the truth I hated to admit. I didn't know why I had been brought back here, or what I was meant to do.I hated being kept in the dark.

A chill ran over me—not from the cold, but something deeper. Wrong. Unnatural.

Be alert, Storm-Born. Danger approaches.

The words came as a whisper in my skull, sharp as ice. My skin prickled. I shifted, stretching to glance around, but the hall was empty.

Only shadows stirred in the corners.

And then I heard it.

A soft footstep. The scrape of leather. The whisper of steel.

I shot to my feet, heart hammering. I had been a fool, I had come down here unarmed, in nothing but my underdress. My throat worked as I tried to swallow my panic.

"Who is there?" My voice cracked out sharper than I intended. There was no answer.

A knife flashed from the shadows, aimed at my throat.

I threw myself sideways, crashing into a bench, sprawling across the floor. Pain lanced up my hip, but I scrambled backward as the figure lunged again. His hood was drawn, his face hidden in shadows. Another blade gleamed in his hand.

My pulse spiked. Instinct took over. Training. Survival.

I reached toward the embers—heat, light, strength. Words Freydis had taught me hissed from my lips.

"Veil me. Shield me."

Smoke curled from the fire, swirling around me like wings. The veins beneath my skin burned bright with magic. Blue and silver lightning lacing through my arms, my chest. For a heartbeat, I glowed. The hearth roared white-hot, searing the dark.

My attacker reeled, cursing, shielding his eyes.

I screamed.

"Skúli!"

But my focus slipped, the magic stuttered, and the smoke dissolved. My attacker's hand closed on my arm, iron tight, dragging me across the stones. My shoulder slammed against a table leg. I gasped, scrambling backward but he loomed over me, grinning.

He had won.

I screamed again, desperate, clutching the first weapon my hands found–a forgotten knife near the benches. My fingers wrapped around the hilt like it was a lifeline.

"You think that is going to save you, witch?" His voice was a snarl. "You have no idea what forces you are playing with. He always wins."

"Skargrim?"

The hall doors slammed open.

Steel sang.

Skúli hit the man like a storm wind, blade flashing. Fury burned across his face, raw and lethal. My attacker barely got his blade up before Skúli disarmed him with a twist, his sword pressed against the man's throat.

"Who sent you?" Skúli's voice was like death itself.

The man spat blood, sneering. No answer. His jaw clenched and foam bubbled at his lips.

Poison.

He collapsed at Skúli's feet, lifeless.

The hall went too quiet, too still. I pressed a shaking hand to my chest, my breath shallow. The furs I'd wrapped around myself lay discarded on the stones. My vision swam, my body heavy from magic pulled too fast.

Skúli turned, eyes finding me. Not angry but frightened. For me.

"Alura–"

"I am fine," I whispered, though it was a lie. My voice shook. "You came."

"You called."

My throat tightened. I swallowed bile. "I think he meant to kill you."

Skúli's gaze lingered on the body, then the fire, then me. His voice was low. "No. He meant to kill you."

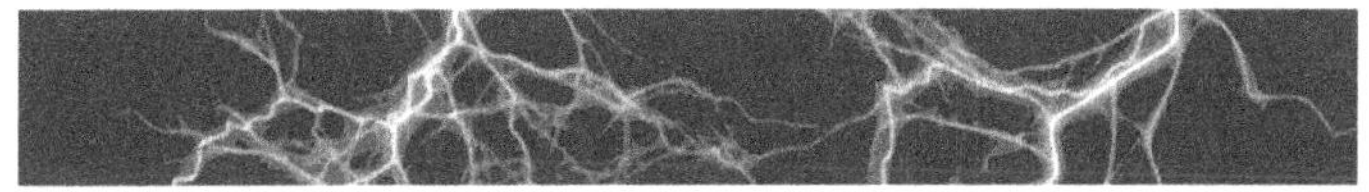

Skúli bolted the heavy door of his chambers behind us. Shadows danced up the stone walls, the fire's glow unable to chase them away.

I stumbled to the hearth, clutching myself, still shivering. The cold was bone-deep, but worse was the tremor I couldn't stop. The knowledge of how close I had come to death.

Behind me Skúli paced like a caged wolf. Agitated. His silence was sharp, volatile.

"Stop it."

He froze. His voice cracked like thunder. "You should not have been alone."

"I did not think–"

"Exactly!" His fury lashed. "You did not think!"

I whirled on him, teeth bared. "What, should I not breathe without your permission now?"

The firelight caught the storm in his eyes. "He had poison in his mouth, Alura. He was watching. Waiting. If I had been slower–"

"I saved myself," I cut in, chest heaving. "I called my magic."

"And lost it in a breath!" His fists shook, veins popping out on his arms. "It drained you. You can barely stand!"

"I am not your responsibility." The words left my mouth sharp as glass.

"Yes, you are!" His voice shattered against the stone. He spun away, bracing against the wall, trembling with restraint. "Gods have mercy, Alura..." His voice broke. "I cannot lose you too."

The words landed heavy between us.

My breath stilled. "What did you say?"

He didn't turn. "Forget it."

"No." I stepped closer, heart pounding. "Say it again."

When he turned, his face was stripped of its armour. No scowl. No mask. Just grief and terror laid bare.

"You are not a tool," he said hoarsely. "Not to me. Not anymore. You were given to me as a thrall, a slave. But you always have had a choice here. I will not sacrifice you to anyone's prophecy." His eyes burnt into mine. "If someone wants you dead...they will not get another chance."

Something inside me broke open.

I reached for him without thinking. He caught my hand, his grip strong, grounding. Then, slowly, as if afraid I might vanish, he drew me closer. My chest pressed against him, his breath hot against my brow.

"Alura," he whispered, my name torn from him like a prayer.

I closed the space, leaning into him until our foreheads touched, breaths mingling in the hush between us. He smelled of smoke and snow and iron, of safety carved out of chaos. My hand trembled in his, but he steadied it, lifting our joined fingers to his mouth.

His lips brushed across my knuckles in a reverence that undid me.

I let out a shaking breath, and he wrapped an arm around me, gathering me into the breadth of him. His strength caged me, but it was not a prison–it was a shelter.

He held me as though I were breakable, precious, as though the weight of his grief and fury could not reach me if he could only hold on tightly enough.

My forehead slid against his until our temples touched, until I could feel the thunder of his pulse answering the wild call of my own. His breath caught, ragged, as though this closeness was as much a wound as a balm.

For the first time, I felt what it was to be chosen. Not for power or prophecy, not for what I could endure. But simply, devastatingly, for myself.

CHAPTER TWENTY-EIGHT

ALURA

We didn't sleep.

Skúli sat silently in the chair by the fire, sharpening his blades, the rasp of steel on whetstone steady and unyielding. I lay on the furs draped over his bed, watching the shadows dance across his face.

"Who would want me dead?" I asked softly.

He looked up, our gazes locking. "I do not know. Yet."

"It was not random."

"No it was not." He sighed, wiping the blade clean before setting it aside. "Could be Skargrim. Could be one of the old bloodlines, afraid of what you are. What you stand for. What you might become."

I reached for the necklace at my throat, the dreki pendant cool on my fingers as they held it tight like it could tether me. "Could be about you too."

He went still.

I sat up, my voice sharper now. "They call you the Shamed One, but that man…he aimed like he knew something. Like he wanted to strike before a truth came to light. And if our fates are bound—"

I didn't finish. Skúli didn't speak.

"What are you not telling me?"

He stiffened, his breath catching, and for a moment I thought he might shut me out. His silence was louder than any answer.

"It does not matter," he said, low and fierce. "What matters is this. You. No one touches you. No one takes you. Not while I still draw breath."

I leaned forwards, unwilling to let it go. "Then tell me. Why do they call you the Shamed One? What is it you are hiding?"

His jaw worked, teeth clenched against words he didn't want to say. At last, his voice broke like gravel. "Because I am wrong. Wolf-Marked. Cursed. They saw it as a stain, a reminder of what should have been royal blood—spoiled. Some people believe I killed my family over it."

My chest tightened. "That is not shameful. That is fear."

He gave a bitter laugh, hollow like a cracked bell. "Fear and shame are two sides of the same blade. To them, I was proof of the gods' displeasure. Ulfhednar are not meant to rule. Neither are berserkers. We are too unstable. Too dangerous. A king must sit steady, not run under the moon with blood on his teeth."

I swallowed hard. "So you are..."

"The true heir." His voice dropped. "Not just to Drakensvar. To all of it. Every cursed crown on this cursed continent." He spat the words like poison. His gaze flicked toward the door, toward the shadows, as if even the walls might betray him. "My mother was queen before Skargrim's wife. I was born when the blood of the old kings still ran pure. And Skargrim buried it with that name–Shamed One. Easier to say I was unfit than to admit the crown had passed into weaker hands."

The weight of his words crashed over me like cold water.

Suddenly, so much made sense–the way he never knelt, why the people still looked to him like a leader, the heaviness in his eyes when he thought no one noticed. The whispers of destiny that seemed to coil around us, pulling tighter with every breath.

"You did not tell me." My voice was barely a whisper.

"No." His gaze found mine, wearily. "But I am telling you now. And if *they* knew that you knew the truth...you would be hunted alongside me."

My heart lurched. This wasn't just a confession. It was a death sentence, placed into my hands.

Silence fell, heavy but different. Not prince and thrall. Not warrior and seidr. Something else. Something more dangerous.

"I will not let anyone take you," he said, softly.

And for the first time, I believed him.

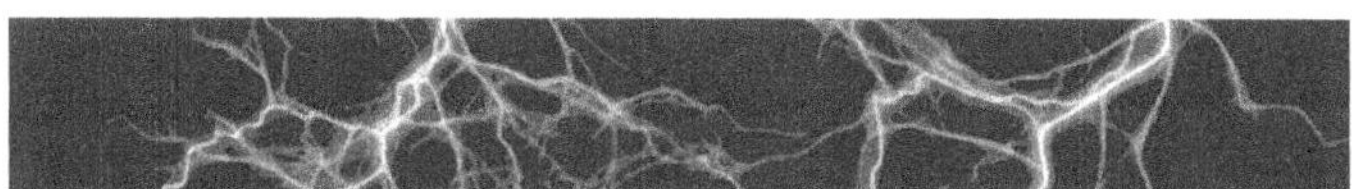

The days after Solstice fell back into rhythm. My holiday was over, and I was expected in Freydis's workshop from dawn until dusk. Before, I'd been given weekends free. Now, there was no such luxury.

Word had spread about the attack. Some townsfolk whispered about me in fear, others in awe. A few came to me directly, asking for blessings, calling me *storm-marked*.

Freydis seemed satisfied. I could mend most wounds without thought, and in the afternoons we worked on channeling my Seidr for deeper injuries. Today, she had me carving protective runes for every household in Drakensvar. It was tradition, she said, renewed each year—but her strength waned with age, and though her fingers remained deft enough to paint the symbols, it fell to me to carve them.

Bone in hand, I scored wood and stone, rune after rune, until my hands ached and my eyes blurred. There were thousands to finish before the raids.

The weather held mild, but each passing day pulled us closer to the crossing. Closer to war. My throat tightened. Not everyone would return. Some would fall on foreign soil, crying the gods' names with their last breath, praying their sacrifice would win them Valhalla.

"Focus." Freydis's voice snapped me back.

"Sorry."

She eyed me with her hawk's gaze. "What weighs on you, girl?"

I rolled my eyes at *girl*.

"Did something happen at Solstice?" she asked, lips curving in a knowing grin.

"I suppose," I said, shrugging.

I bent back to my carving, sliding the finished rune across for her to paint. She didn't stop.

"And your control?"

"Fine."

"You called on it." It was not a question.

I nodded. "It was defensive."

Her brush didn't pause. "And you and Skúli?"

I stilled. "What of us?"

"Are you two... working well together?"

What did she mean by *together*?

"I suppose. We are learning. Trying." The words felt thin compared to what it really was. How could I explain the pull? The way in one moment he ignored me, and in the next he would tear the world apart to protect me? "He is infuriating."

"Men always are, girl."

"Is that why you never married?" I shot back, hoping to turn her attention.

She laughed. "I never married because I took vows as a priestess. I never wanted a husband. Could you imagine? Now you and Skúli, however..."

She trailed off, mischief glinting in her eyes.

"Me and Skúli?" I asked, warily.

"There is potential. Strong blood. Strong power. You could reinstate the line of succession."

I nearly choked. "What—children? I thought you warned me away from him!"

"Do you ever listen?" She teased. "Of course it is a mistake. But mistakes change the world."

"You are contradictory," I muttered.

"Wisdom often is," she said breezily. "The gods rarely speak in straight lines."

I bent over the next rune, but her words hung heavy. Children. Legacy. It felt like something from another woman's life—not mine.

"I do not know what I feel," I admitted softly. "Some days he makes me want to scream. Others..." I faltered, voice trembling. "Others I feel like I am standing too close to a raging fire. And I do not know if it will burn me or consume me."

Freydis hummed, setting her brush aside. Her gaze sharpened, the priestess shining through the frailness of her frame.

"You do not have to decide today. Or tomorrow. But remember—magic, power, love... They are not separate things. Not for women like us. They all demand a price."

I lifted my eyes to hers. "And how do I know if it is worth paying?"

Her mouth curved faintly. "You cannot. Not until it is already spent."

Then she returned to her painting as if nothing had passed between us. As if she hadn't just placed another weight in my hands.

I sat in silence, candlelight flickering over our work, and wondered how much more the gods would ask me to give.

CHAPTER TWENTY-NINE

ALURA

The great hall of Drakensvar glowed like the heart of a forge.

Winter pressed against the stone outer walls, but inside, the air was alive with firelight and laughter, the thrum of drums, and the smokey tang of roasting boar. Pine boughs draped the beams overhead, their needles shining with frost brought in from the cold, while shields lay against the walls like a gallery of scars and victories. Tonight, though, the shields were not meant to remind anyone of blood. Tonight was for peace.

The visiting settlement's delegation filled one side of the long tables, their furs and cloaks mingling with Drakensvar's own. Tankards clashed in toasts, and the tension that had once sparked between the two cities was drowned beneath mead and music.

Astrid was the first to seize the joy of it.

She was already on the cleared stretch of floor between benches, hands caught with one of the visiting women as the musicians played a tune. Her laughter carried high above, wild and carefree, and her hair shone like fire in the firelight as she spun. When she turned, I caught the sharp gleam in her eyes, the same flame that always seemed to burn hotter when she had an audience.

"Your friend looks as though she is trying to set the hall ablaze," Eirik said beside me, tipping his mug toward Astrid as she whirled past.

I smiled despite myself. "I think she might."

He grinned, that familiar mischievous tilt to his mouth. "Good. Let her burn them all down. I would wager that even half drunk warriors will think twice before crossing a woman who dances like that."

"Who are these people?" I asked, turning back to Eirik.

"The nobles of Vargheim," he said smoothly, lifting his cup as though toasting his own words. "That is where Skúli sent me over the summer. I negotiated this peace."

"You?" The word slipped out sharper than I intended, laced with more skepticism than courtesy.

"Yes, me," He replied without offense, his grin only broadening. "I am known for my...persuasive nature."

I arched my brow. "Persuasive. That is what we are calling it now?"

Eirik leaned a little closer, lowering his voice so that only I could hear him over the hall's noise. "Persuasive, charming, dangerous. Depends on who you ask. The Jarls of Vargheim would swear they bent for reason and diplomacy." His smile edged toward wickedness. "But their daughters might tell a different tale."

"Astrid and Skúli are right, you are insufferable."

"Perhaps," he said lightly, tipping his head in a mock concession. "But you cannot deny the results. Look around you, no blood spilled, no swords drawn. Only music and feasting. That, Little Storm, is the mark of my brilliance."

I laughed softly at the use of the new nickname, warmth threading through me despite myself.

But as the sound left my lips, my gaze strayed toward the high seat at the dais. The laughter died there. Skúli sat there alone, his broad shoulders filling the carved chair as though it were made for him alone. His black cloak had slipped from one side, baring his muscular arm as he leaned forward to hear one of the visiting elders. His face was serious, though not unfriendly. It was the face of a man holding his ground while the world demanded requests and bargains be made.

He looked older tonight, somehow. Less the wild wolf who had brought me here and more the chieftain who bore the weight of hundreds of lives on his back.

And the people noticed.

Already, three different men and one sharp-voiced woman had approached him, tankard in hand, their talk turning with sly ease toward alliance, trade and marriage. I caught fragments when the noise of the hall lulled.

"A daughter of good stock."

"...strong ties for the future."

"You cannot lead alone forever."

Each word settled in me like stone.

Eirik must have noticed my staring because he leaned closer again. "If you keep looking at him like that, Little Storm, he might actually notice you."

Heat rushed to my cheeks. "I was not–"

"Oh, you were." His grin widened. "But do not worry. I will help you."

Before I could ask what he meant, he reached across the table, snagging a small carved board and set it down between us. I recognised the pieces scattered on it–little black and white stones, some already chipped from use.

"What is this?"

"A game," Eirik said as though it were obvious. "Hnefatafl. War on a board. Easier than war on the sea, and no one dies when you lose. Well-" his eyes sparkled with wicked humour "-except maybe your pride."

He began arranging the pieces, gesturing for me to copy him. "Here. You are the king in the middle. You have got to escape to the edges while I try to trap you. Simple enough."

"Simple," I repeated, though I was doubtful it was as simple as he made it out to be.

Eirik leaned in closer, almost conspiratorily, lowering his voice further. "More importantly, it puts you in Skúli's line of sight. Watch."

I glanced up instinctively and found Skúli's gaze flicking our way. His brows drew together slightly, as if wondering what on earth I was doing hunched over a game board with Eirik.

"You are impossible," I groaned.

"You are welcome."

We began moving our pieces, each turn a battle of wit and words. Eirik narrated each move with dramatic flair, loud enough to be overheard but sly enough to sound like natural banter. We threw taunts at each other while I tried to escape his pieces. Eirik laughed when he captured my pieces one by one.

"You are not playing fair."

"Alura, war is not fair," he rebuked.

I slid a stone across the board, making way for the edge he left unguarded.

"Ah! The queen makes her daring escape! But will her enemies tie her noose?"

I bit my lip, trying not to laugh. "You are ridiculous."

"Ridiculously brilliant. Keep playing."

And so we continued, Eirik's voice carried just enough to snag Skúli's attention whenever he wasn't occupied with yet another would-be-ally pressing cups and suggestions into his hands. Each time Skúli's gaze landed on us, something pulled me toward him.

But the moment was shattered by a shriek.

At first I thought it was part of the revelry. Then the shriek turned into a chorus of yells, followed by a crash and the unmistakable sound of plates scattering.

I saw it a heartbeat later, the blue of scaley legs skittering across the table, claws scattering bread and sending roasted meat tumbling to the floor.

The dreki lizard was back.

Its frill snapped open, a brilliant fan of amber–like the sunset–as it hissed at a serving boy who dropped a whole fish in terror.

The hall erupted.

Men leapt to their feet, some shouting with laughter, others cursing as tankard spilled and food flew. One woman tried to swat the creature away with a spoon, only for the lizard to dart under her skirts, sending her shrieking on top of the table.

Astrid abandoned her dancing to howl with laughter, doubling over while the musicians kept playing as though the chaos were part of the entertainment.

"By the gods," I muttered, pushing back from the bench.

Eirik was already grinning ear to ear. "Best feast I have been to all year."

The dreki scrambled across the board between us, scattering the carved stone in all directions before launching itself toward the high table.

I saw Skúli rise at once, his chair scraping back. The lizard skittered up onto the platform, straight toward the venison. With startling speed, he caught it mid-lunge, one massive hand closing around the creature's middle. It wiggled furiously, frill flaring, but Skúli only held it aloft with a resigned expression that made the entire hall roar with laughter.

"Alura," he called over, voice rich. "I believe I have found your lucky dreki."

My face went hot.

Half the eyes in the hall turned toward me.

Mortification pinned me to the bench for a heartbeat too long. Then, because there was no escape, I forced myself to cross the floor under the weight of their stares, muttering under my breath.

Eyes pinned me down, it felt like everyone was staring at me. But out of the corner of my eye, I saw a shadow moving quickly, almost gone as soon as it was there. I shrugged it off.

Skúli was grinning openly by the time I reached him, holding the furious, flailing lizard out to me like some sort of prize.

"Better keep hold of it this time, before it eats half my hall."

Laughter rippled again around us, but this time it felt softer. Not cruel mockery but a shared amusement. I took the lizard carefully, cradling it to my chest before walking back over to Eirik.

Astrid was there waiting by the time I got back, her face red from laughter. "Gods, is that what I think it is?" I let her look at the lizard, she reached out to pet it but it flared its frill at her, making her jerk back. "That is a rare kind, Alura. I have not seen one of that kind before."

The feast slowly righted itself, though the chaos left an aftertaste of humour that lingered through the night. More toasts were made, more songs were sung. The hall brimmed with warmth, but the noise pressed heavy against my skull after a while and I found myself slipping away toward the doors.

Outside, the night struck cold and sharp.

Snow dusted the courtyard stones, glittering beneath the moon, and my breath curled white in the air. The muffled thunder of the feast dimmed behind the heavy doors, leaving only the distant howl of wolves across the mountains.

I closed my eyes for just a moment, savouring the quiet.

"You always flee when the noise grows too loud."

His voice came low, close.

I opened my eyes to find Skúli beside me, shadows sculpting the hard lines of his face. The firelight from the hall cast a faint glow through the cracks of the doorway.

"I needed air," I said softly.

His gaze searched mine, unreadable, before he nodded. "Mm. So did I."

We stood in silence, the cold brushing against us. The weight of the hall–of peace talks, alliances, marriage proposals–seemed to fall away, leaving only us.

"I saw you playing with Eirik," he said at last, voice rough.

My lips curved despite the nerves fluttering in my chest. "He said it might draw your attention."

"And did it?"

I felt my heart beating in my throat. "Yes."

He stepped closer. Not much, just enough that I could feel the heat radiating off him. Enough that the air seemed thinner. His hand lifted, hesitated, then he brushed a strand of hair from my cheek.

I leaned in, just a bit.

And then the doors to the hall burst open with a crash.

Eirik stumbled out, half laughing, half coughing from the fumes within. "There you are! I thought wolves had eaten you both!"

The moment shattered like glass.

I stepped back swiftly, clutching the lizard tighter under my arm, while Skúli's jaw clenched as though he were grinding down words.

Eirik blinked between us, oblivious and grinned. "Come on, Little Storm. They are bringing out another round of drinks, and Astrid is demanding you dance. Do not let her dance alone."

I managed a nod, though my throat still felt tight, my lips tingled with the almost-kiss that hadn't been.

Skúli said nothing, only turned back toward the hall. But as he pushed open the door, I caught the fleeting glance he cast over his shoulder. A look heavy enough to steal the breath from my lungs.

And then the noise swallowed us again.

CHAPTER THIRTY

ALURA

The great hall had finally grown quiet. The last echoes of laughter and clattering mugs from the feast had faded. Outside, the wind whispered along the ramparts, carrying the faint scent of snow from the peaks above. I moved cautiously, my cloak drawn tight, ears straining for any hint of someone else awake.

Something had felt wrong ever since the lizard incident. I had taken the dreki to my room, Skúli muttering about how mischievous it was, but I couldn't stop thinking about the shadows I'd glimpsed earlier. Someone who had lingered too long, whose gaze followed me.

It wasn't just curiosity.

It was intent.

I hugged the darkness like a shield, slipping toward the kitchen, hoping to catch a glimpse of whoever it was. My pulse began to drum in my ears, but I forced myself to move silently, footsteps muffled on the stone. The same way a messenger would move if they were carrying secrets to Skargrim.

A flicker of motion ahead made me freeze.

I pressed myself behind a pillar, breathing shallowly. A figure slipped past the shadows, hood drawn low, hands gloves, moving quickly toward the stables.

I followed.

Careful. Quiet. Keeping to the walls, weaving through the dying torchlight.

Then, the hair on the back of my neck prickled.

I was being watched.

I froze, my instincts screaming. I caught a glint–something metallic out of the corner of my eye. Someone was behind me, tailing my steps. I could feel the weight of their gaze like a hand on my shoulder.

"Not tonight," I whispered under my breath.

I started moving again, keeping my steps deliberate but quick. The figure behind me mirrored my movements, quiet as a shadow. My heartbeat quickened, my skin prickling with the thrill of danger. I had always trusted my instincts, and they screamed now that this was bad.

Dangerous.

A low growl broke the tense silence. I whipped around, reaching for the nearest weapon. A small knife I had tucked in my belt.

Björn emerged from the darkness, the massive wolf's coat brushing against the torchlight, eyes bright and alert. He bared his teeth, letting out a snarl that rolled through the hall like thunder.

The shadowed figure froze...then bolted, glancing back only once before vanishing around a corner.

I sagged against the wall, adrenaline hammering through me. "Björn," I whispered, relief spreading through my voice.

The wolf nuzzled my shoulder, heavy and warm. I ran my hands through his thick fur, shivering not from the cold but from the fear that gripped me.

"You are reckless."

I spun to see Skúli stepping out of the darkness at the far end of the hall. His expression was hard, eyes flashing with something I rarely saw.

Fear, laced with anger.

"I...I thought-" I began, but he crossed the space between us in long strides.

"You thought what, Alura? That you could slip through the night without danger?"

His voice was low, tense, but there was a trembling under it that I recognised.

Worry.

I tried to explain, but my words faltered. "I saw someone," I admitted. "Someone who... I thought they might be–"

"They were following you." He didn't need me to finish. His eyes were dark, focused, and there was that edge of frustration that made my pulse catch in ways that had nothing to do with fear.

"I was not hurt," I said softly.

"No," he said, stepping closer. "But you could have been. Do you understand that?"

I did. More than I wanted to admit.

"I can take care of myself."

Skúli's jaw tightened. "Maybe. But not against everything. Not against them. Not against what is coming."

I swallowed, standing, stepping slightly closer despite the tension between us. "Then help me."

Something shifted in his gaze, softening just enough that I could see it .The anger, the worry–it melted into something else completely. Desire. Relief. Something raw and unspoken.

"Alura," he whispered.

I took another step closer. "Yes?"

His hand reached up, brushing a stray strand of hair from my face. The simple touch made my stomach flip. "You cannot put yourself in danger like that."

"I was not thinking," I admitted. "I just–"

Before I could finish, he closed the gap between us. His forehead pressing to mine, our breaths mingling in the cold night air of the hall. Every instinct in me screamed for me to stop, to pull away. I didn't.

His hand cradled my cheek, warm and grounding, while the other settled at the small of my back, pulling me closer until there was no space left between us.

"Alura," he murmured again, voice rough. "You do not know what you are to me."

I blinked, caught off guard. "I think I do..."

He let out a bitter laugh. "Fuck it."

Before I could react, he pressed his lip to mine. Hard. Demanding. Electric.

I pressed into him, hands clutching at his chest as the kiss deepened, hot and sudden. My stormlight flared without warning, streaks of silver and violet snaking along my veins, illuminating the hall in sharp bursts of light.

"Alura," he muttered against my lips, but there was no hesitation in the kiss. Only urgency, recklessness.

I gasped as the surge of magic reacted to our closeness. Sparks danced across my fingers, curling around us like flames. Björn's low growls echoed through the halls but I couldn't think.

Couldn't breathe.

Couldn't stop.

Skúli's hands roamed, one hand moving from my cheek to cradle the back of my head, the other sliding up my back. His breath was ragged, and there was a flicker of wildness in him that mirrored my chaos.

And then he pulled back. Just far enough to tilt his head, eyes locking with mine, dangerous and full of warning.

"We cannot do that again," he said, voice low but fierce. "We are bound by fate, Alura. This...us...it is a trap that the gods have set for us. Cruel. And it will tear us apart if we do not...control ourselves."

I reached for him again, desperate. "But I–"

"I know what you feel," he snapped, cutting me off. "I feel it too. But the power you wield...it is volatile. If you lose control again, it will not just be you in danger. You risk everything. Me. Us. Everyone we care about."

The magic throbbed inside me, reacting to my frustration, my desire, my fear. A flare of violet lightning lit up the room.

"I do not care,' I muttered, voice trembling.

"You should." He exhaled sharply, leaning his forehead to mine. I could feel his helplessness of feeling bound by fate. "Do you understand what this means? What will happen if you do not control it?""Yes," I whispered, almost breaking under him, the magic, the moment.

"Then we stop." He gritted his teeth, forcing himself back, breaking contact. "We stop. Before we rip ourselves apart. Before the gods do."

I rested my forehead against his chest, feeling his heart beating under my hands.

Skúli let out a heavy breath, hands tightening on my shoulders. "I cannot lose you, Alura. Not now. Not ever. But neither of us can ignore what is coming."

"Then what do we do?"

He shook his head, frustrated by the conflict. "We survive. We fight. We stay alive…apart, if we must."

I tilted my head, glancing up at him. "Even if it kills us?"

"Especially if it kills us," he murmured.

And then, he kissed me again. Not slow or tender, but desperate. I didn't resist. I couldn't. My magic flared again, bright and wild, and I felt the raw power of us igniting. A reminder that our connection was dangerous and unstoppable.

When we finally broke apart, gasping, he rested his forehead against mine once more, voice rough and hoarse. "This is madness. And yet, it is all I want. You must promise me something."

"Anything," I breathed.

"Promise me you will not lose control like that again."

I nodded. "I promise," I said, pushing my magic back down. I didn't fully believe the promise I had made, not when the fire between us burned so bright.

Skúli pressed a quick kiss to my temple, then straightened, moving away just enough to leave space, yet the heat of him lingered.

"Good," he muttered, voice tight with restraint. "Now go back to bed. Get rest. Tomorrow–tomorrow we deal with the world, not each other."

I watched him go, chest still pounding, fingers tingling with leftover sparks of magic. The hall was quiet again, but the tension remained—between us, in me, in the air, in the stormlight that refused to fade completely.

And I knew it was far from over.

CHAPTER THIRTY-ONE
Skúli

The clang of steel echoed through the courtyard, each strike ringing against the stone like a heartbeat. Sweat burned in my eyes and slicked hair to my forehead, but I did not pause. Not now. Not while the men of Drakensvar relied on me to make them ready for the raid.

I watched as Torbjörn swung his axe with all the force of a seasoned raider, and then corrected him. "Again!" I barked. "Stirke with conviction, or strike alone! You cannot falter when the enemy crosses the battlefield."

A chorus of grunts and curses followed, and I shook my head. Half of these men thought they were ready for battle because they had survived raids or border skirmishes. They were not ready. Not for what was coming. Not for the inevitability of the King's armies.

I moved along the lines, inspecting stances, checking grips, observing breaths. Every detail mattered. Every motion could mean life or death. When I reached Eirik, I had to suppress a grin. The man's defiance was almost enviable, even if it might get him killed faster than most.

"Eirik," I called out of the clamor of the courtyard. "Focus your eyes on the opponent, not the sky, the clouds, or the pretty girls in the hall. This is not Solstice. This is survival."

He smirked. "I always survive, Skúli. Do not worry about me."

I narrowed my eyes, but did not argue. He would survive, through stubbornness and luck, nothing more. Luck was fleeting. Skill was eternal. And skill was what I was trying to instill here.

The day wore on, the run rising higher, casting shadows across the frosty training yard. My muscles ached, but I could not stop. I could not rest. I would not allow even one man to falter.

By mid-afternoon, the men were drenched in sweat and exhaustion, but they were stronger, faster, sharper. I allowed a rare smile.

"Enough for now," I called and the clanging of metal ceased. The courtyard went quiet except for heavy breaths and the occasional groan.

I took a moment to wipe my hands, feeling the sting of blisters forming on my palms. It would be nothing tomorrow, and nothing the day after. Pain was only temporary. Survival was more important.

Astrid approached, light-footed, deliberate and graceful. She had been watching for hours, and I knew why. The way her eyes tracked me, the way her fingers curled around the edge of her cloak. It was not a concern for all the men, but for me and Eirik.

"Astrid," I said, voice neutral and measured. "How can I help you?"

Her expression did not waver. She stepped closer, hands clasped behind her back, chin tilted in that stubborn way that always made me feel like she was wiser beyond her years.

"You are pushing them hard." She glanced at Eirik who was joking with a greener warrior. "You know they can handle it."

"They must," I said, letting the words hang. "There is no mercy in war."

Her eyes narrowed, sharply. "And you? How will you handle it?"

I ignored the question, but my hands tightened slightly on the handle of my blade. It was easier to command than to confront my own heart. Easier to correct flaws in technique than flaws in destiny.

She sighed, the sound heavy with concern. "You are taking Alura with you."

"Yes," I replied carefully. "I was told to take her."

Astrid's lips parted, her hands clenching into fists. "Her power...it is not stable. Do you know what that would mean?"

I exhaled. "I know what her power means. But she has proven herself capable. She will survive. I will make sure of it."

She shook her head, frustration flashing. "And what about you?" She asked sharply. "What about your life? The blood claim? The crown? Everything could be lost."

"Everything I am, Astrid, is tied to her." My voice was hard, carrying the weight of the truth. "I cannot turn back. Not now. I was never meant to rule."

She stepped back, taking a breath. "And what about me?"

"What about you?"

"Am I coming?"

"No." I eyed her carefully. "Astrid, you are the last of us. The last of your kind too. It is not safe for you outside Drakensvar, you know this."

"I can fight!"

"I know." I drew in a sharp breath. "There is no one I would rather fight side by side with. But our people need you."

Almost reluctantly, she said, "Then you leave me with no choice. I must stay."

Astrid was too precious to risk, no matter how much she hated me for it.

"You will stay." My tone was final. "You will train. For the day the King comes for us all, you will be ready to defend what is ours."

Astrid's lips twitched, with restrained frustration. "And Alura? What about her?"

My jaw tightened. The memory of last night burned fresh in my mind. The stolen, desperate kisses, the surge of magic that had flared around her like a living thing. The danger. The temptation. How impossible it was.

"She cannot—nothing can happen," I said, voice low. "Not between us. Fate has tied her to me in ways that are cruel. Dangerous. Merciless. We cannot give in. We must not."

She tilted her head, searching my eyes. "You kissed her," she said plainly.

I did not deny it. I would not.

"I did. And it was a mistake. Or perhaps...necessary. But it cannot happen again. Not while we are bound by the gods' plans. Not while her power could consume everything."

Astrid's expression softened slightly, though the fire behind her eyes remained. "Then you understand why I fear for her. Why I fear for all of you. She is a force of nature. And you–you are drawn to her in ways I cannot understand."

I stepped closer, lowering my voice to a level that could cut through stone. "Then trust me to keep her safe," I said, and I meant every word. "I will do whatever is necessary to protect her, even if it costs me everything."

Astrid's eyes searched mine for a long moment, and I saw in them both skepticism and a flicker of relief. She nodded finally, stepping back.

"Then I will stay behind," she said. "And you... you make sure nothing happens to her, or to you. Nothing."

I exhaled, running a hand through my hair, the weight of leadership settling like iron on my shoulders.

"I will not fail her," I said, though the thought of last night's kiss, of her soft, defiant expression, of the stormlight coursing through her veins, made it impossible to feel unburdened.

The courtyard was quiet now, the men returning from their drills, weapons slung and armor glinting in the waning light. I watched them carefully, making mental notes, measuring their stamina, their courage, their readiness. Every man, every decision mattered. Every life could tip the balance.

Astrid lingered nearby, but she did not interfere, and I did not expect her to. Her loyalty, her intelligence, her grace—all of it was unmatched. She was the last of her line, and I could not risk her life in the coming storm.

I turned to the warriors, shouting instructions, demonstrating strikes, correcting stances, forcing precision from exhaustion. And yet, in the back of my mind, I could not escape her gaze, her questions, the weight of what had happened with Alura.

The kiss haunted me. Not because I regretted it—it was everything I wanted—but because it was a reminder of how dangerous desire could be when fate itself was working against us.

Alura's stormlight had flared with her passion, with her fear, with the heat of us together. If I was not careful, if she was not careful, it would consume everything in its path. And I could not allow that.

Later, when the courtyard was quiet again, I found Alura tending to the dreki lizard, feeding it scraps and murmuring softly. She looked up at me, eyes wide, cheeks flushed.

"Skúli," she said softly, almost a whisper, "I did not think you would come out here."

"I always come for you," I said, voice low, almost gruff. "Even when you think no one is watching. Even when you are in danger. Even when you act reckless."

Her lips curved into a smile, though it did not reach her eyes. "I... I just wanted to make sure I was not being followed."

I stepped closer, keeping my distance, though every inch between us felt charged. "And were you?" I asked.

She nodded. "I think...someone was. But Björn..."

"I know," I said, eyes narrowing. "I saw him. He did well."

Her gaze flicked to mine, searching, challenging. "And you?"

I swallowed, heart hammering. I could not afford to fail her. Not now. Not ever

Her fingers brushed against the lizard, and I saw the flare of stormlight in her veins once more. She was fire and storm and danger all in one. And I was drawn to it, even as I knew how impossible it was.

I wanted to reach for her, to kiss her again, to feel that connection flare between us. But I restrained myself, reminding myself of the cruel, merciless hand of fate.

I exhaled sharply, turning away, voice firm. "Tomorrow, we begin the real preparation. You get rest. I will not allow you to burn yourself out here."

She nodded reluctantly, watching me go. And I walked away, heart tight, mind racing, knowing that the moment from last night had changed everything.

I could not deny it. I wanted her. I wanted her like nothing I had ever wanted in my life. But desire was a dangerous thing, and fate... fate was a cruel, unyielding enemy.

And we were bound by it, stormborn and wolfblood, caught in a web we could not escape.

CHAPTER THIRTY-TWO
ALURA

The snow whipped against the great hall's doors like icy fingers. The storm outside made the walls feel impossibly thick and safe, and the hearth blazed as though it knew it had to hold back the winter's bite. The air inside smelled of pine, roasted meat, and the faint tang of mead. Warmth curled around me like a familiar cloak, but it did nothing to dull the ache of worry that clung in the back of my mind.

Eirik had commandeered a bench at the center of the hall and perched himself like a king, one boot dangling over the edge, tankard in hand, gesturing wildly as he told his latest tale.

"And there I was," he roared, voice echoing off the stone walls, "racing a dreki hatchling across the frozen river! Barefoot, of course, because my boots froze halfway there. It squealed, flapped its wings like mad, and I—naturally—won by a full horse-length!"

Laughter rolled through the hall. Astrid leaned toward me, her lips twitching despite her best effort to look disinterested. She murmured, though I could hear the faint edge of amusement, "Mostly true. Sort of. I mean, the hatchling did race, but Eirik did not exactly win by skill alone."

I squinted at Eirik. "You raced a dreki hatchling across a river? In winter? And survived?"

He puffed out his chest and threw up a dramatic shrug. "A minor inconvenience! The thrill of a near-freezing death is hardly enough to deter a man of wit and talent. You see, Alura, it is about strategy—cleverness—and the sheer terror of losing!"

Björn, as if sensing that Eirik was stealing the spotlight, yipped loudly and leapt onto Eirik's chest. The wiry wolf's claws slipped on the polished wood, and Eirik nearly toppled off the bench, taking his dinner plate down to the floor.

"Björn! Down, you little thief!" he shouted, flailing wildly. The hall erupted in laughter, some doubling over as Eirik wrestled the wolf off him.

I couldn't help laughing. "He is impossible," I said to Astrid.

She smirked. "Yes, but entertaining. And terrifying, in equal measure."

Eirik, now free from Björn, threw his arms wide, eyes sparkling with mischief. "And that, my dear ladies, is only the beginning. I once defeated three berserkers in a drinking contest by pretending to pass out, then stealthily stealing their mead while they celebrated my 'loss.' Masterful, no?"

I raised an eyebrow. "And this actually happened?"

He leaned forward, lowering his voice as though revealing a great secret. "Alura, my dear, truth is always stranger than stories. The more impossible it seems, the more likely it actually occurred. Astrid knows this. Ask her."

Astrid rolled her eyes but didn't hide her grin. "Some of it is true. The rest...is mostly an exaggeration."

I leaned back, trying to hide the smile tugging at my lips. "So the ridiculous ones—the ones I almost choke on my mead hearing—those are true?"

Eirik banged his tankard for emphasis. "Exactly! Only a fool would dismiss the impossible first. Reality is too mundane to be remembered."

Skúli, who had been leaning against the pillar at the far end of the hall, arms crossed, watched silently. Stoic, unyielding, like a rock. But when Eirik flopped onto the table to act out being chased by wolves, I caught the corner of a smile twitching at the edge of his mouth. Just a hint, barely there—but enough to make my chest warm.

I sipped my mead and shook my head. Skúli's restraint had always unnerved me, and yet tonight, the faintest shift of expression made me feel like he was letting me in—just a little.

"Ah, but you have not heard the best one!" Eirik exclaimed, flipping onto his stomach for dramatic effect. "I seduced a jarl's daughter to be run out of the village! The scandal, the outrage! And I—naturally—emerged victorious, for who else could win such a battle of wits and charm?"

I blinked. "That one is probably true, right? Or... maybe not?"

Astrid laughed quietly. "Mostly exaggerated. The jarl's daughter part? Definitely true. The being run out of town? Embellished."

I shook my head, laughing harder. "You make the most ridiculous stories sound believable."

Eirik puffed out his chest. "And that, Alura, is why my legend grows with every retelling!"

Björn yipped again, apparently offended at being ignored, and attempted to leap onto Eirik's back this time. Eirik flailed dramatically, nearly tipping over the table. "Björn! You traitorous beast!"

Astrid muttered, barely hiding her laughter. "One day he is going to hurt himself for real."

I whispered to her, "Or set himself on fire."

Eirik gasped theatrically. "Alura! Such treachery! How dare you accuse me!"

I shrugged. "Merely stating facts."

Eirik shot me a look of mock outrage, and I could barely stop myself from laughing. He had this absurd talent for drawing attention, chaos, and amusement all at once.

Through it all, I kept glancing at Skúli. He hadn't moved, not much. But his eyes—sharp, calculating—kept flicking toward me, scanning the hall, noting everything, taking in everything. The laughter, the flailing, the chaos. His jaw tightened for a moment, then relaxed. That faint twitch of a smile returned.

My stomach fluttered. I knew him well enough to know he was amused, and yet the moment was fleeting. Duty, fate, and something larger than any of us pressed down on his shoulders. The tension between us, always simmering under the surface, threatened to boil over.

I took a careful sip of mead, trying not to let my awareness of him show. But I couldn't help it. Each glance, each flicker of amusement, sent heat creeping across my cheeks.

Eirik's voice cut through my thoughts again. "And then—then, I had to fight a pack of wolves while balancing a dreki hatchling on my shoulders! Barefoot. Naturally.

It was the height of heroism, the apex of adventure, and I—of course—triumphed!"

I groaned and clutched my mug. "You are insane."

Björn, clearly unamused by being ignored, yipped again and leapt onto Eirik's lap. Eirik groaned. "Björn! Must you interfere with my legend?" The wolf flopped over, tail wagging, oblivious.

Skúli's eyes flicked toward me again. That faint smirk lingered. I felt my chest tighten in response, though I couldn't explain why. There was something about the way he allowed himself that single moment of amusement—it felt like permission for me to enjoy it too.

The storm outside howled, rattling the world outside. I watched the snow swirl in chaotic spirals beyond the doors, but the warmth, the laughter, the ridiculousness of Eirik's storytelling, and even Skúli's subtle reactions made the hall feel like a haven from everything else.

I caught Skúli's gaze once more, and for a fleeting heartbeat, it felt like the storm outside didn't exist. That he wasn't a prince, a leader, or bound by fate. Just a man, and I... I was just me, here with him.

Then the moment passed, and he straightened, back to his usual stoic self. Duty pressed against him again, and I felt the weight of it reflected in the tension in his shoulders.

But for now, we had this. Laughter. Firelight. Snow-storm outside. Eirik spinning tales too ridiculous to be true, Björn causing chaos, Astrid grinning knowingly. And me, watching, laughing, and secretly hoping that Skúli's rare, fleeting amusement was just for me.

For now, it was enough.

CHAPTER THIRTY-THREE

ALURA

The training yard was frozen over with snow, the flakes still falling, caught in the brazier's light like drifting embers. My breath curled while in the air as I tightened the bindings on my wrist. The wooden sword felt heavy in my hand, colder than it should, as though the storm had seeped into the grain.

Skúli stood across from me, dark cloak tossed aside, broad shoulders squared. He was already watching me, unreadable as ever, that same damned stillness he carried into battle, into arguments, into moments I wanted–needed–him to say something more.

"Again," he said simply.

I lifted my practice sword and shifted my shield, setting my stance the way he had drilled into me a hundred times before. Knees bent, feet steady, weight centered.

My arms already ached, but I wasn't going to let him see that. Not tonight. Not after the way he had barely looked at me since we had kissed.

We circled each other, the snow crunching beneath our boots. My hair clung damply to my cheek, loose from its braid. Skúli moved first–always faster than a man of his size should be–striking at my shoulder. I brought my blade up to catch it, wood clashing hard against wood.

"Too slow," he said, tone clipped.

I gritted my teeth. "I know that."

"Then fix it."

Another strike. I blocked, but it was too late. His sword knocked mine down toward the snow. I jerked back, heart pounding, anger sharp and hot in my chest."

"Again," he said.

"I am trying," I snapped.

"Trying gets you killed." His voice was flat, but there was something burning underneath it.

"I have magic, I do not need a blade."

"If you want to stand in the shield wall, you do not use your magic. You do not get to be almost fast enough. You have to be faster."

His words cut sharper than a blade. Not because they weren't true, but because he always delivered them like they were final. Like I was one of his soldiers. As though he hadn't seen me use my stormlight magic.

I lunged, striking harder than I had meant to. He parried easily, but the force vibrated up his arm, and for once he blinked, surprised.

"You do not trust me," I said, voice low, the words slipping out before I could stop them.

Skúli stilled. "This is not about trust."

"Of course it is," I hissed. My chest rose and fell, my breaths sharp in the cold air. "Every time you look at me, it is like I am something you have to stop from shattering. You train me like I am a child, then expect me to stay in the camp while you go to war. You do not believe I can fight."

His jaw tightened. He shifted his grip on his sword but I didn't advance. "I believe you can fight. That does not mean I want you to."

The way he said it–quiet and unyielding–struck harder than a blade ever could. I wanted to scream at him, shake him, or force him to say what lay beneath his stone exterior. Because I knew. I knew he cared.

My heart ached. "You would rather I stand aside and watch you bleed, is that it? Pretend I am not here? Pretend I do not need the same choices you get to make?"

He said nothing. Just stood there, looming, his eyes dark and unreadable. Still.

That silence was worse than an insult.

"Go fuck yourself," I snarled.

Fury clawed up my throat, light flashing out of the corner of my eyes. I lunged, swinging hard enough to rattle his arm as he caught my blow on the rim of his shield. Sparks flew where wood met wood. He grunted, driven half a step back, but still he refused to answer me.

"Say it!" I snarled, striking again. "Say you think of me as weak. Say you want me locked away while you fight all the battles that should be ours together."

Skúli shoved against my sword, forcing me back with raw strength. "Enough."

But it only lit my temper higher. I spun, coming at him again, raining down another strike. He blocked, turning me aside, but I felt the tremor in his stance.

"You think your silence will shield me?" I spat, panting. "It does not. It makes the wound deeper."

"Alura–"

"NO!" I cut him off, slashing upward with a fury that nearly jarred the sword from my hand when he parried. "Do not say my name like that. As if it will calm me. As if you care. As if you love me."

The word hung in the air like a blade suspended above us, sharp enough to kill. His eyes widened–just for a moment–before hardening again. He pressed his weight into the lock of our swords until my knees threatened to buckle.

"You do not understand what you are saying." His voice was rough, uneven.

"Oh, I understand," I hissed, wrenching myself free and staggering back. My lungs burned, my pulse roared in my ears. "I see the way you look at me and then turn me away. You carry all your fear and grief like armour. You would chain me to the hearth for my own good while you throw yourself to bears and serpents. You think that is protection? That is cowardice."

"Cowardice?" His voice cracked like a whip, the hall's shadows seeming to deepen with the force of it. His sword slammed against mine in a sudden, brutal arc that forced me to stumble backward. "You think that I fear battle? I have bled more than you can imagine. I do not fear dying."

"Then you fear me," I flung back, the words sharp and vicious. I drove forward, my blade slashing, desperate to make him feel even a fraction of the storm inside. "You fear what it means to care for me. To admit it. To stand beside me."

His jaw clenched. For a heartbeat I thought he might say everything that I knew he buried. Instead, he tore his gaze away.

"This is not a burden you are meant to carry," he ground out, voice low but edged with steel. His eyes burned, fierce and pained all at once. "I cannot lose you too. I will not watch you offer yourself piece by piece until nothing remains."

His hand twitched as if he wanted to reach for me, but he stilled. "And if you would force me to stand by, if you would make me endure that again..." His face hardened to stone. "Then I cannot. I will not allow it.""I am not her."

"I know! But we are bound by fate. Whatever is coming...whatever I feel, whatever I want...none of it matters if I must watch you destroy yourself."

His words rang in the cold air, heavy as bell tolling. For a moment, I couldn't breathe, the air between us thickened. I swallowed.

"You speak as though I am already ash," I whispered, my voice trembling. "As if my life is nothing but a shadow of hers. Do you not see how you chain yourself with this fear of yours?"

His mouth pressed into a grim line, his silence was answer enough.

"You think to cage me because you are afraid to hurt again? Then hear me, Skúli, I would rather die a thousand deaths than wither."

I turned my back to him, dropping my sword. Behind me, I heard only his ragged breathing, a man choking on words he couldn't say.

"Perhaps you should have left me in chains," I spat. "Then you would not have to watch me stay. You would not have to torture yourself."

CHAPTER
THIRTY-FOUR
ALURA

My chamber's doors slammed behind me, shaking the furniture with a finality that I could feel in my chest. My breath came in ragged bursts, stormlight flickering faintly in my vision from the anger I could not yet release. I leaned against the door, shoulders trembling, palms pressing against the cold wood, trying to draw steady breaths.

A soft rustle drew my attention. At first, I thought it was the wind on the window, whistling through the cracks in the sill. Then I saw it, movement across the floor.

"Not now," I muttered, brushing a hand across my forehead, only to see the familiar glint of the dreki lizard's scales catching the firelight. The little creature emerged from the shadows, tiptoeing across the floor, frill flicking in curiosity and amusement.

It crawled gently up my leg, curling itself in my arm. Its warm, scaled body rose and fell with tiny breaths, as though it were mocking the storm still inside me.

I exhaled, and for the first time in what felt like hours, my shoulders loosened. I whispered, almost to myself, "At least you do not argue with me."

My hands ran along its warm back, tracing the ridges of its spines. It chirped softly, a small content sound, as though it understood the fury I carry and simply refused to comment.

I sank down on the edge of my bed, drawing the creature closer, feeling the tension ebb as I let myself feel its warmth. My mind replayed the fight, his words, the weight behind them. I could still see his jaw set, feel the intensity in his stance, taste the fire in his eyes.

Minutes passed, or maybe an hour, I lost track of time. Caught between relief and frustration. Then my gaze fell to the doorway. A shadow lingered there, subtle. Almost imperceptible against the candlelight. I stiffened, my heart leaping.

But there was nothing, just the shine of wood. My chest tightened. I walked over and there, just inside the threshold was my practice sword. Oiled, gleaming in the flickering light. No note. No sign of explanation. Yet this screamed of him.

I knelt, running my fingers along the smooth wood, and my chest tightened further. He didn't need to say anything, the gesture said everything. He cared. He wanted me ready. He wanted me safe.

The dreki lizard chirped softly, nudging its frill against my chin and I laughed quietly, finally letting some of the tension leave my body. It felt absurdly comforting, this small creature. More reliable than men sometimes.

I stroked its head, whispering, "You are the only one who does not make things complicated."

And yet, everything was complicated. My heart, my feelings, our fate, the raids, the shadows creeping over the future. Skúli's fears, his burdens, the way he did not allow himself to trust me with them.

The anger still lingered. I wanted to shake him, to demand that he trust me, that he let me stand with him, that he admit what he felt before it was too late. But the little dreki lizard twitched its frill against me, reminding me of steadiness, patience...survival.

I whispered to it again, "Soon. Soon he will understand."

Outside, snow began to drift heavier, drifting down in thick, wet flakes that stuck to the windows. Inside, the warmth of the fire mingled with the soft rhythm of the dreki's breathing became a fragile sanctuary.

The polished sword remained at the doorway, a promise, a tether I could hold onto while the rest of the world was threatening to collapse. As I traced the edges of the practice blade with my fingers I realised that he might not say it, he might not act on it, but his care was there, in every inch of wood, in every shadow of the yard, in every step he took to keep me alive.

Tomorrow will come. There will be training and arguments, with battles, with war, and with him. And I would face it all, armed with more than just a sword.

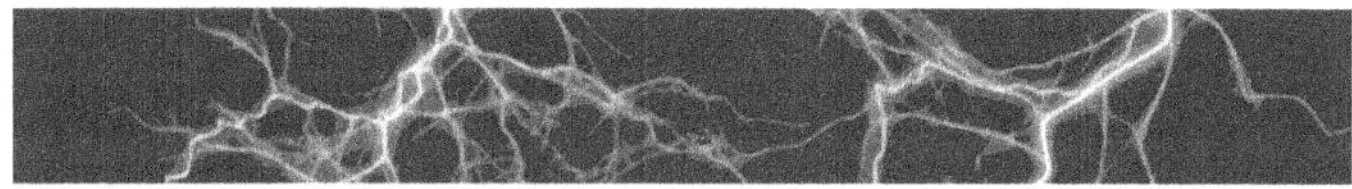

The storm outside had softened into a steady drizzle of snow, draping the stone walls in a ghostly shimmer. I had spent what felt like hours sitting with the dreki lizard on my lap, its warmth seeping into my cold, stiff fingers. By the time I set it down, coiled in a nest of blankets, I realized the hours had passed unnoticed.

Dinner would be late. The hall would be empty by now. I hesitated, wondering if I could face Skúli without my anger flaring again, without the weight of words unsaid hanging between us.

I wrapped my cloak tightly around my shoulders and crept down the staircase. My boots made soft sounds against the stone. The flickering torchlight threw long shadows, and for a moment, I imagined Skúli standing in one of them. Watching. Waiting.

I wasn't wrong.

He was already in the great hall, seated at the head of the table. The wooden boards gleamed from fresh polish, candlelight dancing off the edges. His eyes caught mine as I emerged from the stairs.

I froze mid-step, caught between wanting to retreat and wanting to stride forward, demanding that he meet my eyes without his armour. He, in turn, rose slightly, letting the tension in his shoulders ease a little.

"Alura," he said softly, carrying just enough warmth to make my heart leap.

I forced myself to take a step. "I did not mean to sneak."

He shook his head, a faint smile tugging at the corners of his mouth. "I am glad you came. I...I owe you an apology."

"An apology? From the great Skúli himself?"

He exhaled slowly, the sound rumbling. "Yes. For earlier. For the way I–" he stopped, jaw clenching. "For everything. I let my fear blind me. That was not fair."

I opened my mouth but he held up a hand. "I cannot...I cannot promise it will not happen again," he said honestly. "But know that my intentions–as flawed as they are–are to keep you safe. Always."

A warmth bloomed in my chest, despite the lingering storm inside me. I wanted to throw myself into his arms, to let me share the burden. But the memory of the way he told me we could not be together after our kiss kept me at bay.

"I understand," I said quietly, thinking of the way my power bloomed when we fought earlier. "I do."

The moment stretched between us, just two broken people trying to navigate fear and desire. And then, like an arrow tearing through still air, Eirik's voice cut across the hall.

"Ah! Look who decided to join the living!" He bellowed, shoving his chair back so violently the legs screeched across stone. "And here I thought I had to send a search party!"

I blinked. Skúli's jaw tightened, the twitch betraying his annoyance, though his eyes glimmered with humour.

I sighed, pressing my palm to my face. "Had to be him."

Eirik grinned, unabashed. "What? I only interrupted the most intense brooding session I had ever seen. You two looked like you were about to set fire to the snow with your feelings."

Skúli's eyes found mine and I couldn't help but smile. There was a wordless acknowledgement between us. A reminder that we were still tethered.

I slid into the seat across from Eirik, careful to keep my composure. Skúli adjusted in his seat, close enough that the warmth radiating from his body reached me. A quiet reassurance that words were not always needed.

Eirik leaned over dramatically, pointing at me. "She is still fuming is she not? I can see it in the glow of her eyes. Do not worry, I will make sure you two do not...combust before dessert."

CHAPTER THIRTY-FIVE
ALURA

Winter had eased. The snow on the peaks lessened by the day, and the sun shone brighter, a pale, promising light that filtered through the clouds. Any snow that landed in the courtyard was no more than slush by the time the sun had fully risen, and I knew it was time. The world outside still held the bite of frost, but the storm's grip has loosened. Still, that warmth was only a reminder that what lay ahead could burn hotter, sharper, and more deadly than the cold ever had.

There was no celebration to mark our departure–just the quiet churn of preparation, the steady hum of dread and duty that clung to the air like mist. No banners waved, no horns sounded. Drakensvar itself held its breath.

We had received word from King Skargrim that morning. A raven had arrived just after dawn, bearing his seal and his command. We were to depart tomorrow. The parchment smelled faintly of smoke and ink, official and unyielding.

Skúli had stormed off in one of his brooding moods the moment he received it, muttering something about false kings giving bad orders and leading good men to their deaths. We did not see him again until later, and even then, only in fleeting glimpses.

I stepped onto the docks, the slush squishing beneath my boots. Smoke drifted from a nearby forge, acrid and sharp, mingling with the briny scent of the sea. The rhythmic clink of hammers against steel carried across the harbor, slow, purposeful, like a funeral bell.

Skúli and Eirik were inspecting blades, checking shield straps and armour. Our eyes met for a fraction of a second. In that silent exchange, I thought I saw an apology, or perhaps a farewell. I looked away too quickly to decipher it.

Around the docks, the energy was taut. Younger warriors paced like restless wolves, their shoulders squared in false bravado. One laughed too loudly, fingers hovering over the hilt of his sword. Another had tied a fresh red cloth to his axe handle–a token from a lover perhaps.

The older warriors moved slower, more deliberate. Voices low, they whispered of the coast we would soon face.

"Cursed that shore. Last time we landed near the black cliffs, the ground itself seemed to bleed."

"They drink the blood of their enemies."

"Not men. Demons."

The murmurs clawed at me, but still, they sharpened blades, coiled ropes, and loaded provisions. Duty outweighed sense. Men often preferred swinging their swords to lying idle, even knowing the stakes.

I adjusted the grip on the basket Freydis had packed for me. Dried herbs, rolls of linen, jars of thick salve and tinctures. My healer's kit for the journey. It felt too light for the weight it carried.

Some of the men glanced at me as I passed. Whispers followed in my wake, though I pretended not to notice. I was the Storm-Born. Their fear and awe clung to me like a second cloak.

I reached the boat and set down my basket. The sails were still furled, the hull humming with quiet tension. Tomorrow we will be at sea. And after that...only the gods knew.

"Is that everything?"

I spun. Skúli stood behind me, a faint smudge of soot streaking his cheek, hair damp and clinging to his temples. He looked exhausted, the weight of the coming days etched into every line of his face.

"For the wounded," I said quietly, regretting slipping with the words. "If there are wounded."

"There will be," he said simply, but not unkindly. "But less if we are careful."

"What do you need me to do?" I asked, following as he led me toward the forge.

The warmth of the fire hit us as soon as we entered, the scent of oil and singed leather thick in the air. Outside, the docks buzzed with preparation, but here it felt like the heart of something grim and necessary.

"I need you to rebind these hilts," he said, pulling a coil of leather from a shelf. "Half the men let their gear rot between seasons."

He handed me the cord and demonstrated the technique. I fumbled at first, but gradually found the rhythm, knotting with care under his watchful gaze.

Eirik leaned against the anvil, polishing a blade with a cloth that looked suspiciously like part of his tunic. "Careful, Alura. If you keep being useful we will start expecting things from you," he teased.

"She is already doing more than you," Skúli muttered, his voice low, almost a growl.

"You wound me, old friend." Eirik dramatically clutched his chest. "First you steal my drink, now my pride."

I focused on the task at hand, the repetitive motion soothing my racing thoughts. The forge's heat, the scent of fire and metal, and the precision of binding leather to steel grounded me.

Skúli's eyes flicked to mine occasionally, each glance a small reminder that we were here together.

"Should you not be doing something useful?" He asked without looking up.

"I *am* doing something useful."

"Supervising?" Skúli scoffed.

"I will have you know, I ran a trading crew once," Eirik said, hands wide. "Kept it running for weeks."

"And?" Skúli asked, prompting him to continue.

"Well. They mutinied. But only because they were jealous of my excellent leadership skills."

I couldn't help but snort. A few younger warriors chuckled as well. I bit down a smile.

"See, *she* believes me," Eirik said, pointing at me as though I had just validated his tall tale.

"I believe you are full of shit," I replied without looking up from my work.

Skúli gave me a sideways glance, his mouth twitching up into a smirl. "She is already doing more than you," he muttered again playfully, he stood to check a line of spears laid out for inspection.

Eirik followed him like a shadow, still grinning. "Admit it, you have gone soft. First you start letting a woman-"

He didn't get to finish.

"He is not letting me do anything." I rose to stretch out my aching legs, my voice cool. "I am not a dog on a leash."

That earned a low whistle from Eirik. "Apologies. I did not mean to say you were not terrifying in your own right."

"She is," Skúli agreed. But his voice had changed, it was lower, like he wasn't joking. "And she has earned the right to stand with us. More than you, some days."

Eirik clutched his chest again. "The betrayal."

"If you do not start helping," Skúli said with a grin, "I will have you mucking out horse stalls, every day, for a year."

Eirik groaned, collapsing onto a nearby barrel. "Fine. I will sharpen something. But if I cramp my hands, it is on you."

"Good," Skúli said, lips twitching. "If you die that means I will have peace for once."

I watched the two of them move together, in sync, bickering like brothers. There was a bond between them that no amount of time could rust away, forged in blood and shared scars. Their banter is like shields, not weapons. Armour against what they knew lay ahead.

Skúli's glances toward me never failed, brief and careful, but enough to make my chest ache with a mix of hope and fear.

I realised then how fragile these moments were. Tomorrow, we would sail into uncertainty, where blood and fire might claim everything. But for now, in the forge's warmth, with the scent of metal and smoke and leather, we were alive, together.

I allowed myself a small, quiet hope. Perhaps, just for a moment, the world could wait.

CHAPTER THIRTY-SIX
ALURA

The hearth fire spread a warm amber glow across the stone as the four of us gathered for our last meal together before the raid. It was simple, salted meat, thick stew, crusty bread and a jug of dark ale. This was not a celebration. This was a farewell, unspoken but understood.

A quiet settled between us, heavy, not uncomfortable but charged. Each glance, each tilt of a head carried the weight of unspoken fears and prayers. Tonight we had made a sacrifice to the gods. Skúli, in his white ceremonial tunic, had slit the goat's throat in the courtyard. Swift, precise, almost painless. The crimson blood pooled in the basin, ready to sanctify our departure tomorrow.

Eirik broke the silence with dramatic flair, raising his cup. "If this is my last meal, I would like to lodge a complaint with the gods."

Astrid rolled her eyes. "You would complain in Valhalla if they did not have your favourite stew."

"You are right," he smirked, winking at her. "If I am going to die tomorrow, I want to do it knowing I had one last decent meal with people who do not bore me to death first."

Astrid jabbed him in the side, trying to mask her worry. "You say that every time you drink."

"Because every time *might* be the last," Eirik said with dramatic flourish. "And let me tell you, Alura, these two have dragged me into enough cursed raids and haunted shores that I deserve this speech."

Skúli didn't laugh. He tore a piece of bread in half and handed a piece to me, his fingers brushing mine a moment too long. "Eat. You will need your strength."

"I am not the one charging onto a cursed shore," I said, taking the bread anyway. Skúli had told me that I would be staying on the boat while they claimed the beach. That it would be safer there.

Astrid stiffened. "You have heard the rumours then?"

Eirik snorted, pouring more ale. "That the coast is cursed? That warriors who go there do not come back? The trees whisper the words of the dead? Pfft. Every raid has its tales. Children need to learn fear."

Skúli's mouth pressed into a grim line. "These are not children's tales."

Astrid's voice was soft. "We are all cursed. Is that not what warriors are? People too stubborn to die, too proud to run?"

I swallowed hard, the unease rising. "What do you mean?"

"The island is not marked on most maps. Locals call it Blót-jörð. Sacrificial ground. Skargrim wants it as a base for future raids. Gold, a stronghold. But no one who has tried has returned whole. If at all."

"Then why go?" I whispered.

"Because a king commands it," Skúli said flatly.

Eirik snorted again. "A false king."

No one argued. The fire crackled between us. Astrid poked at her stew without eating. "The younger ones see glory and plunder. The others...they pray tonight. The way warriors do when they fear their last sunset."

Eirik leaned back in his chair, swirling his ale. "Ah but this will be nothing. There was this one time I outwitted the spirits of the Northern Marshes."

"Oh, here we go," Astrid said dryly.

Eirik paid her no mind. "They say no mortal can cross without losing their mind or soul. I walked straight through, blindfolded, carrying only a single loaf of bread and a goat's hoof for luck."

Astrid raised an eyebrow. "Blindfolded? And you still made it?"

"Made it?" Eirik asked, throwing his hands up as if outraged she doubted him. "I danced with the spirits, told them my life's secrets, sang them a lullaby, and they *applauded* my courage! They offered me riches and power, but I–yes, I–politely declined, because I had a raid to attend and a perfectly respectable stew waiting for me."

Skúli shook his head, dryly muttering, "You have no shame."

"I have style," Eirik corrected, giving me a wink. "And charm. Do not forget the charm."

I snorted, nearly choking on my stew. "If anyone believes you, it is only because you can keep a straight face while lying."

Eirik tilted his head at me. "Little Storm, my dear, a straight face takes skill. You should appreciate it more."

Astrid rolled her eyes, muttering. "This man should be blood eagled for the horse shit that comes out of his mouth..."

Skúli chuckled. "Are you doing the honours?"

Astrid grinned. "Or at least tied to the mast on the raid."

I laughed softly, grateful. Even with the looming raid, even with the curses whispered about the island, Eirik's ridiculousness was a warm thread weaving through the tension, reminding us that we were still human. Still alive.

Skúli stared into the fire as the mood dampened. "We leave at dawn."

Eirik raised his cup, solemn for once. "Then to dawn...and whatever comes after."

Astrid added, dryly, "And to you lot leaving me behind to pick up the pieces."

I raised my cup, pressing the rim to theirs. "To returning home. Even if the gods do not want us to."

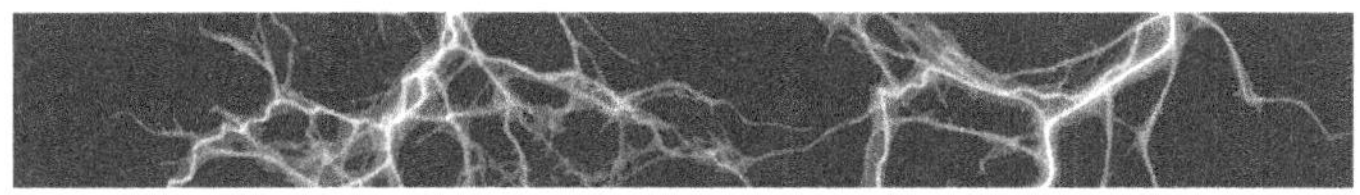

Later the fire had burned low. Only embers remained. Astrid and Eirik had disappeared, Astrid said something about going to the forge. I lingered near the door, my arms wrapped around myself, watching the moonlight sweep across the frostless sky.

Skúli's soft scuff of boots against the stone made me tense. He stopped just a pace behind me.

"You should sleep," I said, not turning to face him.

"I cannot. Not tonight."

Something in his voice made me look back. Shadows played across his scarred face, the moonlight catching the edge of his jaw. His shoulders weren't tense with anger, but restraint. He was holding back.

"I have faced raiders, storms, beasts in the woods," he said quietly. "But I have never been more terrified than to ask you to warm my bed tonight."

I froze for a second, then turned to face him.

"Just for tonight," he continued, step by step, closer, though still careful as if I might attack him. "Before we head to our deaths. Let me have one night where I can pretend I have something left to lose."

My chest tightened. His voice carried neither arrogance nor hope, only the solemnity of a man who knows he may not see many more dawns.

I tilted my head, studying him. "You already have many things to lose."

His eyes darkened at my words, shadow and fire both smoldering there. His mouth opened as if to speak, then he closed it again, the muscle in his jaw working. He looked away for the barest moment, as though my gaze was too much, too dangerous.

"Do you not see?" His voice was hoarse, ragged. "I swore to myself I would never feel this way again. That I could not...I *cannot* lose another. And yet, here you stand." His hand twitched, not quite lifting, as though he wanted to touch me but didn't trust himself to. "I have tried to keep you at a distance. I tried to bury it. But every time I look at you, every time I hear your voice, I forget the vows I made to the dead."

My chest ached with every word he forced out, as though he were bleeding them instead of speaking them.

"I am only asking you for tonight," he went on, lower now, each word stripped of his usual control. "One night where I do not have to hold myself back. One night where I can stop pretending. I beg you, Alura–"

His throat worked, his voice breaking as if the word *beg* broke his pride. "-warm my bed, warm my soul. Let me die tomorrow with the knowledge of how you feel in my arms. Grant me this, if nothing else."

The rawness of it staggered me. He wasn't the unyielding warrior then. He wasn't the man who trained others to kill, who stood before fate as though it could not touch him. He was just Skúli. Flesh, blood and aching.

I swallowed hard, my voice a whisper. "And if we give in to this...if we let it happen, what then? What if I burn the world with what I am, with what we are? What if loving me leaves you nothing but ash?"

His eyes snapped to mine, and there was no hesitation, no falter this time. Only a fierce, devastating certainty.

"Then I will die a happy man," he said, vibrating with truth, "burning with you."

"I might," I whispered. "But you must earn it."

He let himself grin sharply, but the flicker in his eyes betrayed the sincerity beneath. "You would deny a dying man one last wish?"

I lifted my chin, though my breath trembled from the closeness of him. "If you think me so easily swayed, then perhaps you are already dead."

Skúli's breath shuddered out of him, rough as if it tore open his chest to release it. "I have never begged for anything," he admitted. "Not for food when I have starved in long winters. Not for mercy when I bled. Not even to the gods when they took my son from me. But I beg for this. For you. You undo me, Alura. You leave me bare."

The words struck me open. I had thought of myself as strong, but there was no shield for this, no sword to protect me from the man who wore his scars like armour yet tore himself raw at my feet.

My throat closed around the storm of emotion that rose within me. "You think I do not feel the same?" My voice shook. "I ache for you. Every time you hold back, every time you pull away, it kills me a little more. And still, I fear that if I let myself have you, I will lose you quicker."

His jaw tightened, and for a moment I thought he would walk away. That he would leave me here to pick up the pieces alone. Instead, he bent his head, his voice fierce.

"You will not lose me. Not to fear. Not to fate. If the world burns, then I will burn beside you. I do not want a throne, or a crown. I want *this*. I want you. Grant me tonight."

We stepped closer until our chests brushed against one another, until his heat swallowed me. My hands trembled as I slid them up, resting against his jaw, rough with stubble. His eyes searched mine, wide open, no more defenses holding him back.

"You are a fool. A stubborn, reckless fool."

"Then I am your fool," he breathed. "You do not have to, not tonight. You can spend tonight with whoever you wish."

"There is no one else." I took a breath. "Just one night?"

His hand rose, fingers brushing a strand of my silver hair back from my cheek. "If it is all we are permitted, I will take it. I will not beg again, twice is too many."

I chuckled, leaning into him.

"You do not have to beg again," I whispered. "I am yours."

For a heartbeat neither of us moved. The brewing storm between us held its breath. His chest rose against mine, his warmth pulling me under, and when his lips found mine it was not desperation I found. But a reverence that undid me. Slow, unhurried, as though he had all the time in the world, even if we both knew we only had tonight.

My fingers tangled in his hair, his arms wrapped around me, gripping me like I might vanish if he let go. The ache I had carried for so long broke open, spilling into the kiss, into the press of our bodies, into the surrender I had tried hard to deny.

He broke away, resting his forehead against mine.

"Whatever comes next, I want to remember this. You. Tonight. With the gods as my witness."

A breathless chuckle escapes me. "Then let the gods bear witness," I whisper. "Because I want to remember this too."

His breath hitches, a needy moan escaping his lips. "Fuck."

"I want you, not just for comfort, not because we may never have another night." I trembled with the gravity of what I was telling him. "I am choosing this. Choosing you to spend my last night with."

"Then let the world do its worst. Tonight is ours."

CHAPTER THIRTY-SEVEN
ALURA

Skúli carried me to his room. The hearth lay cold, leaving only the moonlight to carve out his features. Shadows clung to him, sharpening the hard lines of his face. When he lowered me, letting me slide slowly down the length of his body, my breath caught. His restraint was a living thing–fragile, furious and desperate.

"Tell me you want this." His voice rasped, strangled, as though he feared the answer.

"I want this."

He stiffened for a moment. Then all his hesitation shattered. He pressed me against the door, his hand wrapping around my throat. Not to choke, but to cradle, a dangerous tenderness. He turned me, keeping his touch at my throat, so my back pressed to his chest. The heat of him burned against me, hard and aching.

His other hand slipped beneath my skirts with an impatient growl at the layers barring him. He shoved fabric aside until his fingers found bare skin, stroking up my thigh.

When they slid higher, brushing against my clit, I gasped, my head falling back against his chest.

Pleasure struck sharp and sudden. My knees trembled as his fingers toyed with me. Gentle, deliberate, devastating. A finger pushed inside me, slow, teasing, making me whimper for more.

"Do not stop," I begged, breathless. My voice broke on the plea. I didn't care if the whole house heard.

He turned my head, capturing my lips with his, muffling my moans as his fingers drove me closer to the edge. His tongue swept mine, hot and claiming, while his palm ground against my clit, giving me something to rock into. He controlled everything–the pace, the pressure, me. And gods, I liked it.

"You are so wet for me," he growled against my lips.

I buckled. My thighs shook, my nail scraping down the wood of the door as he held me upright. His mouth trailed to my neck, teeth grazing the sensitive skin while his hand worked me mercilessly.

"You should see yourself," he whispered, voice breaking with awe. "You look like the night sky. Endless. Untouchable. Burning."

The words barely reached me, drowned in the fire of my body unraveling. My release hit in a violent wave, my cries smothered by his mouth as I shattered in his arms.

When he pulled his hand away, I sagged against the door, shaking, desperate for his touch again. I turned slowly, breath still ragged, and found him watching me like he had stepped too close to the sun. Torture warred with hunger in his eyes.

I stripped off my dress. Then the underdress. Piece by piece, until I stood bare before him, daring him to look, to stop pretending.

That broke the last of his restraint. He seized my mouth in a kiss, all heat and teeth, his body crushing mine, his cock hard against my stomach. He tore his tunic over his head, muscles and scars thrown into silver by the moonlight.

He lifted me easily, tossing me onto the bed. A growl rumbled in his chest as he followed, pinning me beneath him, my wrists trapped above my head. His mouth blazed a trail down my neck, biting, sucking, claiming, until his lips closed around my nipple and I cried out. He teased and tormented me until my body writhed, every nerve alive.

Sweat slicked my skin. Power hummed under it, begging to be released. I swallowed it down, fighting to not lose control.

Skúli didn't notice—or pretended not to. His lips were at my mouth again, his tongue forcing mine open in a kiss that stole every thought from me.

"I have wanted to ask you into my bed for so long," he groaned.

"How long?"

"The first time I saw you."

I laughed breathlessly, but it ended in a gasp as he moved lower, freeing my wrists to spread my thighs apart. His mouth hovered at my core, his hot breath ghosting over me, before his tongue dragged slowly through my folds.

My cry echoed off the stone. He did it again. And again. Until I was convulsing, his hands holding my thighs open wide, his tongue relentless. When his teeth grazed my clit and he growled, the vibration sent me spiraling over the edge once more.

I was still shaking when he moved over me, stroking his cock, thick and impossibly hard. My eyes drank him in, every scar, every line of muscle. He was beautiful. Terrifying. Mine for the night.

"Please," I whispered, raw with need.

That was all he needed. He thrust into me with one sharp stroke, burying himself to the hilt. My back arched, my mouth opening in a wordless moan. He filled me completely, brutally, and it was everything I had imagined and more.

He moved hard and fast, claiming my mouth, my throat, my body. He pinned my wrists again, grounding me as I writhed beneath him, every thrust driving me higher.

"You feel so good," he grunted, each word punctuated by his body slamming into mine. "So. Fucking. Good."

I bit his shoulder, clinging to him with teeth, until he ripped me apart again. Heat flushed my palms, it wasn't just the heat of him but something brighter, wrong. A thread of stormlight bled between my fingers, pale and trembling. I gasped, trying to hide it, trying to shove it back down but it begged to be set free.

Skúli saw, he always saw. His hand threaded with mine. "Alura," he said, his voice stuttering. "Look at me."

I did, though I wanted to hide in shame.

"You are not breaking," he said firmly, still moving inside me. "You are burning. There is a difference."

"What...if I hurt...you?"

He brushed his forehead against mine. "Then let it hurt me. I would rather stand in your beauty than watch you smother it."

Skúli flipped me onto my hands and knees, fisting my hair, pulling my head back as he drove into me from behind. I screamed his name, clawing at the sheets, lost to the storm he created inside me.

Release ripped through me a final time, violent and consuming as silver light lit up the room. Skúli's rhythm faltered, his breath breaking into ragged gasps as he slammed into me one last time. He moaned into my shoulder as he spilled inside me, his teeth sinking into my skin as though he could brand me from the inside out.

When he stilled, he stayed there, trembling against me. Neither of us spoke. Neither of us could.

Finally, he pulled free, collapsing beside me. I thought he would rise, dress and walk away. But instead he gathered me into his arms, tucking me into his chest and pulled the blankets and furs over us both.

He pressed a kiss to my hair, his lips soft.

"Thank you," he whispered, tracing his fingers over my softly fading skin. "For granting a dying man his final wish."

CHAPTER THIRTY-EIGHT

ASTRID

The forge was never truly quiet, even when the rest of Drakensvar slept. Coal breathed in the belly of the hearth, their glow pulsing like the heart of a slumbering god. My hands itched when I laid still too long, my mind raced faster than a storm wind. So I came here. The familiar rhythm of the hammer steadying my breath in ways sleep never could.

The blade before me was not meant for anyone in particular. Just steel, fire and stubbornness. Still, I felt the weight of it in my chest, as though shaping it might shape something inside me too.

The door creaked.

"You could not resist, could you?" Eirik's voice carried inside, warm with mischief. He held up a tankard, foam slopping over his knuckles. "Just happened to be passing by."

I snorted. "At high moon? With ale?"

He grinned, sheepishly. "Well, I thought the forge might be lonely without someone to admire your scowling face."

I set the hammer down. Heat rising in my face from the man leaning on the doorway like he owned the place. "If you spill that near my steel, I will gut you with the dullest knife I can find."

"Ah, a threat. That is how I know you have missed me." He wandered closer, the firelight painting his cheekbones, shadows catching in his pale hair. "Need an extra pair of hands?"

I barked a laugh. "From you? You would crack the temper and ruin it."

He pressed a hand to his chest playfully. "You wounded me, shieldmaiden. I am more than a pretty face."

He shifted the tankard to his other hand, taking the blade gingerly. Too gingerly. The angle was all wrong. With a groan, I wiped my hands and stepped around the anvil.

"Not like that. Here." I reached for his wrist, guiding it steady, adjusting the pressure of his fingers until he held it properly. His skin was warmer than I expected.

The space between us closed without my noticing. His breath brushed against my cheek, carrying mead and smoke. For a heartbeat, the forge was silent.

He leaned ever so slightly closer. "Careful, Astrid. It feels like you are forging more than a blade tonight."

I rolled my eyes, though I did not move away. "Do not ruin the moment with your nonsense."

But my voice was softer than I meant.

He chuckled low in his throat, the sound rumbling through me like distant thunder. Still, he obeyed, and together we drew the file across the steel until it sang with the right edge.

When it was done, he set the blade carefully aside. His grin returned, but it was gentler now, almost shy. "If you ever need someone at your back, Astrid. I will be there. Even if it is just to hand you a hammer."

I swallowed, the words striking deeper than I wanted them to. I managed a scoff, lifting the blade to inspect it. "Then try not to drop it."

The forge was quiet again after he spoke, but not in the way it had been before. The silence was now thick with something I did not want to name. His promise clung to the air like smoke.

If you ever need someone at your back...

I turned the blade in the firelight, pretending to study the evenness of the edge, though my thoughts were nowhere near the steel. My heart thudded against my ribs far more recklessly than my hammer had struck all night. Fool. It was only Eirik. Eirik with his crooked grin and his easy words...who would bleed himself dry for the people he cared about.

Yet my fingers remembered the warmth of his hand when I had guided them ,the way he had stilled under my touch, as if the whole world had narrowed to that one point of contact. I swallowed hard, setting the blade aside.

"Go on then," I muttered, my voice coming out softer than I intended. "Before you start a fire just by standing there."

He chuckled, the sound rough and low. I hated how it curled through me.

"Yes, shieldmaiden. I will leave your sacred place untouched."

His boots scraped against the dirt floor as he turned, lingering at the door. Just before he slipped out into the night, he glanced back at me and for a moment there was no jest in him at all. Just a quiet, unguarded warmth.

The door closed.

I exhaled shakily, pressing a palm to my chest as though I could quiet the blaze there. It was absurd. I had fought men twice my size and never lost my footing. Yet, one infuriating warrior with too much ale and too many words could shake me more than any battle.

The forge crackled, steel cooling on the anvil. I stared at the half-finished blade, realising that my hands were trembling and not from the hammer's strain.

CHAPTER THIRTY-NINE
ALURA

We slept for only a few hours. Dawn pressed at the edges of the horizon, pale light softening the night sky. Soon we would need to reach the docks before Skargrim decided to raid us instead.

Skúli and I walked to the great hall hand in hand. His fingers were rough, calloused, but steady around mine. We didn't speak. We didn't need to.

Astrid looked up first when we entered. Her brow arched as her gaze dropped to our joined hands. "Well," she said, her tone light but knowing. "That explains why you both missed breakfast."

Eirik was less subtle. His grin stretched wicked as a wolf's. "Good morning, lovebirds. Sleep well?" His tone made clear he didn't mean sleep at all.

Heat surged into my cheeks. Skúli rolled his eyes, though I caught the faint curve of a smile tugging at his mouth.

Eirik lounged on the floor by the fire as if he'd rooted himself there, Astrid seated behind him, her nimble fingers braiding his hair.

He jerked his head, and she smacked him. "Stop moving and it will not hurt."

"You keep yanking."

"You are such a baby," Astrid sighed, braiding on. "Your hair is not even long enough to whine this much."

"And yet I suffer," he declared dramatically, his hand over his heart. "Silently."

"You are many things, Eirik," Skúli said dryly. "Silent is not one of them."

"Jealousy is a bitter thing, old friend," Eirik fired back, smug as ever.

Skúli ignored him, turning to me. "Sit. I will do your hair."

"You do not have to—"

"I would like to."

That was that. I sank onto the bench beside Eirik, ignoring his wolfish grin.

"Well, look at this," he muttered. "Matching braids for the happy raiding party. Shall we all wear flowers too?"

Astrid swatted him again, this time hard enough to make him yelp. "Shut your mouth or I will braid it shut."

I bit back a smile as Skúli drew a bone comb through my tangled hair, careful as he worked. He parted smaller strands and braided them close to my scalp with deliberate precision, his touch firm but never rough. Something sticky dragged across my scalp — resin, setting the braids in place.

Then he gathered the rest, weaving the smaller plaits into a single thick braid that pulled tight down the center. His breath brushed warm against my neck, and when he tied the end with leather, he leaned forward and pressed a kiss to the nape of my neck. Light as falling ash.

Intimate. Wordless.

I closed my eyes, letting the warmth soak through me.

"Gods give me strength," Eirik muttered. "If you two start again, I will walk into the sea."

"Good," Astrid snapped, tugging his braid sharply. "Then I will not have to hear you talk anymore."

Skúli exhaled, almost a laugh, brushing loose hair from my shoulder.

"Your turn now," I told him.

He blinked. "You do not have to—"

"I know." I grinned, throwing his own words back at him. "I would like to."

Something flickered in his eyes. Surprise, maybe. Something softer beneath. He sat between my knees, shoulders tense, his hair thick and unruly, silver streaking the temples. I threaded my fingers gently through, untangling knots with care.

"You do not sit still very well," I murmured.

"Not used to being fussed over," he admitted, voice low.

"Well," I teased, sectioning his hair. "You will have to learn."

He gave a quiet huff of amusement.

I worked slowly, weaving each piece with deliberate focus until I bound it tight with leather. Resting my hand on his shoulder, I said, "There. Battle-ready."

He ran a hand over it, lips turning upwards. "It is better than when I do it."

"Of course."

He turned, catching my hand, lacing our fingers together. His voice softened. "You always surprise me."

"And you are still stubborn," I replied, squeezing his hand.

Our eyes met. Fear. Hope. A hundred unspoken things hung between us. Whatever lay ahead, whatever we lost or gained, I wanted him to remember this: he wasn't alone.

Astrid drew my attention with a sharp look, arms full of leather and dark cloth.

"You are not going raiding dressed like that," she said, eyeing my wool dress.

I arched my brow. "What is wrong with this?"

"Nothing," she said, dropping the bundle onto a bench. "If you plan on standing very still indoors. Out there?" She jerked her chin toward the door. "You will trip over the hem, freeze, and die. Not in that order."

"That is... comforting."

"Get changed."

The bundle held worn raiding leathers, supple from use, reinforced stitching at the joints. A black tunic, thick trousers, bracers, and a belt with loops for blades.

"These are yours."

Astrid shrugged. "Were. They do not fit right anymore. And you need them more than I do."

"Astrid—"

"Do not start," she cut me off. "Just take them. You have earned them."

My throat tightened. Wordless, I began changing. Astrid didn't turn away, instead tugging straps snug across my chest, cinching the belt at my waist. She checked the fit like she was fitting armor.

"They suit you," she said at last. "You just need some dirt. Maybe blood."

"Hopefully not," I said dryly.

We shared a long look.

"If we do not come back—"

"You will," she said fiercely. "But if you cannot, make sure they remember you."

I nodded.

She hugged me hard, whispering against my ear, "Watch his back."

"Always."

Then she was gone, barking orders at Eirik.

I stood there a moment longer, the leathers wrapping around me like a second skin.

Skúli joined me, his eyes lingering on me. "Ready?"

I nodded. "As ready as I will ever be."

CHAPTER FORTY
ALURA

The longship cut through the cold sea, its curved prow slicing through the waves like a sharp blade. The rhythmical creak of the boat filled the silence between us, steady as a heartbeat. Spray misted over the side, and the wind bit through my cloak, but I didn't move. I stood at the bow with my hands curled around the wood, watching the horizon inch closer.

Behind me, the men murmured in low voices. Some dozed with their heads bowed, their chins touching their chests. Others sat sharpening blades that didn't need sharpening, oiling armour that had already been checked twice. No one spoke of glory anymore, only the sea and the skies and the whispers of what lay ahead.

The seas were eerily calm and quiet, the waves lapping at the sides of the longships. There were four of them, sailing side by side, each one bearing sword struck shields and freshly painted sails. The smell of salts and pine clung to us. Gulls wheeled overhead, their cries thin and distant, as though even they kept their distance from us.

Eirik was telling a story to a younger warrior, some half-true tale about wrestling a boar in the snow with nothing but a fishhook. The boy laughed too loudly, too often. He was afraid.

Skúli stood braced against the mast. He hadn't spoken since we left. His jaw was set hard; eyes narrowed on the windy sea as if sheer will alone would bend the ocean to his command. His silhouette was sharp against the dull morning sky.

I made my way to him slowly, weaving between barrels, coiled rope and warriors.

"We will reach the coast by nightfall," he said without looking at me.

I nodded. "Do you think they will be waiting?"

He was quiet for a long moment. "I think they know we are coming."

We all knew this was a death sentence.

We stood shoulder to shoulder in the wind. The chill slipping between the gaps in my cloak. He wrapped an arm around me, pressing me into his side. Sharing his warmth.

"Are you afraid?" I ask.

"I am," he admits, voice low. "Not of death. Of losing you."

His expression softens as he drops his gaze to look at me. His eyes are rimmed with exhaustion. "We go into cursed land. The last crew who raided this coast vanished."

I swallow. "Then we come back with ours."

He gave a small, dry smile. "Always so sure."

"No," I say. "I have hope."

Hope is a fool's game out here. We're sailing into a known cursed land but with no knowledge of what lies ahead. It's foolish but I trust Skúli. We all do.

Skúli reached out, brushing a damp strand of hair from my cheek, his fingers lingering for longer than necessary. Shivers run down my body from where we connect and I close my eyes and lean into it, just for a moment.

"Always so full of hope." His expression changes into something painful. "If anything happens-"

"Please, do not start."

"Alura-"

"We do not speak of endings. Not here. Not now," I said firmly.

He didn't argue. Just stood beside me, silent again. His gaze snapped back to the horizon as the wind picked up and the boat surged forward.

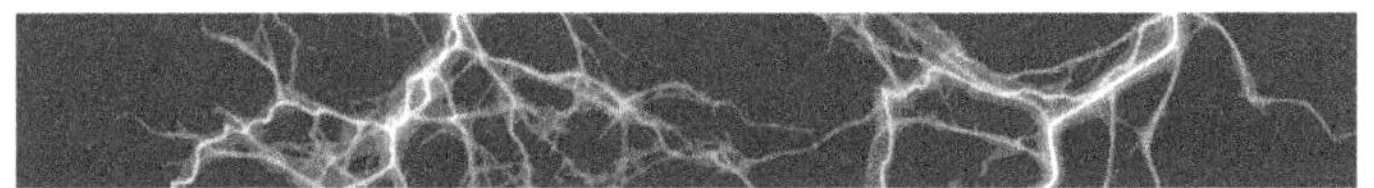

The mist clung to the sea like an infant on its mother. No birds cried overhead. No waves lapped at the boat in welcome. The oars moved in an unsettling union, the creaking of wood echoing out into the nothingness.

I stood on the boat, silent, my cloak wrapped around me, the salty air stinging my cracked lips. Skúli stood beside me, one hand resting on the head of his axe, his face grim and unreadable. Eirik stood at the helm, his usually smug grin absent, replaced with a clenched jaw and eyes fixed forward.

The land ahead emerged like a wound in the fog. Jagged cliffs, dark sand and a low forest just beyond the shore. It would have been beautiful, but there was something wrong. The air was too still. The scent of rot clinging faintly to the wind.

"Gods," a nearby warrior whispered. "It is too quiet."

There was no ringing of alarm bells. No cries from the shores. No people fleeing or preparing to defend their shores.

"They are watching," Skúli said softly, his voice a low growl. "I can feel it."

His wolf bristled by his side. Björn's green eyes were fixed on something past the trees, something we couldn't see.

"We all knew this place was cursed," Eirik added. "That no one who comes here leaves the same."

The boat crashed against the shore, jolting us forward for a second as we hit the dark sand. Weapons were drawn in silence, shields slung into place. Skúli was the first to disembark. Crashing into the motionless water before stepping foot onto the sand. The fog parted just enough to reveal the first line of trees, the dark silhouettes of ancient standing stones just beyond.

My fingers twitch toward my belt, touching the pouch of herbs. There was something here, something calling to me. Something old and waiting.

Eirik turned to me for a moment. "Stay on the boat Alura. We are going to need your skills. It would be a shame to lose you before we can make use of them."

The rest of the warriors followed. I stayed, waiting, barely able to breathe.

Then came the sound. One long, guttural cry from a horn within the trees.

"Shields!" I heard Skúli bark out.

The woods erupted.

Figures charged from the treeline, wild-eyed warriors with painted skin and snarling mouths. They moved like demons, like shadows that had been waiting to defend this place. War cries echoed across the beach as steel met steel and the water ran red.

I ducked low, calling on the flicker of magic I had access to in this dark place. I felt my skin crackle as I watched Skúli. He was a force to be reckoned with, whirling his axe with deadly precision. Every motion was practiced, brutal. Björn was by his side, lunging at the nearest threats and tearing at their throats. The two fought in sync, a force to be reckoned with.

Eirik fought like the seasoned mad man he was, laughing in the face of danger as his adrenaline kicked in. His blade flashed with a feral grace, every swing was wide and merciless, yet somehow always landing true. Where another man would have flinched from the press of steel and the spray of blood, Eirik leaned into it, teeth bared in something too wild to be called a smile. His laughter rose above the clash of swords, brazen and unshakable. It was not the laughter of a fool, but of a man who had long made his peace with death and dared it to catch him.

The air was thick with the stench of blood and earth, churned up by boots and bodies. The sand turned red beneath them, soaked with seawater and gore. The enemies came in waves. Fierce, fast and utterly without fear.

I watched Skúli's axe rise and fall in punishing arcs, each swing ending a life. His shield slick with blood, his jaw clenched, his eyes wild.

"To your left!" I cried out, not able to help myself.

He turned just in time to block a spear thrust, shoving the attacker backward and splitting his skull with a sickening crack. My stomach churned as I watched it play out.

Eirik bellowed from somewhere down on the beach, laughter rolling between curses. "If I die here brother, I will haunt you to the end of your days." He paused for a moment before adding, "And after them too."

A horn sounded from deeper within the trees—lower, longer this time. Reinforcements.

"Shield wall!" Skúli commanded.

The warriors clumped together, their shields overlapping in a pattern that would make it difficult to break through. The back two rows of warriors hoisted their shields above the heads of the men in front of them. They protected each other with their lives. Their trust in each other is both staggering and admirable.

Every one of my breaths was tight with adrenaline and magic. I could feel it rising within me, defending me. The stormlight curled around my fingers, wild and unpredictable. It begged to be let loose.

A second wave broke from the treeline—large men this time, cloaked in fur and bone, faces masked with war paint and blood. Some wielded rusted axes, others had curved blades that caught the dawn light.

One barrelled towards the shield wall. A giant of a man, snarling like a beast. He smashed into the shield wall before a small gap opened, and he was killed. Someone had thrust their sword straight through his throat.

"We hold the line!" Skúli roared above the sound of battle. "We do not fall back!"

This time when the enemy charged, it was all of them. They did not falter. They fought like men possessed.

My breath misted in the chill, and I squinted into the rapidly brightening treeline. There was something there. I was sure of it.

The shield wall groaned under the weight of the assault. Blades scraped and clanged against metal and wood. Spears jabbed through narrow gaps. The warriors behind the wall grunted with effort, sweat streaking down their brows despite the cold. One man screamed as an axe slipped under his shield and found the soft flesh of his thigh. But he didn't fall. The man beside him caught his weight, held the line.

It was not bravery alone that kept them upright. It was a necessity. They knew, all of them, that if one link broke the whole wall would fall.

A hammer struck Skúli's shield, shuddering through the line. He didn't flinch. His boots dug into the sand, his shoulder firm against the man beside him. Blood ran from a cut above his brow, but his eyes were clear, sharp.

"Hold!" He bellowed.

Another crash.

The enemy were battering them like the tide in a storm. Wave after wave. But the shield wall held.

An arrow whizzed past my head, the sickening whistle of it flying past before it buried itself just steps from where I was. Panic began to set in. I was told to stay on the boat. I'd die if I left it. Another arrow whistled past my ear, closer this time.

I'd die if I stayed.

No. I will not die. Not today.

I leapt down from the boat, my feet crashing into the water. Skúli turned his head, shooting me a glare before beckoning me over, to stand behind them.

I moved along the rear flank, stormlight whispering through my body like living fire. My heart pounded, not just from fear but from something else. Something buried deep in the bones of the land beneath our feet.

"Not yet," Skúli's voice said, soothing me. "Keep it locked down. Just for now."

The treeline shimmered.

Just a flicker, like the air had rippled.

Then again.

"Something is wrong," I murmured to myself.

A scream tore from the left flank. Not a normal scream of pain or rage. But horror.

I turned. The outermost men were falling. Not from blades but from something unseen. One man writhed, clawing at his face as if trying to rip something off his skin. Another simply dropped, eyes wide, blood leaking from his nose and ears.

"Reinforce the left flank!" Skúli barked.

Eirik was already moving along with the young warrior he'd been spouting bullshit stories to. They dragged another warrior into formation even as his knees buckled beneath them.

"Magic!" I cried out, my voice getting lost in the chaos. "It is not just warriors! There is something in the trees!"

As if summoned by my words, a low groan rolled through the woods. The air grew colder. The enemy paused, just for a heartbeat, as if even they feared what approached.

Then a figure stepped from the treeline.

It wasn't a man.

It wore the shape of one. Tall, gaunt, draped in tattered hides and feathers. But its face was bone. Not painted, but real bone, its eyes black and gleaming. Large antlers adorned its head. More followed it. Not many, but enough.

Sorcerers. Shamans. Whatever name they were once called by, they were wrong now. Twisted. Corrupted.

Skúli's voice cut through the silence. "Alura."

I stepped towards him. "I see them."

"Time to unleash it."

I nodded. A lump formed in my throat as I raised my hands above us. Stormlight surged from them in a brilliant arc, lashing across the space between the shield wall and the forest like a whip of lightning. It stuck one of the bone-masked sorcerers dead on. He screamed. Not in pain but fury. It staggered, cloak smouldering.

It didn't fall.

Skúli cursed. "Again!"

Raising my hands again, I didn't hold back. The power roared out of me, cracking the sky, splitting the sand and roots of trees. The forest recoiled. One of the shamans dropped to their knees, clawing at its chest.

The line surged.

Steel clashed against steel. Magic met madness.

The shield wall held, barely. Each second bought was paid for in blood. My hands shook. Not from fear. From power.

The magic inside me churned like a storm given flesh. It pulled at my insides, begging to be used, begging to be released. The shield wall was faltering even though the warriors held like gods themselves. Unmoving, bleeding, determined.

It wasn't enough.

The sorcerers pushed forward, snarling incantations in a guttural tongue, their hands etched in symbols of blood and ash. The ground cracked beneath them. The air itself began to bend.

Skúli roared something. My name maybe. But I couldn't hear him. I stepped forward.

I didn't even need to raise my hands this time. The stormlight exploded from my centre, a crackling ring of silver-blue that swept around the entire formation of warriors like a tidal wave. The shield wall, the fighters behind us, even the wounded. All of us, encased in a dome of living, thrumming energy.

One of the sorcerers hurled a jagged bolt of black fire towards us. It struck the barrier, then rebounded, slamming back into the caster and sending them sprawling.

Gasps rang out from behind me.

Eirik looked at me, eyes wide. "Gods, Alura..."

"Do not," I say, concentrating on holding the shield in place.

"How long can you hold it?" Skúli asked, a tender note in his voice for just a moment.

"I...do not...know," I strained out, never taking my eyes off the enemy. "Do not break formation. Just kill them."

Another enemy charged. Then another. They slammed into the shield, hammering with corrupted magic, their chants becoming frenzied.

I braced. The barrier held.

I poured more into it. More magic. More of myself. It was like trying to hold back a forest fire with just a bucket of water. My ears rang. My legs trembled.

I heard...voices.

Whispers.

At first, they were too faint to make out. But with every word they grew louder and louder.

Burn it all.

Sacrifice them to the old gods, to the forest.

Let go. Break them.

"No," I hissed, struggling to maintain concentration.

A prickle of pain stabbed through my temple, sharp and hot. Thick, hot fluid began to flow out of my nose. I didn't bother to wipe it, just letting it flow. Blinking hard against the pulse behind my eyes.

The warriors surged forward behind the safety of the dome, battering back the enemy with renewed force. One of the bone-masked sorcerers dropped, gurgling on his own blood. Then another.

One by one, they fell.

The final one shrieked something in that old, guttural tongue and raised both arms, calling on something darker.

I stepped forward, opening my palm.

The stormlight gathered, then surged like a spear through the shield. It tore across the space between them and struck the last sorcerer.

A scream followed that echoed for miles.

Then, silence.

The treeline stilled. The sorcerer collapsed. The enemy retreated, the madness in their eyes fading as quickly as it had come. What was left of them turned and fled, vanishing into the trees.

I fell to my knees.

The barrier flickered. Then shattered, raining sparks down on the warriors like falling stars. He was beside me in a heartbeat. Skúli's arms wrapped around me, steadying me before I could fall forwards.

"I have you," he said, his voice rough. "You are alright."

"I heard them," I murmured. "The dead. The storm. Whatever is inside of me. It spoke to me."

Skúli glanced at Eirik, whose face had lost its usual mischief. I tried to stand, but my legs buckled. He caught me again.

"You saved us," he whispered. "All of us. But you need to stop. Whatever that was…it almost broke you."

"It tried, it did not win," I whispered, my voice cracking. "But it was close."

Even in the stillness that followed, surrounded by friends, I knew something had changed inside of me. Something I might not be able to undo.

CHAPTER FORTY-ONE
ALURA

The battlefield stank of blood and churned earth. Crows circled overhead, already beginning to gather. The dead were everywhere. Enemies. Friends. Family.

I stood near the edge of the treeline, breathing hard. My fingertips smoked faintly, the last shreds of stormlight flickering around them before fading into the cold air.

I blinked once. Then twice. Trying to clear whatever it was my head was trying to make me see. It wasn't there. Not really.

A voice murmured in my head. Distant. Unintelligible, like someone speaking under water. I clutched my head, shaking it to clear them.

"Alura?" Skúli's voice came from behind me, and it sounded so very far away. When I turned, I swayed. He caught me before I could fall. Again.

"Your nose..." His voice was tight.

I reached up. Blood. Warm, sticky blood smeared across my face. "I am fine," I rasped. "I just…just need a moment."

"No, you are not," Skúli said firmly. "Gods, what did you do?"

"What you asked me to," I snap, heatedly. "I shielded us. The shield wall would have broken. We would have all died."

"You are barely standing."

Eirik joined us, his face contorted into concern. He looked between the two of us, then at the dead enemy sorcerer lying not far off.

"You took on *that*," he said, pointing with his chin. "With just your magic?"

I nodded. We all fell silent.

Then Eirik spoke again, softer. Full of gratitude. "You saved us. That is no small thing." Then he sighed dramatically. "I suppose I owe you my life."

Skúli looked at me, his eyes searching my face with something darker than concern. Fear. I recoiled from him, terrified of the possibility that he could fear me.

"The price of magic is too steep." His voice is gruff. "You need to rest."

Skúli dragged me to an abandoned shack, just beyond the edge of the battlefield. The firepit was cold and the roof sagged but it was a shelter. He cleared the broken wood from one corner while I sat, still trembling. My limbs ached; my head throbbed with pressure.

Like something was trying to break free.

"You need to lie down."

"I am fine," I muttered.

He crouched before me, hands on my knees. "You are bleeding, your eyes are distant, and you have not taken a full breath since we got off that gods-damned beach."

"I said I am *fine.*"

He narrows his eyes. "No. You are not. Lie down."

His voice was firm. No bark. No thunder. Just care, wrapped in command. It made me angrier than shouting would have.

"I am not one of your warriors. You do not get to order me around!"

"No you are not," he said calmly. "But I will force you if I have to."

The threat shouldn't have made my heart lurch but it did. I turned away from him, laying down stiffly. I let my head hit the rolled cloak we were using for a pillow. The world titled slightly. The whispers grew louder in the corners of my mind—still muffled.

"Stop hovering," I snapped.

"I am not hovering."

"You are."

He was quiet for a moment. I cracked an eye open. He sat near my feet, leaning against the wall, arms crossed, staring into the empty hearth.

I hated the silence. It caged me in, like the whispers.

"Are you afraid of me now?" I asked into the silence.

He didn't answer right away. "I am afraid for you."

"That is not what I asked."

He looked at me, finally. Something crossing his features that was hard to distinguish. "Fine. Yes. You bled from your nose, your body lit up like a wildfire and you looked like you were not inside your own body."

"I was. I am."

"Then what were you staring at when you turned toward the trees?"

I said nothing. What could I say? The wind moved through the cracks in the walls. The voices hissed again. Urging. Yearning.

"You need rest," he said. "You need to stop using it before it eats you alive."

"I cannot." My voice cracked. "If I stop, I do not know what will happen. I do not know what I am without it."

I pressed the palms of my hands into my eyes, the headache blooming behind them like the mother of all migraines.

"Alura-"

"I said I am *fine,*" I snapped, sitting up. "Just stop. Stop coddling me."

He didn't flinch. Just watched me. His face was unreadable.

After a moment, he said, "I am not coddling you. I am holding onto you." He leaned forward. "You are strong. But do not lie to me and say this is not hurting you."

My eyes met his and something within me softened. For a second, the storm within me pulled back.

"I am scared," I whispered. "There is something inside me. Something that was not there before."

He moved beside me, wordless and pulled me into his arms. "Let me help. I will help shield you from it. For as long as you let me."

I let my forehead rest against his chest, letting my fingers curl into the leather of his armour. And for a while, the storm was quiet.

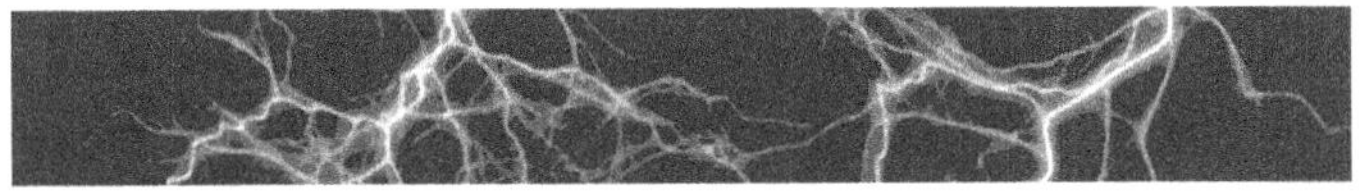

Blood lingered in my nose when I woke.

My head pounded, like I was hungover, but there was something more to it. Distant bells were ringing in my head, chiming out of sync.

Skúli wasn't in the shack when I woke. He'd draped his cloak over me and left a waterskin nearby. The fire pit had been coaxed to life, letting a steady warmth wash over me.

They still needed me.

I grabbed my bag, my hands moving in practised motions. Salves, poultices, clean linens. I say each thing as I touch them, mentally preparing. My limbs felt like stone and something within me still ached, but I forced myself to get up. People were bleeding. Dying. And I couldn't rest while others suffered.

Outside, the camp sprawled in uneven clusters of movement. Smoke drifted from hastily built fires. The wounded sat in groups—some being tended, others not yet seen.

Eyes followed me as I stepped out into the light.

Not all. But enough.

I knelt beside the first man I found. His arm had been sliced from shoulder to wrist, already crusting with blood. I didn't speak, just began cleaning the wound. He winced, but didn't pull away.

"I thought you were a shieldmaiden," he rasped.

"I am a healer."

"Not anymore." He looked at me, nodding slowly. "We would all be dead if not for you."

"Maybe," I say, my hands faintly trembling. "Or maybe I just bought time."

He didn't reply. I move onto the next warrior. And the next.

Some avoided my gaze. Not wanting to look too hard at whatever it was I had become in that moment...and the ones after. Others watched too long. A few whispered when they thought I wasn't listening.

"Did you see it? She glowed."

"No rune or charm does that. That was something else."

"...witch."

The story slithered through camp. Not screamed or spat. But spoken all the same.

I pressed a bandage to a gut wound, tied it tight. A girl no older than sixteen grunted in pain but gave me a nod of thanks.

"Some of the men think you are a god now," Eirik said casually. Lounging over by a driftwood fire, watching the flames turn green every so often. "Others are a little worried you might turn them into toads."

"I would start with you," I replied, rolling my eyes.

He grinned. "Fair." Then more seriously, "Skúli told everyone that you kept the line from falling. That you shielded us. It means something. Even if they do not know what to call it."

I press a hand to my temple. "What if it gets worse? What if next time I cannot stop it?"

Eirik gave me a sad smile, his eyes darting to meet mine. "Then we hold the line. For *you*. Like you did for us."

For a moment, I didn't say anything. I just breathed. Just listened to the rustle of wind, the crackle of nearby fires. The voices were quieter now.

But they weren't gone.

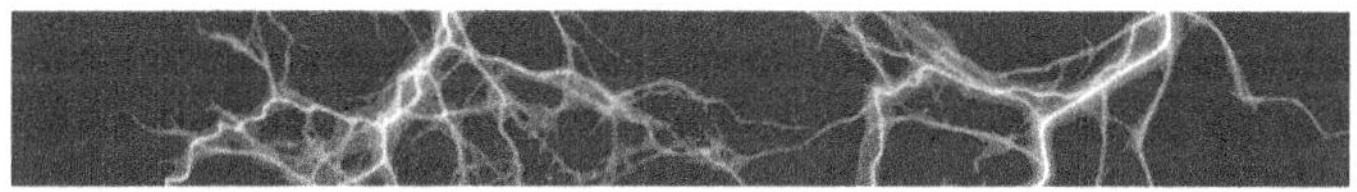

When Skúli finally emerged from the trees he had mud up to his knees and a dried streak of blood across his brow. He had that same certainty he always had, but he paused for a moment when he saw me.

"You should be resting," he said quietly.

"So should you."

His mouth twisted in reluctant amusement, but it faded as he looked past me to the battlefield. The crows were thicker now, circling, perching. Watching.

"We lost six," he says. "Two more might not see morning."

I follow his gaze. "And the others?"

"Holding. Thanks to you."

I crossed my arms, hugging my middle. "Some of them are afraid of me."

"They are fools then."

"You were," I whispered. "Maybe they are right to be afraid."

He turned to face me, his brow furrowing. "It was for a moment, Alura. A terrifying moment. You kept us standing. You saved us all."

"I did," I say slowly. "But the voices, Skúli. They do not stop. As long as I breathe, they whisper. I do not even know where they are." I take a shaky breath. "What if this magic is just a slow death with a prettier face?"

His hand found my shoulder. "Then we fight to the death. Together."

I look up at him. "You did not even flinch."

"I have faced worse things than a woman with power." His voice was low. "But I have never met one who used it to shield the men beside her."

My throat ached. "What if I become something they should be afraid of?"

"Then I will shield them. I will remind you who you are. I will protect you." His lips curl into a smirk. "And if that fails, I will let you terrify me into submission."

I let out a shaky laugh, looking over the camp. It was beginning to quiet. Fire lit, meals passed around. They were trying.

I leaned into him a little. "They think I am a god."

"You are. But not for the reasons they think."

I closed my eyes, and for a brief moment, the voices dimmed to a murmur. Not gone. But bearable.

"I am glad it was you beside me," I said softly.

"I am glad I was too." He kissed my temple, grounding me. Until a shriek from inside the canopy of trees startled me.

CHAPTER FORTY-TWO
ALURA

The shriek tore through dusk like a blade—high, inhuman and close.

My breath caught. Skúli shifted instantly, one hand going to the hilt of his axe, the other pulling me to his side. Around the firepit, heads snapped towards the treeline, and the soft murmur of evening conversation died as it snuffed out by sudden wind.

Another cry echoed. Then silence.

Not birds. Not animals. It was something else.

Eirik was already on his feet, his half-eaten bowl of stew forgotten at his feet. "Sounded like it came from the north edge," he said, voice tight.

"It is too soon for another attack," someone muttered nearby.

"Not if they did not flee," said another. "Not if something was left behind."

A low wind stirred through the trees. Warm despite the season, wrong somehow. The air felt heavy, like before a storm, charged with that prickling energy. I tasted copper at the back of my throat, and my skull pulsed once, hard.

The voices, quiet only moments ago, began to murmur again. Faint at first, then insistent. Urgent.

Let it out. Let it out. Let it BURN.

I shook my head, trying to clear the thoughts, teeth gritted. Skúli looked at me with concern.

"What is it?" He asked quietly.

"I do not know," I whispered. "But something is coming. I can feel it."

Shouts rang out at the northern watch post. A horn sounded—short, clipped. A Warning.

Weapons were drawn. Campfires doused. Warriors rushed to their positions, some barefoot, others still buttoning tunics. No one waited for orders.

"We hold the line again," Skúli said grimly, eyes scanning the woods. "Eirik takes the flank. Alura--"

"I am coming," I said.

His jaw clenched. "Only if you hold back."

"I cannot promise that," I whispered. "Not if it is like before. I will not stay back—hold back if there is something I can do to help."

He cursed under his breath but nodded, pressing a quick kiss to my temple. "Then do not die. That is an order."

Together we moved toward the edge of the camp, toward the place where firelight met shadows and where something ancient stirred behind the trees. The last thing I saw before the first arrow flew was a figure on the ridge, tall, thin and fiery orange hair that hung just below its shoulders.

Arrows whistled through the air, but none found home in a target. They embedded harmlessly in the ground or thudded into tree trunks. A few were twisted, malformed, or made of brittle wood that cracked in impact.

It made no sense.

"Why fire and miss?" Eirik muttered beside me, blade drawn.

"You are meant to be taking the flank," Skúli growled, his brow furrowed as he took in what was happening.

"Figured I would protect our best weapon instead."

Skúli narrowed his eyes at the treeline. "We are meant to be looking the wrong way."

Behind us, a scream tore through camp.

We spun as warriors scrambled to reposition, trying to determine where the real attack was coming from. But there was no pattern. Shadows moved in every direction. Illusions, reflections of warriors we had already killed earlier in the day flickered in and out of view, laughing before vanishing into smoke. Some men lunged at them, only to fall into traps strung with bone chimes that sand with unsettling laughter.

A drumbeat began, low and ominous. Not from our side. My breath hitched as the erratic; mocking sound flooded around us. It sounded like it was being played by a child who didn't know rhythm but loved the noise.

Then laughter again. Too high, too gleeful for a battle-field.

Then they appeared. Warriors dressed in skins and bones, some crawling on all fours, howling at the rapidly rising moon. Others moved in an unnatural march, almost dragging their feet as they jerked with weapons raised. Bjorn growled at them.

"They are playing with us," I told no one in particular. "It is a sick game."

Skúli grunted in confirmation. Eirik stiffened beside me, raising his sword and shield with a shaky confidence.

"What do we do?" Eirik asked, his voice no longer play-ful.

"We fight," Skúli growled. "Shield wall!"

The warriors all got into formation, the echo of wood slapping against wood as they all huddled together, over-lapping their shields. Skúli pulled me to the back of it just before another reign of arrows flew. This time they did hit. But as they hit, they dissolved into smoke.

The enemy warriors charged, and I almost stopped breathing, turning stiff. There was a feral howl that the enemy unleashed as they battered against us.

"Brace!"

The command was so fluid, so natural to Skúli in a way that only belonged to a seasoned warrior. I wondered for a second how long he'd been fighting for. How many raids had he been on? How many had failed?

The enemy gnashed their teeth as their weapons battered against us, yelling with an unhinged rage as they tried to thrust their weapons between the shields. But our warriors held on. They braced as their leader had told them to, putting all their faith into him.

"Brace!"

There was a yell from further down the shield wall. Someone had been struck. Warriors reassigned themselves, holding the wall as the enemy continued their assault against us.

From somewhere beyond, a shrieking cackle sounded out to me. It shifted in pitch, reaching a level that made me need to block my ears. No one even flinched.

"The forest is screaming," I shouted above the keening sound echoing in my head. Skúli caught my eye for just a moment and nodded.

Then, I felt it. That sliver of magic that was so like my own yet so different. Calling out to me, begging me to tap into it. I couldn't tell if it was coming from the earth or the sky...or something else—someone else.

I glanced back up to the figure on the ridge. I couldn't be sure, but it looked almost as if they were smiling. Like they were a puppeteer, and the enemies were their puppets. They were orchestrating this entire thing. If we wanted to get out of here alive then I needed to get up there.

"Skúli!" I shouted, crying out over the noise of battle.

He looked at me, just for a second. "Not now, Alura. I am a bit busy."

He grunted as he braced his own shield in the wall. I looked around, trying to see if there was anyone else who could take me. Anyone else who could get me up there, I wouldn't dare go alone. Not like this.

I still didn't have control over my power, over myself. And I didn't trust myself not to succumb to the voices that now lived in my head.

Yes. Yes. Over there. Go to him.

I tensed. A familiar hand landed on my shoulder, and I looked to my side. Eirik's face was grim but also knowing.

"What is the plan?" He didn't hesitate, didn't tell me to stay put. "You have a plan, right?"

I nod. "I need to get up to that ridge," I pointed out where the fire-haired person stood.

"Why?"

"They are controlling this entire thing. I need to get there. I need to stop them." I looked into his eyes trying to see any semblance of fear or a sign that it was a bad plan.

He just nodded. "Gods be good, Skúli is going to kill me." He gave me a firm look. "You stay with me, understand? Step where I step. Always stay with me. Do not leave my protection."

"I will."

We raced around the back of the shield wall, Eirik muttered something about not living long enough to make it back home. I heard Skúli shouting orders to the warriors. I turned back just in time to see them open the shield wall, creating a tunnel for the enemy to funnel into. They struck the enemy down, moving to cage them in so there was nowhere to run.

"Eyes forward Alura," Eirik said hastily, grabbing me by my vest and dragging me toward our goal. "Looking behind us will only get us killed. Did he not teach you anything?"

Eirik scoffed for a moment before he turned serious again. We made our way through the trees, careful to avoid the sound traps, careful to avoid pits and nets. My heart hammered in my chest and my throat grew dry.

I didn't have a full plan. Not really. I was still formulating it in my mind. I just knew that I needed to get up there. I had to stop this madness.

And only I could do it.

An arrow flew towards us, whistling, but Eirik raised his shield, and I ducked behind him. It splintered upon contact, falling at his feet in shards. Then a feral warrior emerged, dressed in nothing but a skin that was still dripping blood. He growled at us, a low, feral sound, baring his broken and cracked teeth at us before he lunged.

Eirik moved into position, taking a few steps forward and slamming his shield into the enemy. It staggered back, dazed for a moment before its fingers curled around a bone-hilted dagger. It unsheathed it and began circling us. Eirik didn't stop moving, mirroring its movements so that he was always between me and whatever it was.

Maybe it used to be human, but not anymore.

Then it disappeared into the smoke. I whirled around, trying to find where it had gone. Eirik cursed, doing the same. We were disorientated, confused as to how it just disappeared like that. It was not right, not natural.

I must have turned a dozen times before it reappeared, lunging at me with the bone knife. I put my hands up before I could stop myself, but no magic came. I take a half-step back and the knife sliced through my hand.

It grabbed at my wrist, licking the dripping blood from my wound then howled like an animal that was going in for the kill. I reached down to my belt slowly, gripping the knife that was sheathed there and drew it out. It seemed more interested in licking my wound rather than killing me, so I took that opportunity to get the perfect angle.

The perfect shot.

I thrusted my knife through its ribs, angling it in such a way that I knew I'd gotten its heart. It looked at me for a moment, its eyes red and its face covered in filth and blood. Then it dissipated, turning into smoke that blew away in the breeze.

"What the fuck was that?" Eirik asked, breathless and horrified.

"I do not know," I admitted.

We pushed on, moving between the trees as I clutched my blade in my hand. I'd almost asked Eirik to take me back. To take me back by Skúli's side, to protection and warmth. But I could still hear the clang of battle, the cries and the shouts. It wasn't safe there; it wouldn't be until I got to the ridge.

Another enemy appeared out of the shadows, material-ising inside them and then racing at us. Eirik didn't hesitate this time. He braced his shield, raising his sword and within moments the sword was buried into the enemy's chest.

The deeper we pushed into the trees, the darker it got, and the more unsettled I began to feel. There was dark magic here, the kind that called out to me in waves.

Onwards. Onwards to your destiny.

You can fulfill it. The prophecy or the demise.

BURN THEM ALL.

"Are you okay?" Eirik whispered, scanning the trees as I began to clutch my head.

I gritted my teeth and nodded. "Yes," I lied. "Keep going."

We reached the bottom of the ridge, and I stared up at it in awe. I needed to climb that damn thing and I needed to not get killed in the process. My breathing was already coming out in painful heaves. Fear and exhaustion were beginning to kick in.

A rustle echoed out from behind us, twigs snapping under our feet. Eirik and I both whirled around, looking at the five new enemies that were emerging.

Eirik shot me a quick look. "You get up on that ridge. You do what you need to do to end this. So, we can go home. Understood?"

I nod.

"Tell me you understand, Alura."

"I-I understand," I stutter, glancing at Eirik's grim face.

"You go, you end this. Like a real shieldmaiden. Astrid will be so proud that you have earnt that armour."

His voice was thick with emotion, but I did as he said and began the climb up the ridge.

"And Alura?" Eirik called out to me one last time. "Do not die, Skúli will kill me."

CHAPTER FORTY-THREE
ALURA

The ridge was steep, a trail of churned mud and blood winding up through the trees. The battle still raged behind me, off in the distance I could hear Skúli's roar, the clash of shields and steel echoing like a war drum.

The air was different up here.

Thinner. Still. Wrong.

Eirik fought like a storm at my back, cutting down the shadows that slipped between the trees, ducking low to block the curved blade of a masked warrior that had almost taken me in the side. He'd shoved me up the slope, blood streaming from his brow.

"Go!" He barked. "I will hold them! Do not turn back!"

I turned, doing as he said and pressing forwards into the last rays of faint light. The stones beneath my boots hummed faintly, a vibration that I felt in my bones more than heard. The trees parted into a narrow crest lined with stones that hummed faintly with power. Runes had been carved into them, but they shifted when I looked too long.

At the centre, waiting, was *him*.

He looked like a man, but the longer I stared, the less certain I became. He felt like a storm that laughed.

He stood tall and lean, wrapped in red and black, his shoulders draped in a fox-fur cloak. His face was mostly hidden behind a mask—one side grinning, the other twisted in anguish.

"Well," he said lightly, applauding slowly. "You climbed after all."

My magic sparked instinctively, crawling up my arms in jagged threads. My wound throbbed, blood slick and warm against my skin.

"Well done, Storm-Born," he said, his voice silken and strange. "Your warriors fight well, but it was you I wanted to see."

"Who are you?" I demanded. My stormlight curled around my hands again, ready. My skull throbbed. "Why did you do this?"

"Because I *could*," he replied with a shrug, stepping lightly from stone to stone. "Because mischief is a kind of truth. A reflection. A disruption. And you, little storm, are a *great* disruption."

Something in me twisted at how he used Eirik's nickname for me. Somehow he knew that was what Eirik had been calling me and now he was trying to use it against me.

I took a step forward, magic sparking around my feet. "You killed my people."

Anger, fear, wrath. It all swirled around inside of me, creating something new. Something dangerous.

"I tested them," he corrected, tilting his head. "Some passed-" A pause as he squinted his eyes at me. "Some did not."

"Why?" I hissed. "What do you want?"

He spread his arms. "To see what you *are*, of course. To see the great Storm-Born in all her glory."

My breath caught.

"What have you done to this place?" I demanded.

He tilted his head, his mask catching the dim light. One side was grinning, the other twisted in agony.

"I corrected imbalance," he said. "The forest was choking on silence. I reminded it how to scream."

"You turned people into monsters."

"I revealed what they were willing to become." His gaze sharpened on me. "There is a difference."

Anger flared within me, hot and bright, lightning seeking to release. The runes beneath my feet pulsed in response. Once, twice. Then, cracked.

He noticed. His breath caught, just slightly.

"Oh," he murmured, something like delight creeping into his voice. "You feel them, don't you?"

I looked down. The stones were splitting where my blood had dripped, the runes unraveling like frayed thread.

"What did you do?" I whispered. Not to him, but to myself.

"Me?" He laughed softly. "Nothing. You did this."

The storm inside me surged, answering the fear, the fury, the aching in my bones. The voices I had fought back rose—not shouting, but guiding.

Yes. Like that. Break it.

"You were bound," I said, the truth sitting heavy on my chest. "This place was holding you."

"Was."

The final rune shattered.

The sound was not stone breaking. It was something older giving way. The forest exhaled. For one terrible moment, the world tilted.

Then, he was in front of me, closer than before, close enough that I could feel the heat beneath his skin, the wrongness of him.

"You have no idea," he said quietly, "what power you carry. What storms shaped you. The gods gave their blood to light the world. But you?" His voice softened. "You hold it. Wild. Untethered. No one ever taught it how to choose."

"You are lying."

He circled me now, slow and deliberate, trying to make me feel small.

"Am I?" He murmured, now behind me. "Or is it that your own gods are liars? You feel it, do you not? The pull. The cost. The voices. The *truths* buried beneath their silence."

"Stay away from me," I said, though my feet wouldn't move.

"Our great thunder god never told you what storms cost," he went on, almost gently. "So let me."

He reached out—not to touch me, but my magic itself. Agony ripped through me as my magic flared blinding white, lightning arced from my hands into the stones, into the sky, into him. It should have burned him.

Instead, he laughed.

"Stop," I whispered as the pain shifted, twisted, re-shaped. Like lightning being forced through a broken path. I screamed as the storm recoiled inward, branding itself into my bones.

I collapsed to my knees, gasping. He stood over me, whole, unburned, mask gleaming. "I did not take your power," he said softly. "I would never insult Thor so deeply."

My blood ran cold.

"I taught it something," he continued. "I taught it to answer desperation. To grow strongest when sacrifice is required."

"No," I whispered.

"Yes," he said, delighted. "Now every choice you make will matter. Someone will always pay the price."

He leaned down, voice brushing my ear. "Sometimes, Little Storm…that someone will be you."

"I can *show* you," he said, his voice low, tempting me. "You and I, we are not so different. You break rules. I write my own. They fear us both."

"No," I said louder. "I am nothing like you. I do not hurt people. I do not use them as puppets. I will save them."

He was close now, so close I could hear his breath behind the mask. "Not yet," he whispered. "But soon."

"Who are you?" My voice is breathless, my heart hammering in my chest. Fire danced beneath my skin.

"No one. Just a joker."

He vanished. Not in a burst of smoke or fire. Just gone—like the air swallowed him whole.

Below the ridge, the battle was beginning to come to an end. The shadow warriors started to disappear as they stopped fighting and our warriors struck them.

I knew now that this wasn't just a raid. It was a game. And we were the pieces.

* * *

The ridge behind me felt like a scar carved into the land. I stumbled back through the woods, legs aching, the stormlight dulled back to faint flickers beneath my skin. Every breath scraped my lungs. Every shadow made my skin crawl.

When I broke through the tree line and back down towards the store, the battle had quietened. Smoke rose from scattered fires. Those of us that were still standing were limping or collapsed near the surf, weapons slack in their hands, blood on their faces.

I made myself useful, tending to the wounded as I'd been taught to do. I was halfway through stitching a finger back together when I felt him behind me. He waited patiently, not quite hovering but not giving me space either. I focused on my work, ignoring his looming presence. Ignoring the way the warrior in front of me squirmed by whatever it was he saw on Skúli's face.

I focused on sewing the skin back together and the warrior in front of me grits his teeth, refusing to make a sound of pain in front of his leader. I had to give him extra credit for that. I finish up the suture, closing it and snipping off the end. Then I wrapped a bandage around it to try and keep it clean.

Once I was happy, I stood again. The young warrior gave me a nod of thanks and I went to move onto the next person who was waiting for help, but Skúli moved in front of me, blocking off my path.

His face was contorted into something reminiscent of pain and fury. "You left." He gritted his teeth. "You were meant to stay with the wall, and you left."

"I did what I had to do to save us."

"Did you use magic again?" The words were meant to be caring, thoughtful even. But they came out in a panicked anger.

"No," I lied. I hadn't meant to use what little magic I had up on the ridge, it had just burst out of me. As if reacting to my lie, the storm inside me lit up. Only briefly. Just for a second. "No."

He looked at me, like he was trying to determine whether I was telling the truth. A part of him must have decided it didn't matter, he enveloped me in his arms. Eirik limped towards us, blood streaking his temple, one hand pressed to his ribs, Bjorn by his side.

"Well," he said hoarsely. "I wish I had gotten a reunion like that."

I made a face at him, still wrapped in Skúli's arms.

"Get your own shieldmaiden," Skúli grunted.

"I was so worried," he murmured into my hair. "So, fucking worried, Alura. Do not ever do that to me again."

"I cannot promise that." My voice was small and broken. "I cannot promise anything."

He pulled back to look at me just as wet tears began to fall onto my cheeks. He used a thumb to brush one away. "I know. The life of a warrior is not easy. The choices we must make are not always easy."

"That was a cursed mess," Eirik continues as if we weren't having a moment.

"It was not a raid. It was staged. Controlled." I turned to Skúli and said, "I spoke with him."

"Who?"

"The man who did all of this-" I gestured around us "-I met him. He said we were the same. That...I was like him."

"You are nothing like him," he reassured me with a growl.

"I think I am," I whispered. I step out of his hold, putting my tools away in their little bag. "I think he is right but not in the way he thinks."

"I do not follow."

"I felt his magic. It is different from mine but it feels the same. Similar." I took a deep breath. "I think we are made of the same thing."

Skúli gazed at me, trying to see something within myself that I couldn't. Trying to determine if I was telling him the truth or if I was correct. It was futile. I knew it was. It wasn't something that anyone around me would be able to see. It was something only I could feel. Buried deep within my soul.

"That is how you could sense the forest." It wasn't a question; it was him understanding what I was telling him. I nodded. "He was using his magic on the forest, and you could feel it."

"I felt it as soon as I stepped off the boat. I just could not figure out what it was. Skúli, this place is haunted but not in the way that we think. It is haunted by something older and far more dangerous. Someone is here, pulling the strings, weaving fate. Their magic is what made its people into...whatever they are now."

He pursed his lips, letting what I've told him sink in. Then finally he said, "No man could have done this."

"No," I say, agreeing. "Not a man. A god."

"Yeah?" Eirik said, looking around at the eerily still tree-line. "Well, let us make sure we do not stick around to see what they do next."

Skúli nodded grimly. "We leave at first light. I want everyone who can walk back on the boat before the sun rises above the trees."

"And the ones that cannot?" I ask.

He hesitated for just a moment. "We carry them."

Eirik let out a laugh, clapping Skúli back as he came to stand by him. "You are getting soft."

"You will see how soft I am when I make you row us back home." His lips pulled up into a small grin. "Alone."

We made camp right there on the beach. The tide rolling in slow and black under the fractured moonlight. The wounded were tendered, the battle over and the dead laid in rows. There were fewer of us now.

I sat with Skúli and Eirik around the low-burning fire, our backs to the sea, our faces toward the haunted woods. No one said much. But we didn't have to.

We'd survived, for now.

CHAPTER FORTY-FOUR
SKÚLI

The smell of smoke and ash clung to the air, sharp and metallic, even as the first pale light of dawn began to touch the horizon. The bodies of foreign warriors and fallen friends alike lay scattered across the field. Each one carried a story I would never hear, a life snuffed out too soon. I had no words for it—only the ache in my chest that never seemed to fade.

I kept a hand on Alura's back, feeling her warmth against me, the faint tremor in her shoulders as she moved among the wounded. My own fingers itched to sweep through her hair, to hold her tighter, but there were too many tasks demanding attention—too many lives that needed saving before we could think of ourselves.

"You should not be here," I said, voice low, careful, almost a growl as I caught her lingering near a fallen warrior.

Her eyes met mine, fierce even in exhaustion. "I cannot stay away," she said. "Not when there is still life to mend."

I wanted to argue, to tell her the storm inside her frightened me, that the power she carried could take her from me before I could even blink. But I did not, I held it to myself. I could only brush a thumb along her knuckles, grounding her, and hope she felt the same tether that held me together.

"I know," I said. "But stay close. Do not let me lose you—to yourself, or to them."

She nodded, the faintest ghost of a smile touching her lips before she turned back to the wounded. I let her go, only for a moment.

When the pyres were lit, the flames roaring to life and consuming the dead, I held her in my arms. My eyes caught every flicker of stormlight that shimmered faintly at her fingertips, each pulse making my stomach tighten with worry. She noticed it too, and she glanced at me, uncertain.

"I will be careful," she whispered.

I believed her. I had to. Still, I drew her closer into my side, wrapping my arms around her as we watched the smoke curl into the sky. Her head rested against my chest, her hands clutching mine, small and warm.

"You are alive," I murmured, more to myself than her. "And I will not let anything take you."

Her breath caught slightly at my words, and I felt the pulse of her stormlight again. Just a flicker, fleeting—but enough to remind me of the danger she carried within her.

"I am still here," she said, lifting her face to mine, her silver hair brushing my cheek.

"And I am here with you," I whispered back, pressing a slow, lingering kiss to her temple. "No storms, no fires, nothing will take you from me."

Even as I said it, the words felt like a vow forged too quickly.

For a moment, the world narrowed to just the two of us. The crash of waves against the shore, the low crackle of distant flames, the groans of the wounded—all faded beneath the rhythm of our breathing. I tilted her chin up and kissed her lips softly, reverently, tasting the salt and iron of sweat and fear, the sweetness of life that clung to her.

She leaned into me, lips parting slightly, and I could feel the tremor of exhaustion, of adrenaline, of something deeper—longing, desire, fear—running through her. I pressed my forehead to hers, letting my hand trail along her jawline, grounding her, grounding myself.

"Whatever comes," I said, voice low and certain, "I will burn beside you. If the world falls, I will be there. Only you and me."

Her eyes glimmered, reflecting the rising sun, the firelight, the unspoken promise between us. She pressed herself closer, letting the warmth of my body shield her.

"Only us," she whispered.

The longboat waited, creaking against the tide, and I helped the wounded aboard first. Eirik and the others moved efficiently, but my focus never left Alura. She climbed in with a grace I knew hid the ache in her legs, the weight of the day pressing on her shoulders.

I felt every injury around us—the stiff way Eirik rolled his shoulders at the oars, the silent grimace worn by a shieldmaiden, the hollow stare of a mere boy who had lost his father on the shore.

I slid into the boat beside Alura, wrapping an arm around her waist. Her head rested against my chest, and I felt the faint tremor of her power ripple through the air again. Just a spark, no more. But it was enough to set my teeth on edge.

Enough to remind me that this peace was fragile.

"We will make it home," I whispered, more to steady my own nerves than hers. "We will see Drakensvar again, alive."

She tilted her face up, and for the briefest moment, the smoke and ash and bloodshed were gone. "I believe you," she said.

The wind tugged at our hair, carrying the tang of salt and the faint scent of fire. I held her tighter, afraid to let go, afraid that even a single heartbeat of distance might mean losing her.

The shore receded behind us, leaving only smoke and memory. But even as the sun rose, gilding the waves in gold and silver, I could feel it—something lurking in the edges of the horizon. A shadow that moved too deliberately, too patiently.

I tightened my grip on her, feeling the storm pulse faintly under her skin again. And I knew, with a certainty that made my chest ache, that the battle was far from over—but the cost had only begun to reveal itself.

"Hold on," I murmured, voice almost lost in the wind. "Whatever comes next... we will face it together."

Alura pressed closer, whispering, "Together."

And as the longboat cut through the water, the shadows lurking beyond the dawn did not fade. They shifted.

The war had only just begun.

I knew then that whatever hand had touched our fate, it would not release us gently.

ACKNOWLEDGEMENTS

I would like to thank everyone who has been a part of making Seidr's and Swords into what it is today.

To my beautiful partners, thank you for listening to me ramble about this idea and the process of turning it into a full book for the last year. I'm sorry I've driven everyone in the house absolutely crazy, but I promise it'll only last forever. The support you've both given me has been amazing, from helping me developmentally edit to coming up with Eirik's jokes and stories.

To my family, who have always supported my crazy ideas.

To my friends for never getting annoyed by my incessant rambling, for being the first reader's and always being my cheer squad.

For my beta reader, Jeff, who made me realise that this was well worth the amount of tears and screaming into the void.

And finally to my cover designer, Okenneth from Inspire Designs. You truly made Seidr's and Swords come together by just using the vibes and trust I'd handed over.

Without you guys, this never would have been the book I dreamed it could be.

ABOUT THE AUTHOR

Marie Leforte grew up in Australia's capital, where her love for storytelling began long before she could spell the word *literature*. From childhood notebooks to published novels, she's been chasing the magic of words ever since.

Now based in rural New South Wales, Marie shares her days with her partners, children, and a lively menagerie of animals.

When she isn't weaving worlds filled with prophecy, love, and myth, she can usually be found with a book in hand, an energy drink nearby, and laughter echoing through the house.

9 781763 731127